"I'm sorry about that misunderstanding we had, Mr. Dickens," Keely said.

"But I thought we understood each other perfectly, Ms. LaRoux," he replied. "It was obvious to both of us that working together would be impossible."

"Not impossible," she countered. "Difficult, perhaps, but certainly not impossible. And I'm perfectly willing to accept the fact that a talented photographer like you would be worth every minute of difficulty you caused." That didn't come out quite right, she thought, biting down on her bottom lip.

"What's *your* talent, Ms. LaRoux?" There was a glitter in his eyes.

"I beg your pardon?"

"You just expressed that you would be willing to put up with me because of the work I'd produce. But why on earth should I put up with you?" A slow smile eased across his lips. "Like I said, what do you have to offer me in return?"

Dear Reader,

Spellbinders! That's what we're striving for. The editors at Silhouette are determined to capture your imagination and win your heart with every single book we publish. Each month, six Special Editions are chosen with *you* in mind.

Our authors are our inspiration. Writers such as Nora Roberts, Tracy Sinclair, Kathleen Eagle, Carole Halston and Linda Howard—to name but a few—are masters at creating endearing characters and heartrending love stories. Their characters are everyday people—just like you and me—whose lives have been touched by love, whose dreams and desires suddenly come true!

So find a cozy, quiet place to read, and create your own special moment with a Silhouette Special Edition.

Sincerely,

The Editors
SILHOUETTE BOOKS

BEVLYN MARSHALL
Lonely at the Top

Silhouette Special Edition

Published by Silhouette Books New York

America's Publisher of Contemporary Romance

To Bruce, the love of my life

SILHOUETTE BOOKS
300 East 42nd St., New York, N.Y. 10017

Copyright © 1987 by Bevlyn Marshall Kaukas

ISBN: 0-373-09407-8

First Silhouette Books printing September 1987

America's Publisher of Contemporary Romance

Printed in the U.S.A.

BEVLYN MARSHALL,

a Connecticut resident, has had a varied career in fashion, public relations and marketing but finds writing the most challenging and satisfying occupation. When she's not at her typewriter, she enjoys tennis, needlepoint, long walks with her husband and toy spaniel, and reading. She believes that people who read are rarely bored or lonely because the private pleasure of a good book is one of life's most rewarding pastimes.

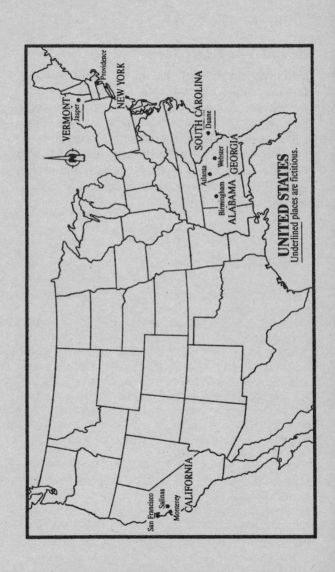

UNITED STATES
Underlined places are fictitious.

Chapter One

When Keely LaRoux strode into the lobby of The Citation Company on Monday morning, the heels of her sensible black pumps tapped a sure, steady beat against the glossy marble floor. Though small-boned and slender, she had long since learned to radiate self-confidence and authority. The tilt of her chin, the set of her shoulders, the smooth, rhythmic swing of her leather attaché case all demonstrated that she meant business. Beneath this cool exterior butterflies rioted in her stomach, but she gave no outward signs of nervousness. It was a big day for her, her first as the company's director of corporate communications. At thirty, not only was she the youngest director at Citation, but also the only female one. Ten years of hard work had finally paid off.

Keely expected to work even harder in the future. Her game plan was to become a vice president before she was forty. She looked the image of corporate success in her navy wool Brooks Brothers blazer and straight skirt, her white silk broadcloth shirt and paisley foulard tie, cleverly twisted beneath her shirt collar to look like a rosette. The Golden Fleece brass buttons on her blazer were the flashiest part of her outfit and perfectly acceptable. Yet despite her conservative dress and petite figure, she couldn't avoid standing out in the crowd. Her thick, short crop of red hair was like a bright, bobbing buoy in the sea of gray and blue pinstripes sweeping through the Citation lobby during morning rush hour.

Harry, the night guard, caught her attention by waving both arms, and Keely smiled and headed toward him. They had become good friends over the years. When Keely worked late, which was often, Harry would stop by her office during his rounds for a chat. He was an easygoing, unpretentious fellow and reminded Keely of the folks in her little hometown of Jasper, Vermont.

"How come you're still hanging around here, Harry? Don't you have better things to do?" she asked him, repeating almost verbatim the question he often posed to her with fatherly concern.

His plump face creased into a wide grin. "I've been waiting around for a phone call from my son-in-law. Now I'm waiting for hospital visiting hours to begin."

Keely knew exactly what he was talking about, since he had talked about nothing else for the past month or so. "Your daughter's had the baby! Don't keep me in suspense, Harry. Girl or boy?"

His smile spread even wider. "Sugar and spice and everything nice."

"So you're finally a grandpa. Congratulations!" Keely gave him a little peck on the cheek. The distant memory of her own father flashed across her mind. Unlike Harry, he hadn't been much of a family man. In fact, he had deserted his family when Keely was twelve and two of her four brothers were still in diapers.

Harry pulled a cigar out of his pocket and handed it to Keely. It had a pink band around it, declaring, in gold script, *It's A Girl*. "Congratulations to you, too, honey. I heard about your promotion."

Keely was surprised, since she had only heard about it herself late Friday afternoon. Then she remembered that news traveled fast around Citation headquarters, even faster than it spread in the little town of Jasper.

"The rate you're going, you'll end up president of this company," Harry went on.

Keely laughed and pretended to puff on the cigar. "I don't think Mr. Wellfleet is ready to give up that position quite yet."

"Well, you've got plenty of time, honey."

"Not this morning, I don't," she said, glancing at her watch. It seemed there was never enough time for anything, even a pleasant chat. "I've got to go, Harry. I'm having my first staff meeting this morning, and I want to prepare for it. I'm a little nervous." She'd never admit that to anybody in the company but Harry.

"Don't worry, honey. You can handle it."

"Thanks for the vote of confidence, Harry," she said, sincerely appreciating it. As she hurried to the elevators she hoped the department staff would be as supportive. She was reasonably sure they would be. Except for Peter Plack, that was. It had been rumored that he would be named director when Clay Johnson retired. Not because Plack was the best person for the job, but because he and the president's son had been fraternity brothers in college. Keely was proud that she had been chosen instead, on merit rather than connections.

Her new office was located on the tenth floor, and when she entered it she found Edith Hamilton clearing out the drawers of the teak desk.

"Good morning, Ms. LaRoux," the elderly woman said, her voice guarded. "I'm getting Mr. Johnson's office in order for you. I mean *your* office, of course." She added a ship's barometer to a carton containing sailing magazines, stationery bearing Clay Johnson's name, and an assortment of flotsam that collects in desk drawers over the years. "I know I should have done this sooner, but I just couldn't seem to get to it. It's hard to believe that Mr. Johnson won't be coming back."

Edith had been Johnson's secretary for fifteen years, and Keely could understand her feelings. "We'll all miss him," she said sympathetically. It was true enough. Johnson had been a most agreeable boss if also an extremely ineffectual one, especially these past few years as he cared more and more about sailing his boat than steering his department in the right direction. It was Keely who had taken on many of the responsibilities he'd neglected.

Without glancing at Keely, Edith slammed shut the desk drawers. "I've ordered stationery with your new title on it, Ms. LaRoux," she said in her clipped, efficient voice. "I saw to that as soon as I read Mr. Wellfleet's memo regarding your promotion."

"Thank you, Edith." There was no missing the tension emanating from the older woman, and Keely tried to mollify it. "And since when am I Ms. LaRoux to you? You've called me Keely for almost ten years." She smiled warmly, but Edith did not respond.

"That was before you became my boss. Of course that's only temporary, until you can find your own secretary." Edith busied herself with taping up the box.

Keely was taken aback by Edith's cold demeanor. They had always gotten along well and shared a mutual respect. Or so Keely thought. But it was clear that Edith wasn't pleased with her promotion. This upset Keely because she had learned to value Edith's sound judgment in business.

"Actually, I had hoped you'd stay on as my secretary," Keely told her. "Unless you object to having me as your boss, that is." Keely believed in being direct when she sensed a problem and appreciated that quality in others.

"I assumed you'd want a younger secretary, being so young yourself," Edith replied, tucking a stray strand of gray hair into her smooth bun.

Keely's green eyes widened in surprise. "I want someone who knows the ropes. Someone whose opinions I trust. And that someone is you, Edith Hamilton."

Edith pushed up her bifocals and gave Keely a penetrating look. Apparently she was satisfied with what she saw because a lovely smile suddenly softened her severe countenance. "I'm glad you feel that way. And here I was worried that you'd expect me to retire like Mr. Johnson."

"Oh, Edith, of course not." Keely's impulse was to hug the other woman reassuringly, but she contained it. People at Citation didn't go around hugging one another. "And I was beginning to worry that you resented my promotion."

"What nonsense. There's no one who deserves it more than you. You got where you are by always doing a good job, not by playing politics like certain other managers in this department." It was obvious she was referring to Peter Plack. "There's nothing I'd like better than to assist you, Ms. La-Roux."

"Then it's settled," Keely said, extending her hand. "And no more of this Ms. LaRoux business, okay, Edith? We've been friends a long time."

"Well, it is company policy to call directors by their last—"

"Hang company policy! We'll do things our way in this department." For once Keely couldn't care less that her rebellious streak was, as usual, jutting out just when she was doing her best to fit into the corporate mold.

"Very well, Keely."

The two women shook hands, laughing a little over their misunderstanding. Then Edith took away the box containing Clay Johnson's personal belongings, leaving Keely alone in her new corner office.

She paced it awhile, trying to get acclimated, then gazed out the huge tinted windows. She had a bird's-eye view of Madison Avenue and watched the stream of traffic below, musing about how far she'd come.

She'd started working for Citation when she was still in high school to supplement the meager family income. The Citation factory in Jasper manufactured parts for power lawn mowers, one of the many products the huge corporation produced. Keely had worked on the assembly line part-time. After graduation she got a full-time job there as a secretary, volunteered for any additional responsibilities that came up and eventually produced an award-winning employee newsletter. That got the attention of corporate executives in New York, and she received an offer to transfer to Citation headquarters. It was an offer too tempting to refuse, although the increase in salary didn't go as far as she'd thought it would in New York City. Struggling to make ends meet had fired her ambition. It still did.

She walked behind the wide desk and tried out the gray leather swivel chair. It seemed a little big for her small frame. Well, she would adjust to it, she told herself. Just as she had always adjusted. It hadn't been easy for her, a small-town girl, to fit into the tightly structured corporate world. Citation had been a giant manufacturing company for over fifty years, producing everything from nuts and bolts to hair dryers. It could still almost boggle Keely's mind to envision the extent of its factories and products. Not that she would ever let on that she was a little in awe of it all. But it still thrilled her to realize that she, little Keely LaRoux from Jasper, was now an executive at Citation headquarters.

She snapped open her attaché case and took out her leather-bound appointment book, the gold Cross fountain pen she had bought herself on Saturday to celebrate her promotion and a silver-framed photograph of a pretty girl with long red hair.

Keely placed the picture on her desk and smiled, immediately feeling more at home in her new office. People usually assumed it was a picture of Keely herself as a child, and she had become used to their surprised reactions when she told them it was her daughter, Joy. Because of her slight build, lightly freckled face and short, rather boyish haircut, Keely looked much younger than she was. Certainly not old enough to have an eleven-year-old child.

"Joy of my life," she murmured now, giving a last glance at the photograph before settling down to work. She was immersed in jotting down points she wanted to cover during her first staff meeting as director when Peter Plack barged into her office. She looked up from her yellow writing pad, her eyes slightly narrowed in irritation.

Peter was an attractive man in his mid-thirties, groomed to perfection. He held a dozen long-stemmed roses against the vest of his natty charcoal-gray suit.

"That harridan outside your office tried to keep me out, but I simply had to give you this tribute." He bowed formally, offering the roses. "Congratulations on your promotion, Red."

Keely despised that nickname. She was self-conscious about the gaudy brightness of her coppery hair in this conservative corporate setting and had even considered dyeing it a more muted shade. But she could never bring herself to change what was so much a natural part of her. She didn't make an issue of Plack calling her Red, but she couldn't ignore his reference to Edith.

"Mrs. Hamilton is not a harridan, Peter. She's a professional doing her job." Not really wanting to, she accepted the roses. "Thank you. How nice," she said politely but without much enthusiasm. She disliked the man and knew he'd felt the same about her ever since she rejected his amorous advances. Plack was a married man constantly on the make, which Keely found despicable. She had told him as much.

"Just a little something to show my goodwill," he said through a tight smile. "It's no secret that I expected the job, but I guess our illustrious president, in all his infinite wisdom, thought it would be good public relations to have a token female as a director."

Keely willed herself to remain cool and collected. "I was promoted on the basis of merit, not sex," she replied.

"Of course you were, babe." He winked. "The fact that you have much prettier legs than I do had nothing to do with it. Although I'm sure Wellfleet noticed them often enough."

Keely tossed the roses onto her desk. "Careful, Plack," she warned, her voice low and steady. "That innuendo is way out of line, and you know it."

His small brown eyes widened to demonstrate innocence. "Hey, can't a guy give a little compliment to his new boss lady? All I said was that you have a great pair of legs, Red."

"Fine." She raised her hands, palms up, to signal the end of the discussion. She wasn't going to waste her breath arguing with him. She had more important matters to deal with right now. "Since we're both busy, I won't keep you any longer, Pete. I'll see you at the staff meeting in an hour."

Although she had dismissed him, he did not leave. Instead, he picked up her new Cross pen and examined it intently. "About that staff meeting, Keely. I don't believe I can make it. I have another meeting scheduled with our ad agency rep, and I'd really hate to cancel it."

Keely just bet he would. She knew that the agency representative he was meeting was an eager-to-please young woman with wavy blond hair and a curvaceous figure. "Reschedule it," she advised softly. "The meeting I called has top priority."

He balked, losing his cool. "Since when do you tell me what to do, LaRoux?"

"Since I was promoted over you, Pete." She tried to keep her tone gentle. As much as she disliked the man, and as much as she wanted to make it clear that she was now his boss, she did not relish lording it over him. Still, she knew it was important to stress her authority if she was going to maintain it in the long run.

She stood up, hoping that would spur him to leave. His cold, small eyes slid over her figure. "You sure don't waste time throwing your weight around, do you, Red? All hundred and five pounds of you, I estimate."

He was off by a pound, but Keely didn't correct him. She raised her chin to look taller. "Just be at that meeting," she ordered. He nodded curtly and turned to go, but she was forced to call him back. "My pen, please, Pete." It had not escaped her attention that he had slid her expensive pen into his jacket pocket.

Caught in his casual theft, he took the pen out and slapped it into her waiting palm. His eyes glittered with hatred. "Sorry. An honest mistake. I have one just like it." He left, red faced, slamming the door behind him.

Keely regretted the incident, knowing it would deepen Plack's resentment of her. He could be a formidable enemy, a real snake in the grass when it came to office politics. As she tried to concentrate on her work, the insinuating scent of the roses he'd given her began to irritate her. Her first impulse was to throw them out, but she thought better of it. The innocent flowers were really very lovely. Costly, too.

Keely had learned the value of frugality growing up poor on a farm. Her mother never threw anything away. Not even rags, which she braided into rugs. No one had ever given her mother expensive roses. For that matter, Keely had never received roses from an admirer before. The trouble was that Plack was not an admirer but a man who would prefer to see her fail rather than succeed. She could not tolerate the presence of his insincere gift in her office a moment longer.

And then it occurred to her how to put the flowers to a better use. She picked up the phone and called down to the lobby to find out if Harry was still there. He was just about to leave for the hospital, but she urged him to wait a moment longer. Grabbing the lush bouquet, she hurried out to the elevator. When she reached the lobby she presented them to a surprised Harry.

"For your daughter," she explained. Seeing his pleased smile made the roses beautiful again, and the ill will of the original gift bearer was erased.

"That's real thoughtful of you," Harry said, cradling the bouquet in his arms as if practicing holding his new grandchild. "They must have cost you a pretty penny."

"I didn't buy them," Keely was obligated to admit, not wanting to take undeserved credit. "But I think your daughter will appreciate them more than I did."

She gave Harry a hearty pat on the back and headed for the elevators again, eager to get back to her desk. She hoped there would be no further interruptions before her staff meeting.

She stepped into an empty waiting car. As she was pushing her floor button she heard a demanding male voice order her to hold the car for him. But it was too late. The doors were already closing, and Keely was not inclined to take orders from some unseen man. Suddenly a long, plaid-flanneled arm pushed through the narrow opening, and the doors retracted. If they hadn't, his arm could have been crushed. Who did he think he was? Keely wondered. Superman? She glared at him when he boarded the elevator. He glared right back.

"Didn't you hear me call to hold the car, lady?"

"Not in time, I didn't," she replied curtly, and turned away from him, giving her full attention to the button panel.

Her one brief glance at him had seared every detail of his appearance into her brain, and she had no reason to look at him again. Except to gape in admiration, which she wasn't about to do. He was a tall, blond, broad-shouldered man with streaks of gold in his short, thick beard. His eyes were silvery gray and piercing above high, strong cheekbones that were tanned a ruddy brown. She found him so immediately and compellingly appealing that she experienced a melting, sinking sensation as the elevator began to rise. He seemed to fill the cubicle with his presence, and although they were alone in the car she felt crowded, almost stifled.

She had never felt so uncomfortable alone with a man before, which she told herself was ridiculous. She worked with men every day, and some of them were very attractive. But this one was different, or at least his effect on her was. Her heart was beating as if she had just had the fright of her life. She wasn't exactly afraid of *him*; it was her own strong reaction to him that bothered her.

"A beautiful autumn morning, isn't it?" he said. His deep voice was smooth and urbane, belying his rough apparel of plaid shirt, quilted vest, well-worn jeans and hiking boots. He looked more like a lumberjack than a city slicker, and Keely wondered what he was doing here at Citation headquarters. No trees needed cutting down that she was aware of.

Even though she had walked from her apartment to work, she had been too concerned about her promotion to pay attention to the weather. Back home in Vermont, she had relished the vibrancy of autumn. But here in New York tall gray buildings didn't change to vivid golds and oranges like maple trees. Inside these temperature-regulated buildings, one season was much like the others.

"Yes, it is a lovely day," she replied politely, still avoiding looking at him.

"You're the very image of it," he commented. "Does the shade of your hair change with the seasons, or is that beautiful color natural?"

Already on guard, she was quick to take offense at such a personal question. "I don't believe that's any of your business." The artificial primness of her voice rang false in her own ears.

But he didn't seem to mind. He laughed softly. "You're a true redhead, all right. Impatient to close the elevator doors on me. Irritated by a well-meant compliment. I have a penchant for pretty, fiery redheads."

No, he certainly was not a lumberjack, Keely thought. Lumberjacks did not use the word *penchant* with a French pronunciation. She began to resent the pretense of his rough costume. She liked to know exactly who she was dealing with at all times, and this man confused her. "Perhaps all redheads don't have the same inclination for you," she pointed out stiffly.

He laughed again. It seemed every comment she made amused him immensely. "If I could manage to be free tonight, perhaps I could take you out," he said with easy assurance.

She thought his proposal extremely egotistical. If *he* happened to be free! Well, what about her? Didn't it occur to him that she might have other commitments? And she certainly hadn't given him cause to assume she was interested in him. Only a completely self-centered man could interpret her barely civil tone as encouragement. Surely he couldn't hear the wild beating of her heart. She spoke over it.

"I don't go out with strange men who try to pick me up in elevators. This isn't a dating bar, mister."

That should put an end to it, she thought, at the same time wondering why she wanted to put an end to it. As much as this stranger irritated her, he attracted her. That was precisely the reason he irritated her so much. She didn't like the way her body responded to his nearness without her will's permission. The last time it had responded this way she had been eighteen and had fallen head over heels in love. It had changed all her plans for the future. She had promised herself never to be so stupid again.

Apparently her abrupt refusal did put an end to his interest. They continued their journey upward in silence. As each floor number flashed above the doors, the urge to resume their conversation in a friendlier tone flashed in Keely's mind. What would be the harm of going out with a man she found so physically appealing? She imagined how it would feel to have the strong, long arm that had practically crashed through the elevator doors around her shoulders. She pictured his high-boned face dipping to hers until their lips met. She had never kissed a man with a beard before. What would that be like? she wondered.

But except for a brief clearing of her throat, she could not bring herself to break the silence between them. Relief and regret clashed within her when the car stopped on the tenth floor and she stepped out. But as she marched down the long corridor to her office without looking back, a shiver of excitement ran up her spine. She sensed that the bearded stranger was following her.

She hadn't experienced such a flurry of agitation since Royal LaRoux had followed her home from high school. The memory of him made her quicken her step now. She hurried through the reception area, not daring to glance over her shoulder until she reached the haven of her secretary's office. When she did, the big blond man in the plaid flannel shirt was nowhere to be seen.

"Has something gone wrong, Keely?" Edith asked, looking up from her typewriter.

"Of course not," Keely answered more abruptly than she had intended. There was no need to snap at Edith simply because a strange man had disappeared out of her life. "Maybe I feel a little pressed about the staff meeting," she amended.

"I'll make sure there's a fresh pot of coffee in the conference room," Edith volunteered.

Keely waved away that suggestion. "That's not part of your job description, Edith. We can all get our own coffee." When she had been a secretary at Citation, she had often wished someone in authority had realized that.

But Edith was from the old school and believed that it was as right and proper for secretaries to provide coffee as it was for ladies to pour tea. Since she was both, she stood up with a determined set to her face. "It's really no trouble," she insisted, and Keely was wise enough not to object. "Your telephone messages are right there on my desk," Edith added before leaving.

Keely flopped into her secretary's chair and shuffled through them. Absolutely nothing that couldn't wait until the afternoon, she decided. Then she read the last message. MR. WELL-FLEET REQUESTS THAT YOU HAVE LUNCH WITH HIM TODAY, Edith had printed in bold caps. Keely's chest tightened. The last thing she needed on her first day as department director was a luncheon meeting with the president. She was tense enough as it was. Thinking herself alone, she let go a very unladylike expletive.

A booming laugh rang through Edith's office. Keely's eyes darted to the doorway to discover a paragon of bearded blond maleness standing just inside it. "Is that proper language for a corporate secretary to use?" he asked.

"You again!" She was so shocked to see him that she didn't correct his misconception. Her heart jumped for joy. Or maybe it was fear. As she watched him move toward her, the image of a lion stalking his prey sprang to her mind. They were completely alone. "You have some nerve following me," she said defensively.

He paused a few feet from the desk and ran his hand through his golden mane. "Lady, that's the last thing I'd do after getting your negative message loud and clear in the elevator. The receptionist directed me here. This is the corporate communications department, isn't it?"

Keely nodded, still wary. She couldn't imagine what kind of business he could possibly have in her department. "What do you want here?" she asked abruptly.

A wide smile split his beard. "Tell me, did you have to go to charm school to get your job?"

"Look, mister, you may have time to joke around, but I'm very busy."

He sighed. "No, I guess you didn't. Because you would have flunked out for sure. Are you so curt with everyone, or is it just me you find so objectionable?"

The truth was, she did find him objectionable, despite his good looks. She didn't like the way he was dressed or the way his hair was in need of a good trim. She didn't like his self-assurance, his familiar manner or the way he seemed to be laughing at her. He didn't fit in here at Citation, and this rubbed her the wrong way. She had no trouble handling men like Peter Plack, but this one was a different sort entirely. Her sixth sense told her that he was trouble indeed.

"Do you have an appointment with someone?" she asked coolly, ignoring his last remark.

"I'd like to see Clay Johnson. He's been expecting me."

"Oh, has he?" Keely raised a dubious eyebrow. "Well, I guess Mr. Johnson got tired of waiting for you to show up, because he retired last week."

Impatience now flickered in the stranger's light gray eyes. As nonchalant as he appeared to be in dress and behavior, he also radiated a tense energy that Keely had picked up on and found stimulating the moment he had stepped into the elevator. "You know, I'm rather busy myself this morning," he said, irritation giving a cutting edge to his soft, cultured voice. "And I don't appreciate getting the runaround from some flippant secretary. I'd like to see the man who replaced Johnson immediately."

"But a man hasn't replaced him," Keely responded, mentally laughing up the sleeve of her blue blazer. The stranger's demanding, chauvinistic attitude had put the devil into her, and she refused to say more than that.

"How typical of corporations. Slow as molasses," he pronounced with disgust. "Now who in hell am I going to deal with here?"

She found pleasure in annoying him. "The fact is that a new director has been named." She smiled sweetly. "But not a man."

He exhaled with exasperation. "My second guess, then, is that a woman has. Would it be asking too much for you to tell me *her* name?" He folded his arms across his broad chest.

"Not at all. I know it as well as my own. Keely LaRoux."

"You're kidding." Amusement replaced the irritation in his face, and his light eyes sparkled with mirth. "She sounds more like a stripteaser than a corporate executive. But just my luck she's some tough old battle-ax with a mustache."

The fun suddenly went out of the game for Keely. "I happen to be the new director," she stated flatly.

He took in this information without blinking and studied her with his keen, crystal-clear gaze. His eyes were remarkably penetrating, and for one crazy moment Keely wondered if he had X-ray vision and could see through her clothing.

"Well, at least you don't have a mustache," he pronounced. "As a matter of fact, you really could have a brilliant career as a stripteaser, Ms. LaRoux. Maybe you missed your calling."

She refused to let herself blush and fingered a gold button on her jacket. "I'm perfectly happy with my present occupation, thank you. Now, what can I do for you?"

His lips stretched into a grin, and he displayed very white, even teeth. "The question is, what can we do for each other? A lot, I'm sure."

She had expected a little more deference now that he knew she was head of the department, and she didn't appreciate his insinuating attitude. "The only thing you can do for me right now is simply tell me your name and why you're here. You're not as charming as you think you are, you know."

He laughed. "As if *you* could judge, Madame Executive! Okay, let's get down to business. I'm Charles Dickens."

She snorted. "Sure you are. And I'm Jane Austen."

His smile faded. Apparently he didn't like jokes about his name. "Chuck Dickens," he enunciated slowly, as if Keely were deaf or very stupid. "I should think someone in your position would be familiar with my work."

Oh, *Chuck* Dickens, Keely thought. She sat up straighter and raised her chin. She knew who he was, all right. He was one of the most sought-after commercial photographers in New York. His specialty was annual report photography—product pictures of tremendous visual impact that grabbed the attention of investors and shareholders. He certainly was living up to his reputation for arrogance, she noted. Corporate people referred to him as the Pirate because he charged outlandish fees.

"Of course I'm familiar with your work," she said quickly, trying to cover up her embarrassment at not immediately recognizing his name. "I'm just surprised that the great Chuck Dickens has to solicit clients like a door-to-door salesman. If you're looking for work at Citation, why don't you have your agent contact me?" There, she thought, that should put him in his place.

He seemed to consider his place the edge of Edith's desk, where he sat down without further ceremony and leaned toward Keely. He leaned so close that she could feel the heat of his breath on her face when he spoke.

"My dear, charmless Ms. LaRoux," he said softly. "Whether you have the savvy to appreciate it or not, you should be grateful I'm here. I don't solicit work. Clients seek *me* out. Your predecessor, Clay Johnson, knew that much at least. He told me I could write my own ticket if I agreed to shoot Citation's next annual report. I finally agreed."

Johnson had never mentioned that to Keely. Of course he was getting terribly absentminded during the last months before he retired, and Keely had had to bail him out of hot water a number of times. She had gotten used to covering up his mistakes and was beginning to sense that this was yet another one.

"Exactly how large a ticket did you write for yourself, Mr. Dickens?" she asked, her green eyes sharp and distrustful.

"Three thousand a day plus expenses," he tossed out casually.

She had to laugh. Poor, sweet Clay Johnson had really botched things up with this one. That fee was more than triple what the budget allowed, and Keely knew what a stickler Mr. Wellfleet was when it came to budgets. Keely rolled Edith's chair back, away from Dickens's heady nearness. She tried to keep her expression unconcerned.

"Tell me, did you and Mr. Johnson sign a contract?"

Dickens stroked his thick beard impatiently. "Of course not. We had a *gentlemen's* agreement."

Relief eased through Keely. She could extricate her department from this dilemma after all, rather than infuriate the president.

"Well, since I'm not a gentleman, I guess I don't have to uphold the agreement," she told Dickens. "I'm sorry, but that fee is way out of line at the present time. I don't know what Mr. Johnson was thinking of, but there's no way Citation can afford your services, Mr. Dickens." She considered her reply firm but polite enough under the circumstances.

He didn't, though. He stood up abruptly, and the muscle in one taut cheek began to twitch, as if she had slapped him. Other than that, his expression remained impassive. To Keely, though, his anger was almost palpable, and she steeled herself, her insides tightening.

When he finally spoke, however, his voice was almost gentle. "I think you have a lot to learn in your new position, Ms. LaRoux."

Maybe he could have said something more insulting, but because of her own deep apprehensions about her new job, that comment cut her to the quick. "Good day, Mr. Dickens. So sorry we can't do business together and your time here was wasted," she replied in a chirpy, insincere voice.

He shrugged his wide shoulders. "No need to apologize. It was time well spent. After all, I got to meet you, Keely LaRoux. And believe me, it was an experience I never intend to repeat. I wouldn't work on a Citation project you were directing if my livelihood depended on it. Which, luckily, it does not. One of these days you're going to get thrown off that high horse of yours and land smack dab on your cute little—"

"I said goodbye, Mr. Dickens," Keely interrupted, her voice at a much higher pitch than usual.

He shook his leonine head regretfully. "Funny, I never thought I'd meet a redhead I didn't like." Evidently satisfied with this exit line, he walked out the door.

The way her day had started, Keely fully expected her staff of ten to mutiny during the meeting she had called. But when she walked into the conference room her co-workers smiled and congratulated her on her promotion. Their warm support comforted her, and she did not let Peter Plack's cold silence dampen her spirits. At least he had acknowledged her authority by attending.

But when she returned to her office she felt suddenly drained of energy, although it wasn't even noon yet and she still had a luncheon meeting with the president ahead of her. Nagging doubts that she could handle her new position began to gnaw at her. That infuriating Chuck Dickens had made it clear that he didn't think she could. But who was he to judge her? She wasn't usually so curt to people she dealt with in business. But somehow he had made their brief encounter too personal, and she had reacted against the pull he'd had on her emotions. He'd broken through her cool veneer of professionalism, and she didn't like that one bit.

The cold fingers of self-doubt began to squeeze against Keely's temples. Had she dismissed Dickens from the annual report project too abruptly, simply because she was so physically attracted to him? Nonsense, she told herself. She had acted decisively, not reacted emotionally. Clay Johnson had made a grave error in judgment by recruiting such a high-priced photographer, and she had nipped his mistake in the bud. Why lead Dickens on when there was no chance Wellfleet would ever approve such an expenditure?

Part of Keely's success at Citation had to do with her ability to second-guess the president. Not that she knew him that well personally. Johnson had always handled face-to-face meetings with the top man, but Keely had been the one to follow through on his directives. Apparently she had done a good job of it because she had been promoted. Still, she was nervous about meeting with Wellfleet. For a moment she wished Johnson were still director and she were secure in her less visible position as a manager. But that was only for a moment.

Keely glanced at her watch and saw that it was time to face the big cheese. She quickly passed a comb through her short coppery hair and powdered her lightly freckled nose. Had her nose been this shiny during Chuck Dickens's scrutiny of her? She mentally kicked herself for even wondering. What did she care? Their paths would never cross again, thank heaven. She stood up, smoothed down her simple navy skirt as if smoothing down the feathers Dickens had ruffled and, shoulders back, marched out of her office to meet with the president.

Chapter Two

Armstrong Wellfleet was on a diet, which meant that anyone lucky enough to share lunch with him was on a diet, too.

"Please, help yourself, Keely," he said, waving his pudgy hand over a silver platter of crudités.

She chose a carrot stick and chomped on it earnestly, hoping the crunch would cover up the cacophony emanating from her stomach. Keely's stomach always growled furiously when she was nervous.

The president of Citation was a short, burly man in his mid-fifties. His frowns made employees quake. His rare smiles could make their day. He was smiling now. "How do you feel about your promotion?" he asked Keely.

"I'm looking forward to taking on all the challenges of the position," she answered correctly.

"You're the first woman I've ever advanced to director, you know. But I'm the kind of man who keeps up with the times. And there's no law saying a female can't be a vice president here one day. How does that sound to you, Keely?"

"Music to my ears, sir." She immediately feared that her reply had been too glib.

But he chortled. "I like young people with ambition. And you've got plenty of that, it seems. Didn't you manage to attend college at night while you had a full-time job here?"

"Yes, I graduated with honors and have a degree in public relations." Keely assumed he already knew this, but it never hurt to reiterate one's accomplishments and qualifications, she had learned.

"Excellent," he pronounced, passing her a small cut-glass bowl of cottage cheese.

Keely helped herself to a spoonful of it, feeling much more at ease. The president was a most agreeable man, she decided, discounting his reputation as a quick-tempered martinet.

"Citation is a company in the process of change, Keely," he went on. "And it needs up-and-comers like you. Clay Johnson's retirement was way overdue. By the way, get rid of that secretary of his and hire someone young and eager."

"You don't mean Edith Hamilton?" Keely's wide eyes registered both surprise and dismay.

"Yes, that's her name. Out with the old and in with the new."

"But Mrs. Hamilton and I work very well together," Keely protested. "And I find her years of experience with this company invaluable."

"But can she accept new ideas, Keely? Or is she stuck in her ways like Johnson was? No, better to put her out to pasture and get someone new to assist you."

His callous attitude about such a diligent, long-term employee shocked Keely. The last thing she wanted to do was oppose Wellfleet when she was so obviously in his good graces, but she wasn't about to sacrifice Edith Hamilton, either.

"I want her to remain as my secretary, sir," she said firmly.

Wellfleet's thick, bushy eyebrows melded together, and although Keely was intimidated by his harsh glower, she did not allow her gaze to waver under it. If she couldn't make decisions about her own staff, then her title of director would be hollow and meaningless.

"Very well, Keely." His voice had lost all traces of warmth. "I have more important concerns than your choice of a secretary." He patted his mouth with a damask napkin and threw it down. "Let's get on to other business. Namely, the annual report. Producing that publication will be the most important project on your agenda for the next few months."

This was no surprise, and Keely extracted a little notebook from the pocket of her blazer. "I've put some thought into it already," she told him. "And I've jotted down a few ideas I'd like to share with you."

But Wellfleet wasn't interested in sharing ideas, only expounding his own. He raised his hand to silence her and began his speech, no doubt practicing for a stockholder's meeting.

"My chief duty as president of this company is to guide it into the future, Keely. My goal is to develop new product lines utilizing the latest computer technology. And that's the image I want to promote in our upcoming annual report. I want stockbrokers and financial analysts to view Citation as a state-of-the-art company. And how can you help me accomplish that, Keely?"

His question had placed her on the hot seat, and Keely shifted uneasily. She didn't want to be subjected to that glower of his again if she came up with the wrong answer. "What you would like from me is a state-of-the-art annual report," she replied. "A publication that reflects Citation's new high-tech image."

"Bingo!" Wellfleet thumped his pudgy hand on the table, rattling the ice cubes in the Waterford glasses. "And that means exciting graphics and photography. Have you heard of Chuck Dickens?" Keely nodded as a sense of dread enveloped her. "Well, the one thing Johnson managed to do before he retired was get this Dickens to agree to shoot the product pictures for the report. But I'm sure Johnson mentioned that to you before he left."

This time Keely shook her head. There was a sharp ache at the base of her neck, as if she had somehow wrenched it.

"Don't look so tragic, Keely. You can't be expected to know something old Johnson was too absentminded to tell you. But

I'd think you'd be a little more excited about this. Dickens is one of the hottest commercial photographers in New York.''

"He's very expensive, Mr. Wellfleet," Keely pointed out, her voice strained. "There's no way we can afford him on our budget."

"I've decided to increase the budget. This annual report is an extremely important part of my marketing plan. Sure, he's overpriced. He's got the reputation of being a pirate and a real pain in the butt to deal with. But, dammit, if a company wants to change its image, Dickens has the visual perception to put across that message."

"Surely there are other photographers who are easier to work with and just as good." Keely knew she was grasping at straws.

"I want Dickens, and that's final!" With that Armstrong Wellfleet stood up and gave Keely an almost forgiving smile. "You can have any secretary you want, Keely, just so long as you make sure this project is successful. So get in touch with Dickens immediately. I expect you to travel to all the company facilities with him and keep him in line. He'll be taking pictures of some top-secret products, and you know how sensitive that can be. Don't let me down."

Keely stood up, too, and smoothed down her neat navy skirt again. This gesture enabled her to wipe the sweat off her palm before shaking the hand Wellfleet offered her. In that instant she decided she would not tell him that she had already dismissed Dickens. Not quite yet, anyway. Not until she did everything in her power to get him back again.

"Yes, Ms. LaRoux," the bored female voice replied over the telephone. "Mr. Dickens has gotten *all* your messages this afternoon. I'm just the receptionist here. I can't make him return your calls if he doesn't want to. Besides, nobody tells Chuck what to do."

Keely could certainly think of something she'd like to tell Chuck Dickens to do. "If he won't talk to me on the phone, maybe he'll see me in person. I'm coming to his studio."

"Schlepp down here if you want, ma'am," the weary Brooklynese voice replied. "But it won't do you much good. Chuck's off on a shoot right now."

"Where?" Keely demanded. "I'll take a cab there immediately."

"That cab better have wings, lady. He's up in a helicopter taking aerial shots. Listen, next time he checks in, I'll give him your message *again*. Okay?"

Keely hung up the phone and tried to concentrate on other matters. But the image of Chuck Dickens's high-boned, golden-bearded face kept searing her mind. Attractive as it was, it was a face she disliked intensely at this moment.

Edith came into her office with a cup of coffee. "Heard from that photographer yet?" she inquired with concern. Keely had confided her dilemma to Edith, knowing she'd be supportive.

"No, he's up in a helicopter somewhere." She took a gulp of coffee. "I hope it crashes. Wellfleet can't expect me to produce a photographer who no longer exists, can he?"

"Keely LaRoux, bite your tongue," Edith admonished.

"Sorry, that was a nasty thing to say." She pressed her fingertips to her temples. "But my nerves are on edge, waiting to hear from the man."

"Calm down, dear," Edith advised gently. "Whether he agrees to work for you or doesn't, the sun will still rise tomorrow."

"And I may be awakening to it jobless. Wellfleet won't be exactly overjoyed with me if he finds out I practically told Dickens to go to hell. He's not too pleased with me as it is since I dared disagree with him at lunch."

"You did?" Edith asked in a surprised tone. "About what?"

"Oh, it's not important now." She wasn't about to tell her secretary that the president had wanted Keely to replace her.

A deep sigh escaped her. "Why, oh, why did I let that Dickens character get to me? Why did I act so high-handed with him?" They were questions Keely had asked herself a thousand times during the past few hours.

Edith smiled encouragement. "What's done is done. You can be very persuasive, Keely, and when Mr. Dickens calls, I'm sure you'll be able to convince him to accept the assignment again."

"*If* he has the decency to return my calls." The phone rang, and the two women stared at each other. "Wish me luck, Edith," Keely said, picking up the receiver. Edith waved her crossed fingers before leaving the office.

"Ms. LaRoux speaking," she answered coolly, although her heart was thumping madly.

"Hi, Mom" came the reply.

Keely never would have thought it possible, but she was more disappointed than happy to hear her daughter's voice. "Joy, are you calling from school? Is something the matter?"

"Mom, it's after five. I've been at Mrs. Alphonso's for HOURS." Going on twelve, Joy had gotten into the habit of speaking in capital letters. "She's teaching me how to knit a sweater, since you refuse to buy me the one I REALLY want at Bloomingdale's."

"Sweetie, that sweater was over a hundred dollars. I can't afford to spend that much money on something you're going to outgrow or tire of in a few months." It had been their bone of contention for weeks.

"All the OTHER girls at school can afford them."

Keely sent her daughter to an expensive private girls' school on the East Side. It was close to their apartment, and Keely wanted Joy protected and well cared for while she was working. The tuition took a big bite out of her salary, and one of the chief reasons she'd wanted this promotion so badly was to be able to give Joy more. But *not* faddish hundred-dollar sweaters.

"Well, tell your friends that handmade sweaters are much more chic, Joy."

She could imagine Joy rolling her eyes over that statement. She remembered her own mother telling her that the girls at school wouldn't know she was wearing charity clothes. They had, of course, since some of them had donated those very same unwanted clothes to the church. And they had thought it very clever to call her Secondhand Red instead of Secondhand

Rose. This memory made her decide to surprise Joy with the sweater she wanted after all. She didn't want her daughter to feel as humiliated as she once had.

"When are you coming home, Mom?"

"Not late, I hope. But I have to talk to someone before I leave. I'm sure he'll be returning my call soon." Yes, always be optimistic, Keely thought.

Joy sighed deeply. "You're going to be late again, I bet. Well, I'd better go back to my knitting. I dropped a stitch, and Mrs. Alphonso is hunting all over her apartment for it."

Keely laughed. "I love you, sweetie."

"See you when I see you, Mom. Bye."

Lately Joy had stopped telling her mother that she loved her, too. She had become reticent and distant, and Keely hoped it was only a phase she was going through. It seemed that now, more than ever, Joy resented the time Keely spent at work. If only her daughter could understand how much Keely yearned to be with her right now, teaching her how to knit, instead of stuck behind her desk, waiting to hear from some egotistical photographer.

She buzzed the outer office and told Edith to go home. There was no need for her to wait around, too. Edith's husband had suffered a heart attack a few months ago, and Keely knew she was concerned about him.

Well, she was concerned about her daughter, too, she reminded herself. Although Joy was under the excellent supervision of the widow who lived across the hall, it wasn't the same as being with her own mother. Keely began throwing papers into her attaché case. It was obvious that Dickens would never return her calls, and she'd decided to go home, too. But before she snapped off her office light she felt compelled to try to reach him one more time. She dialed his studio number, which was by now engraved in her mind.

"Oh, it's you again," the bored telephone voice responded to her greeting. "Lucky me. I was just about to leave work."

Keely ignored the sarcasm. "Could you please give me Mr. Dickens's home telephone number? I'll try reaching him tonight."

"No way, lady. Strict orders from the boss. It's unlisted."

Keely felt like screaming in frustration. "Please! It's very important that I clear up a misunderstanding we had. Can't you find it in your heart to help me out?" Her tone was pleading. Pride had its place, but not when she was dealing with a recalcitrant receptionist.

"You mean this isn't business? It's personal?" Interest made the flat voice rise a few notes, and Keely was quick to pick that up.

"At this moment Chuck happens to be the most important person in my life. It may be curtains for me if I don't see him soon." Well, that wasn't exactly a lie, Keely told herself, ignoring a stab of guilt as she threw in a little sob.

"Hey, honey, take it easy." The voice was now sympathetic. "Don't do anything rash. Chuck doesn't need any more problems with women right now. Listen, why don't you go down to Lawley's Bar and straighten things out with him before you do something drastic. His heart's in the right place, even though it's never in the same place very long, if you get my drift."

Keely certainly did and was thankful she wasn't one of Dickens's "women," as the receptionist assumed she was. What did he have, a harem? "Lawley's Bar?" she repeated.

"Yeah, that's where he usually hangs out after a shoot. He may be crying in his beer over you right now, honey." The once-bored voice now oozed with pity, as if this was highly unlikely.

Keely thanked her for the advice, slammed down the receiver, rushed out of the office and raced down ten flights of stairs rather than wait for an elevator. It seemed everybody on the block was trying to hail a cab. Keely put two fingers into her mouth and produced a sharp, shrill whistle. A taxi stopped right in front of her.

"Ten dollars says you can't make it to Lawley's Bar in five minutes," she told the driver. During her years in New York she had discovered that such challenges worked better than simply offering a tip. People in the city seemed to thrive on challenges. And Keely LaRoux was one of them.

A few heads turned when she walked into Lawley's. It was one of those pretentious East Side establishments that did its best to imitate an English pub, Keely realized as her eyes skimmed the crowd of artistic-looking people carrying on intense conversations over imported beers. She spotted Chuck Dickens right away. Although he was standing at the back of the room, surrounded by others, he wasn't an easy man to miss. He was taller than most, and more impressive. The black turtleneck and snug jeans he wore made it obvious that there wasn't an extra ounce of flesh on his big-boned, majestic frame. A small but very definite quiver ran through Keely, and she hesitated before approaching him. She forced herself forward before she lost her nerve completely.

"Mr. Dickens," she called as she strode across the room. "May I talk to you a minute?"

She saw a few shocked faces turn toward her and then noticed that Chuck Dickens's long arm was poised in midair. At the instant she called he had released a dart. It now sailed across the room, missed its mark completely and stuck into the wall high above the dart board. Blushing over her blunder, she watched him shrug, take some money from his wallet and hand it to a man who was laughing his head off. Then he turned and began walking toward her. *Stalking* toward her, Keely thought, the image of a dangerous, golden-maned lion again springing to her mind.

"Did I throw off your concentration?" she asked in a much softer voice.

He smiled wryly, displaying his even, white teeth. "Of course not. I *wanted* to hit the wall instead of the bull's-eye. That's much more fun than winning a bet."

"It's my fault you lost it," Keely admitted. "How much was the bet? I'll repay you."

He shook his head. "That wouldn't be fair. There's no guarantee that I would have hit the bull's-eye even if you hadn't blared my name across the room like a foghorn."

"I insist," she said curtly, irritated by his description of her voice, which did tend to be a little low and husky. "Just tell me how much you bet. I'll give you the benefit of the doubt." She opened her small leather shoulder bag to show she meant business. She wanted to nullify this unfortunate incident and not be in his debt when she broached the subject of the Citation project. The last thing she wanted was for him to have the advantage of being chivalrous.

And that's the last thing she got. "Okay," he agreed easily. "The bet was two hundred."

"Two hundred *dollars*?" Keely's green eyes widened. "You bet that much on some stupid dart toss?" She reconsidered her offer. After all, he really *could* have missed. But no, a deal was a deal. She had made it in good faith. "I'll have to give you a check," she said through clenched teeth, taking out her checkbook.

"No problem, Ms. LaRoux. I know where to find you if it bounces." Gallantry did not seem to be part of his makeup. He motioned to an empty table in the corner. "You can sit down here to write it out."

She did, and he sat across from her. She could sense him staring at her as she scrawled out the check, pressing down so hard with her pen that she almost broke the tip off. She didn't enjoy throwing away hard-earned money, especially when the recipient was as highly paid as Chuck Dickens. It crossed her mind that she could have bought her daughter two Bloomingdale's sweaters for the amount his idiotic bet was costing her. She ripped out the check with vehemence and handed it to him.

"Here. Take it!"

He gazed at it for a moment and then gave her a studied look. Then he ripped it up into little pieces and placed them in the ashtray. "I never accept payment for something I haven't actually done," he said. "That's how I run my business and my life."

With that he waved his hand, and a pretty waitress appeared almost immediately. He ordered two dark beers, and although Keely would have preferred a club soda, she thought it best not to object. Under the circumstances, she was grateful that he was willing to tolerate her presence for a while.

She cleared her throat. "I'm sorry about that misunderstanding we had this morning, Mr. Dickens," she began.

"But I thought we understood each other perfectly, Ms. LaRoux. It was obvious to both of us that working together would be impossible.'' His tone and expression were not un-kind, only emotionless, as if he had just observed that rain was predicted and it didn't make much difference to him.

For some reason she did not care to analyze at the moment, his indifference hurt her deeply. ''Not impossible,'' she coun-tered. ''Difficult, perhaps, but certainly not impossible. And I'm perfectly willing to accept the fact that a talented photog-rapher like you would be worth every minute of difficulty you caused.'' That didn't come out quite right, she thought, biting down on her full bottom lip.

''What's *your* talent, Ms. LaRoux?'' His tone remained im-passive, but there was now a glitter in his sharp gray eyes.

''I beg your pardon?''

''You just expressed that you would be willing to put up with me because of the work I'd produce. But why on earth should I put up with you? Like I said, what talent do you have to of-fer me in return?'' A slow smile now eased across his lips.

His insinuation was not lost on her, and she was almost tempted to smile back and tell him he could discover her hid-den talents while they were traveling together. After all, her job was at stake. Why not use whatever sex appeal she had to con-vince him to take on the project?

For the first time in her career, the very idea of doing just that excited her. He had already made it clear that redheads appealed to him. And he certainly appealed to her physically, despite their clash in personalities.

But she didn't smile back. In fact, she frowned.

''Let me level with you, Mr. Dickens. I wouldn't be here if I didn't have to be. But I found out that the president of Cita-tion wants you, and only you, to be the annual report photog-rapher. I didn't tell him that I had dismissed you this morning. I was hoping to convince you to accept the project again be-fore I admitted my mistake to him.''

He tilted back his chair to lean against the wall. ''So con-vince me.'' His profile, Keely noted, was strong and stubborn.

''It'll be up to you to change Citation's image. Which means you'll have complete artistic freedom. We want this to be the most imaginative, dramatic report ever published. Everybody in the business will be talking about it, which will add to your reputation. Don't turn down such a creative opportunity just to spite me for our little run-in earlier today."

"I react on the basis of a lot of emotions, Ms. LaRoux, but never spite," he said evenly. He stared up at the ceiling. "Frankly, the idea of doing something unique appeals to me. Corporate photography is hellishly boring most of the time, but it pays the rent. Can you promise I won't have any jackass executives breathing down my neck during the shoots?"

"I'll make sure of that, since I'll be accompanying you to all the company divisions."

He gave her a sidelong glance, and it occurred to her that she could be one of the jackass executives he had in mind. He stroked his thick golden beard and seemed to think for a moment. "For four thousand a day, I'd consider it."

So he really was a pirate. Keely could actually picture him with a patch over one eye, a gold hoop in one ear, a sword thrust into his belt, his broad chest bare and muscular and . . . She blinked away the image. "That's not fair, Dickens," she objected. "You agreed to three thousand with Johnson."

"But that agreement's history, lady. You made it null and void by ordering me off the project, didn't you? We're renegotiating now."

"Sorry." Keely held firm. "I'm not going to let you rob the company that's employed me for ten years just to make up for my own mistake in judgment. I'd rather face the music and admit my mistake to Wellfleet." She knew, though, that she would have to offer Dickens something more to mollify him for the injury she had caused his professional pride. "What I can do is give you a credit line on the inside back cover of the book." That wasn't usually done in corporate publications.

"Three credit lines. My name, and the address and phone number of my studio," he countered. "On the inside front cover."

She nodded. "You've got it."

He swung his weight forward to get the chair back on four legs and faced her over the table. "It's a deal then. I look forward to working with you, Ms. LaRoux."

She sat back, surprised. It had all been too easy. "What made you change your mind? Before you stormed out of Citation this morning, you made it clear that you didn't think much of me as a director."

"You're right. I didn't," he readily agreed. "But it seems you have a few qualities I like in a business associate. Tracking me down to Lawley's showed a lot of determination. And when you handed over that check, you proved that you didn't back out of a deal. I like people who take responsibility for their errors in judgment. And you really did level with me. I appreciate that. Plus, you were too honest to let me rob the company, even if it meant saving your own skin. Those are traits I admire."

His remarks made her readjust her first impression of him, too. Maybe he wasn't such an egotistical womanizer after all. Maybe they could work well together without sex getting in the way of things. She gave him a friendly smile. "I look forward to working with you, too, Mr. Dickens."

"Why don't you call me Chuck? We really should be a little less formal, since we're going to be traveling together so much." He covered the hand she had placed on the table with his, and the warmth of his touch coursed through her. "And eventually sleeping together, too."

"What?" She snatched her hand from under the tent of his. "Listen, Dickens, that's not part of the deal."

He looked offended. "Why, of course not. I'd hardly expect you to barter your lily-white but no doubt freckled body to get me back on the project. But I knew we were fated to have an affair the moment I stepped into the elevator. So did you." He shrugged, as if it was all so obvious and simple. "Let's not be coy about it, Keely. We're both adults."

A sharp, nervous laugh escaped her throat. "Don't be absurd. I have absolutely no intention of having an affair with you, Mr. Dickens. Let's get that straight from the very beginning. My secretary will be in touch with you about setting up a travel schedule. Good night." She stood up abruptly and almost bumped into the pretty waitress who was bringing them two beers.

Chuck let out a weary sigh. "I assumed you were the type of woman who would appreciate a direct, honest approach, but I guess I was wrong."

"You got that right, at least. You were way off base." She dug into her purse and threw some money onto the table. "That's for my beer." She left without touching the brew.

At the door, though, she was compelled to look back to see if Chuck Dickens was watching her. He wasn't. He and the attractive young waitress were deeply involved in what seemed like a very intimate conversation.

Was he constantly on the make? Keely wondered. The answer was obvious, and she was glad to have been forewarned before they started traveling together. Not that she would have been inclined to succumb to his attraction in the first place, she reminded herself as she hurried out of the bar. She walked up the street toward her apartment, only a few blocks away. She felt like breaking into a run. She was very excited. No matter how difficult Chuck Dickens was going to be, the important thing was that he was back on the project. She glanced at her watch under a street lamp. It was getting late, and Joy was waiting for her. Keely did start to run.

Chapter Three

Aren't you hungry, sweetie?'' Keely asked her daughter, watching Joy push her food around her plate as if it were dog chow.

It was Sunday evening, and Keely had spent the better part of the day preparing a huge pot of French cassoulet. She had made enough to feed an army, or at least Joy and her babysitter, Mrs. Alphonso, next week while she was away on business. She would be taking her first trip with Chuck Dickens tomorrow.

"What's this thing?" Joy asked, poking the tong of her fork at it.

"That's a clove, Joy. Not a poison pellet." Keely immediately regretted the impatience in her voice. She wanted this meal with her daughter to be special and pleasant. "I studded one of the onions with cloves to give the stew extra flavor," she explained. "You're not expected to eat it."

"Good. And I won't eat the onions, either." Joy speared a carrot and nibbled on it daintily.

"I'm going to miss you next week, kiddo," Keely told her.

"Then don't go away."

"I have to, Joy. I explained all that to you already. I don't want to, but it's part of my new job."

Pouting, Joy slumped over her plate, and her long red hair just missed dipping into the pile of white beans she had picked out of the stew with fastidious care. Keely bit back a reprimand to sit up straight and eat every one of those beans. She didn't want Joy to remember her as a nag during her absence.

If only her daughter would try to understand why she had to work so hard, Keely thought. Her primary motivation was to insure a good future for Joy. Sometimes, right before dawn, she would wake up in a cold sweat, worrying about what would become of Joy if anything happened to her. It was difficult to save money in the city, to build up a little nest egg.

Keely was managing to save more since her mother had passed away and her brothers were old enough to support themselves. Not that she had regretted one cent she had sent back to Jasper over the years. She had only wished she had been able to send more.

During her first years in New York, with a baby to support, she had almost been able to hear the wolf scratching at the door. Even now, with her promotion and higher salary, she could still hear his pant during those lonely predawn hours. She had learned long ago that nothing in life was secure. She couldn't afford to make mistakes in her new position, as she almost had concerning Chuck Dickens. One little slip on her way up the corporate ladder could be her last. There were too many wolves disguised in three-piece suits, like Peter Plack, biting at her heels.

"Are you thinking about WORK again, Mom?" Joy asked, breaking into Keely's thoughts.

"Sorry, kiddo." She smiled at her daughter. "Why don't you tell me what's happening at school? You never talk much about it lately."

Joy rolled her big green eyes, which were not quite as dark but almost as vivid as her mother's. "Because it's so BORING. Nothing exciting ever happens to me. Life is such a drag."

At that moment Keely thought her daughter the spitting image of Royal LaRoux, despite the fact that her coloring was her mother's. Joy's father had always been so restless, so discontent.

"Life is what you make it," Keely told her. "I was never bored at your age. I was too busy—"

"Milking cows. And shoveling out the barn. And chopping wood," Joy interrupted in a singsong. "I know, Mom. You already told me how hard it was growing up in the Dark Ages."

Keely smiled indulgently. Maybe she did sound like an old crone at times when she talked about her past. "I'm only thirty years old, dear child. They had actually invented electricity before I was born."

She remembered how she had thought her own mother so old when she had been Joy's age. Of course her mother really had been haggard and worn by too much work, too many debts, too many children. She had put her faith in the wrong kind of man. So had Keely, for that matter, but unlike her mother, she had recovered from the disappointment. Keely maintained the belief that her mother's death three years ago had been caused not by heart failure but by heartbreak. Her heart had never mended properly during the long years after her husband's desertion.

"I bet you had more fun as a kid living on a farm than I do," Joy said. "You had all your brothers and all those animals to keep you company."

"At times I couldn't tell them apart," Keely joked. "But you're right, Joy. There were a lot of good times to make up for the bad."

When she'd first been transferred to New York City from Jasper, she had ached with loneliness for her family. But it had been an opportunity she couldn't pass up. There had been no future for her and Joy in Jasper. In New York, it was limitless.

"I wish we still lived in Vermont," Joy said sulkily. "Then I'd be near all my uncles and cousins. And I would have gotten to know Grandma better before she passed away. Here I don't have anybody but Mrs. Alphonso, who isn't even a relative."

She had pushed all the right buttons to turn on Keely's guilt. "You have *me*, sweetie," she responded in a choked voice. "You have a mother who loves you very much and would give you the world if she could."

"A mother who's never around because she's always working," Joy countered.

Keely sighed. The argument had come full circle, and they were right back where they'd started. She cleared the table and carried the plates to the tiny galley kitchen. Although it was a high-rent apartment in a safe, convenient neighborhood, it was way too small for them. Aside from the breadbox-sized galley kitchen, the two bedrooms were like broom closets, and the living room was not much bigger than a walk-in closet. Maybe she and her growing daughter chafed against each other because of their cramped quarters, Keely thought. They should move to a larger place. Which would cost a lot more.

Again she wished that Joy could understand how important her job was to their future happiness and comfort. Head bent, shoulders drooping, she scraped the uneaten food from both their plates. She didn't have much of an appetite, either, after bickering with Joy. Then she felt her daughter's arms around her.

"I'm sorry I acted like such a spoiled brat, Mom. I know you have to go on this business trip. It's just that I'm going to miss you a whole bunch, kiddo."

"Me, too, kiddo." Keely turned and hugged her daughter tight. "And I'll make it up to you, Joy. Maybe we can go back to Jasper for a vacation next summer. Now that I'm a director, I get three whole weeks off. Would you like to spend them there?"

Joy hesitated. "Europe would be nice, too."

Keely let out an exasperated laugh and tossed a dish towel to her daughter. "You *are* a spoiled brat! Now, help me with these dishes, Miss Fancy Pants. Europe, indeed!"

"My best friend at school is going there with her family next summer, and all she's going to do is BRAG about it when she comes back."

"Fine. And you can brag about how you learned to milk a cow."

They laughed together over the running water filling the sink.

A taxi took Keely to LaGuardia Airport the next morning, and she made sure to get a receipt for her expense account records. There was a definite spring to her step as she hurried down the long corridor to her plane. A sense of excitement coursed through her. This was her first business trip as a Citation executive.

She was determined to make a good impression with the management people she would be meeting at company divisions, so she was wearing her navy Brooks Brothers suit again. It had practically become her uniform, which justified its cost in her mind. One of the expenses Keely most regretted was her business wardrobe, but she knew how important it was to look right in the corporate world. Her freshly washed, slightly wavy hair bounced around her ears. Another necessary expense was the Fifth Avenue salon she patronized to get it styled. But the cut of her hair was just as important as the cut of her suit.

The men at Citation were equally concerned about their haircuts. Quite a difference from her four brothers, who had gathered in the kitchen once a month or so to let Keely shear them with a rusty pair of blunt-edged scissors. Back in those days she had worn her copper hair in a thick braid down her back. One of her chief pleasures had been brushing it at night. The wealth and gleam of it had made her feel rich. But a long, lush crop of wavy red tresses did not suit the business world. She wanted to be taken seriously.

When she reached the departure area her eyes skidded over the people waiting to board the plane. With a twinge of disappointment she immediately discerned that Chuck Dickens wasn't one of them. She hadn't spoken to Dickens since their meeting at Lawley's Bar the week before. There had been no need to; Edith had made all the travel arrangements with him.

She glanced at her watch. She was early, as usual. She perched on the edge of one of the plastic seats, nervous as a teenager fully expecting to be stood up on her first date. Which was ludicrous, she told herself. Dickens hadn't gotten to be such a sought-after photographer by being unreliable. Whatever misgivings Keely had about the man, she somehow sensed that he had integrity. In business, at least. His personal life was another matter—one that didn't concern her, she reminded herself.

One of Keely's cardinal rules of behavior was never to get romantically involved with a business associate. She had seen other women try to use sex to get ahead, and they hadn't lasted long in the corporate scheme of things. Of course, Chuck Dickens wasn't part of the corporate structure. He was a completely independent agent. Which made Keely even more wary. She didn't understand a man like Dickens. Actually, she didn't even like him much. So why was her chest tight with the expectation of seeing him again?

And then she did see him, and her chest got even tighter as he sauntered toward her. From anger, she decided. If she wanted to make a good impression with division managers, having Dickens along wouldn't help. At least he could have taken the trouble to get a decent haircut, she thought as she observed how his shaggy mane brushed the collar of his very wrinkled bush jacket. A bush jacket, no less! His khaki chinos were wrinkled, too. A beat-up canvas camera bag was slung over one of his broad shoulders.

"Greetings, Ms. LaRoux," he called, flashing his big white smile. "Why the frown? I haven't had a chance to make you angry with me yet."

She gave him a cool once-over. "Perhaps you misunderstood where this assignment was taking you, Mr. Dickens. We're traveling to a plant in Duane, South Carolina, not going on an expedition to the Amazon."

He let go his booming, carefree laugh. "Actually, I did wear this jacket to the Amazon once. These are my working clothes, lady. Just like that stuffy suit you're hiding your lovely curves in is yours. But you don't hear me criticizing your outfit, do you?"

"I think I just did," Keely replied dryly. "Listen, Mr. Dickens, I don't mean to be picky, but these plant managers are very conservative. They expect corporate representatives to look the part. I hope you packed a jacket and tie, at least.''

''I don't even own a tie. And I'm my own man, not some corporate lackey.'' He said this easily, without a trace of malice.

''Didn't you bring a suitcase? Surely even free souls like you need clean underwear and pajamas.''

''Don't own pajamas, either. But you'll find that out eventually.'' He ignored her glare. ''Zinko's going through security with the rest of my baggage,'' he added.

''Zinko?'' Keely repeated the name cautiously. Somehow she didn't like the sound of it.

''My assistant, Spike Zinko.'' His light gray eyes sparkled with mischievous glee. ''I can't wait for you to meet him, Ms. LaRoux.''

They didn't have too long to wait. The moment Keely spotted the gawky young man approaching, she knew it could be none other than Spike Zinko in the flesh. Except there wasn't very much flesh on him. He was the tallest, skinniest boy she had ever seen. He was sort of dancing up to them, if his frenetic movements could be termed that. Apparently he was moving to the beat of a rock song on his Sony Walkman. His black jacket was unzipped, exposing a Mickey Mouse T-shirt.

''Hey, Chuck!'' he called from too far away, drawing unnecessary attention to himself. ''How's it going, man? Who's that with you? Your new lady? Where's the big honcho from Citation? Maybe we'll get lucky and he'll miss the flight.''

Chuck motioned Zinko closer. ''Stop shouting, Spike, and take off those damn earphones. This little lady is the big honcho from Citation. So start behaving yourself. She's a firm believer in first impressions.''

Zinko quickly took off the earphones and finger-combed his messy brown hair. A cowlick stood up like a spike at the back of his head. He smiled down at Keely, revealing both his top and bottom gums and two rows of crooked teeth. It was such a wacky, friendly smile that Keely couldn't help but smile back. Still, she was acutely aware of what an odd trio they made—the petite, conservative businesswoman, the big, bearded Viking pirate and this renegade from a punk rock basketball team. Yes, they would definitely make an impression when they arrived at Citation divisions across the country.

They boarded the plane and found their assigned seats, three across. Chuck offered to put Keely's small suitcase on the luggage rack above, but she insisted on doing it herself. When she stood on tiptoe and reached up, her blouse came untucked, exposing her pale, lightly freckled midriff. Feeling Chuck's eyes on her, she quickly stuffed the blouse back into the narrow waistband of her skirt. She buttoned up her jacket and climbed over Zinko's very large feet to her preordained seat in the middle. She felt rather like a little pickle sandwiched between the two men.

Although she would have hated to admit it to anyone, Keely had never traveled by plane before. She paid very close attention when the blasé flight attendant demonstrated how to use the safety equipment. Chuck, meanwhile, leafed through a magazine. Spike put on his earphones and closed his eyes. When the plane took off, Keely gritted her teeth and tensed her muscles to help it defy gravity and stay up. It required her total concentration, but she was willing to give any help she could to the pilot.

"We made it. Maybe you can loosen your grip on my arm a bit now," Chuck suggested softly.

"Oh. Sorry." Keely hadn't realized she'd been clutching his very solid, muscular arm, and she released it immediately.

He reached over and patted the hand she had returned to her lap. "That's okay, Ms. LaRoux. Almost everybody has a fear of flying. We manage to get used to it after awhile. Part of civilized life. Like driving on a freeway. Or riding a subway. Just your normal, everyday fears about staying alive."

"You may as well call me Keely," she suggested lightly. As much as she wanted to maintain a formal business relationship, it seemed silly not to be on a first-name basis now that she had held on to him for dear life. "I suppose everybody calls you Chuck, not Charles."

"Everybody but my father. I was always disappointing Charles to him."

Keely blinked, surprised. "But you're so successful."

"Not as far as he was concerned. I let him down by not going into banking like every Dickens male before me had. I managed to get kicked out of every prep school he pulled strings to get me into. I never went in for formal education. A big waste of time, as far as I'm concerned." He stated this quite proudly.

Keely thought of her own struggle to get a college degree while supporting a child. "It's odd how people who have all the advantages in life don't seem to appreciate them," she said flatly.

Chuck sighed. "You took the words right out of dear old Dad's mouth." He turned his attention back to the magazine on his lap.

Keely hadn't meant her comment to sound like a reprimand, but there was something about Chuck's careless attitude toward life that irritated her. Everything came too easily for him, she concluded. And when things came easy, you didn't value them. Why this would bother her so much, she didn't know. She was never going to be one of Chuck Dickens's easy conquests.

Determined to disregard his presence, she took some work out of her attaché case. She couldn't concentrate on it, though, because she and Chuck were constantly brushing against each other as they shifted position in such tight quarters. Keely was also butting elbows and knees with Spike Zinko on her other side, but for some reason she hardly noticed that.

An attractive flight attendant came down the aisle wheeling a breakfast cart. Although she was a bit harried, she took time to give a wide, lovely smile when Keely looked up. Keely smiled back, then realized the stewardess wasn't looking at her at all.

"Hi, Chuck. Long time no see," she said.

"I haven't been flying domestic lately," he told her. "I've been going to Europe a lot. But I certainly remember your pretty face, Kathy."

Her smile faded. "The name is Betty."

"Isn't that what I said?" He had the grace to look mildly abashed.

"I'm glad I didn't hold my breath waiting for you to call me like you said you would."

Chuck tugged on his golden beard impatiently, but his voice was smooth and kind. "Like I said, Betty, I've been traveling to Europe a lot. I haven't had time to pick up my laundry, let alone have a social life."

What about that cute waitress at Lawley's Bar? Keely was tempted to interject.

"Well, next time you're back in New York, give me a ring," Betty said, somewhat appeased. "If I'm not scheduled to fly then, we could get together."

Never the twain shall meet, Keely found herself wishing. She decided that no matter how attractive Betty was, she still wore too much lipstick.

The flight attendant was a professional and spent no more time flirting with Chuck. She handed out the breakfast trays and continued down the aisle. Zinko, who had been in a world of his own before the food arrived, perked up considerably and devoted his avid attention to the meal. Keely had never seen anyone eat so quickly. He seemed to inhale the food rather than chew it.

"Man, I'm hungry," he said unnecessarily.

Chuck was amused. "You're always starving, Spike. Here, you can have mine, too." He handed his tray across Keely to his assistant. "Growing boy," he whispered to her.

Keely sincerely hoped not. He was too tall already. After he had gobbled up Chuck's portion, she could sense he was eyeing her tray. She took another bite of her bland, rather rubbery scrambled eggs. She had skipped breakfast, and they tasted pretty good to her.

"Don't look at me, Spike," she told him. "I'm not sharing one scrap with you."

Zinko gave his sweet, crooked, gum display of a smile. "That's okay, Ms. LaRoux," he said kindly, as if forgiving her for her supreme selfishness. In the end Keely broke down and gave him half her muffin, all her sausage and her allotment of jam, butter and cream.

The rest of the flight was uneventful. Chuck read. Zinko napped. And Keely managed to forget she was thousands of feet up in the air and jotted down ideas for ongoing Citation projects. But when the pilot announced they would be landing in Greenville shortly, Keely fastened her seat belt and sat rigid and tense.

As the plane began to descend, Chuck casually took her hand in his and squeezed it. She relaxed as warmth flowed through her body. When the plane landed safely, he released her fingers. Neither of them acknowledged the gesture. It simply seemed like the most natural thing to do.

Once the three of them reached the terminal, Chuck and Zinko sprang into action. Zinko went in one direction to claim the baggage; Chuck went in the other to rent a car. Keely followed him to the booth and overheard him request a Lincoln Continental town car. She raised her eyebrows. It was her responsibility to keep their traveling expenses within budget.

"Why such a fancy car?" she asked Chuck.

"That's the only kind I can travel in, Keely," he informed her abruptly, and before she could object further, he was out the glass door to claim the vehicle.

When he pulled the large silver car up to the loading area, Keely climbed into the front seat. She inhaled the rich scent of new leather. Everything about the car was luxurious. It seemed to her a very ostentatious way to travel to the little factory town of Duane.

"I'll let it go this time," she said. "But in the future we'll rent ordinary compact cars to get us to our destinations. This is too expensive."

He tugged on his beard, a sign she now knew indicated impatience or irritation even when his expression didn't. "What's the big deal, Keely? The company is paying for it."

She didn't like his cavalier attitude. "Travel expenses come out of my department budget, which your hefty fee is taking a big enough bite out of already, Mr. Dickens. Since this is the first major project I'm directing on my own, I don't want cost overruns." She didn't add that she was frugal by nature and habit.

Chuck gave her a knowing smile. "All you care about is impressing top management, isn't it? You're one ambitious lady, I'll say that much for you."

Why did it always sound a bit insulting when men called women ambitious? Keely wondered. She clenched her jaw. "Listen, Dickens. I didn't have everything handed to me on a silver platter like you did growing up. My father walked out on us when we were kids. And the only strings my mother ever pulled for me were the ones on her apron. So don't try to put me down by calling me ambitious. Where I come from, it's called survival."

For once Chuck Dickens had no quick comeback. He contemplated Keely quietly, as if recording her indignation with those sharp gray camera-lens eyes of his. She refused to squirm under his scrutiny, but it enraged her even further. She took advantage of his silence and continued her lecture.

"Now, getting back to this car rental issue. Maybe you're used to traveling in such luxury, but I'm not. And since I'm the client and you're working for me, I believe I have the last say in the matter."

She stopped then, not caring for the sound of her own voice. Was there a principle at stake here? Or was she just being small-minded about the whole issue?

Obviously Chuck thought she was. He shook his large blond head slowly, almost wearily.

"Let me explain something to you, Ms. LaRoux," he began in a very patient tone that was as soothing to her as fingernails scraping against a blackboard. But then he paused as Zinko came toward them, pushing a dolly stacked with metal boxes of various sizes. "Well, I won't have to waste time explaining. You'll see for yourself."

Chuck leaned across her, his beard just grazing her cheek like a tingling electrical current, and pressed a button in the glove compartment to open the trunk. He got out of the car, and so did she, more than a little curious. She stood aside and watched as he helped Zinko load the metal cases into the trunk. Then Zinko sped away with the dolly again.

"Where's he going now?" Keely wanted to know.

"To get the rest of my equipment, of course."

"There's more?" She tried not to sound too amazed.

"Plenty more. An assignment like this requires a lot of special setups. And that involves a lot of paraphernalia. Like any journeyman, I always travel with the tools of my trade."

Keely stared into the gaping hole of the big car's roomy trunk. It appeared to her like a huge mouth open and waiting to take in more. "And you need a car this size to transport it all," she said.

"Bingo!" he pronounced. "I can leave everything stored safe and sound and out of sight in the trunk overnight, which saves a lot of time and effort packing and unpacking. And since time is money in this business, it saves a lot of that, too. Which should delight the likes of you, Ms. LaRoux."

Keely did her best not to show how foolish she felt. It occurred to her that he'd intended for her to feel exactly that.

"You could have explained all this to me before I lit into you like that," she told him in a voice that had lost its sharp edge.

"You didn't give me much of a chance to, did you?" He flicked his thumb lightly beneath her firm jaw and smiled. "All I want is a chance with you."

His touch had been brief and playful but had gone deeper than her skin. At that moment, more than anything, she wanted a chance with him, too. "Let's call a truce, okay?"

He nodded. "Truce sounds good. But let me get rid of this for you first." He brushed his hand against the top of her jacket sleeve.

She looked sideways. "What was that?"

"Nothing much. Just that chip on your shoulder."

She couldn't help but laugh. "Thanks. It was getting pretty heavy there," she admitted. She'd always been able to accept teasing about her obvious faults. Having four brothers had trained her well.

"While we're at it, you might as well brush mine off, too," Chuck told her. "You're right. I let you dig a hole for yourself about this car business. I could have spoken up sooner."

She accepted his offer and brushed her hand across his broad shoulder, enjoying the feel of his muscle beneath her fingertips. But he grabbed her hand and brought it down to his chest.

"My chip is right here," he said.

He'd placed her palm over his heart, and she felt the beat of it. She was moved by his gesture and words. "That's not so easy to get rid of," she said wistfully.

"Oh, I don't know. You've already managed to nudge it a little off center. That's a start at least." He smiled softly.

She removed her palm from his chest and immediately missed the warmth of him. She wondered if she'd ever understand this man. He was so distant, so cool at times. And now so endearing. What was he really trying to tell her?

She was about to remind him that they weren't going to start anything between them, but her words of caution remained unspoken. The truth was that she wanted to get to know him better, if only he'd let her. That would indeed be a start.

At that moment Zinko returned with more metal boxes. Chuck helped him unload again. Then he slammed down the trunk with a mighty thud.

"Ready to proceed, Ms. LaRoux?" he asked her.

Keely nodded, but she wasn't at all sure that she was. She sensed she was heading toward unknown territory with this man and there would be no turning back.

Chapter Four

It was a four-hour drive from the airport to their destination of Duane. Chuck drove. Keely sat beside him and studied the map. Spike slept in the back seat. The car floated like a boat along the smooth, rolling two-lane highway. They passed small farms, and Keely noted how rich the bright red soil looked against the deep green pine forests in the background.

"This is good land," she pronounced. "I bet they had fine harvests of corn. Maybe soybean and tobacco."

"For a city gal, you sound like you know what you're talking about," Chuck commented.

"I wasn't always a city gal."

He waited for her to say more, but when she didn't, he didn't prod. He squinted at the bright blue October sky, then pulled a pair of sunglasses from one of the many pockets of his bush jacket. When he slipped them on, Keely missed the sight of his light gray intelligent eyes. Spike began to snore.

"He sleeps a lot, doesn't he?" Keely said.

"Don't worry about Zinko. He's a bundle of energy when he has to be."

"I didn't say I was worried."

"But you are," Chuck insisted. "Because you're judging him by his appearance. I saw how your face fell when you met him at the airport this morning. I must admit that you were very nice to him, though. A hell of a lot nicer than you were to me when we met."

"You were too brash," she told him. "And too self-important when you finally introduced yourself."

Chuck smiled, as if she had complimented him. "You would have been a lot more tolerant of me if I'd fit your stereotyped image of a successful businessman in a three-piece suit. It was my beard and work shirt that put you off."

"It was your manner," Keely reiterated, although she admitted to herself that there was some truth in his observation. "But I do think you go out of your way to dress like a rebel who disdains big business, especially considering the fact that you don't rebel against the high fees corporations offer you."

Chuck's laugh sounded more like a bark. "You have a sharp tongue, lady. I hope you have an equally sharp mind to temper it occasionally."

They drove along in silence after that. Keely wondered why she and Chuck Dickens couldn't have more than a five-minute conversation without clashing, even after calling a truce.

"Look, Keely," he said, finally breaking the silence and pointing to a row of oak trees ahead. Their orange leaves glittered in the sun. "Blazing beauty. They remind me of you."

His unexpected compliment made her heart leap, and she gave him a sidelong glance to see if he was being facetious. She couldn't tell; his eyes were shielded by his dark glasses.

"You travel a lot, don't you?" she said to change the subject.

"Constantly. It seems I've been sleeping in a different bed every night for the past six months."

With a different woman? She bit her tongue before asking that. "That must be quite a disruption in your personal life," she said instead.

"Actually, I don't have much of a personal life," he replied blithely. "My work takes up too much time."

"You're not married then?" She tried to sound very casual.

Her question brought a hoot from the back seat. "Don't mention the word *marriage* to Chuck, Ms. LaRoux. He might drive off the road."

"Go back to sleep, Spike," Chuck told him.

"I can't, man. I'm starving. When are we going to stop for lunch, anyway?" They were passing through a small town. "Hey, that little diner on the left looks like a good place to eat."

Both Keely and Chuck burst out laughing. The diner was called The Three Little Pigs. "We can't pass that up," Chuck said, slowing down.

It was steamy inside, and the odor of fried food hung heavy in the air. As they walked down the narrow aisle to a booth in the back, customers at the counter swiveled their stools and their necks to stare at them. Again Keely was aware of what an odd trio they must make, especially to the natives of this sleepy little southern town. Chuck's camera bag took up half the space on the booth bench, so Keely slid in beside Spike.

"You could have locked your bag in the car," she suggested.

Chuck and Spike both looked at her as if she had said something quite shocking.

"Chuck and his bag are inseparable," Spike informed her.

"I never let my cameras out of my sight," Chuck added with the serious expression of a parent referring to his cherished children.

A waitress wearing house slippers shuffled toward them. She was very plump and fair. "Y'all want something to eat?"

It seemed the most obvious reason for being there, but they all nodded yes. Chuck requested menus.

The girl giggled at his absurd request. "We don't have menus!"

He gave her his wide, pleasant smile. "Then what do you suggest we have, miss? You seem like a young lady with excellent taste."

Her rosy, round face turned even rosier, and she showed off her pretty dimples. "Well, we got hawg hahks today."

"I beg your pardon?" Keely said.

"Hog hocks," Chuck translated. "You know, swine joints. Sounds good, huh?" His eyes were sparkling with impish glee. Clearly he assumed she would consider the dish repellent.

"Sure does to me," Spike declared. "I'll have a double order."

The young waitress turned back to Chuck and simpered sweetly, "You try them, too, mister. It's our specialty."

"Okay. But maybe the lady would be happier with something less exotic."

"Nonsense. Make that three orders, miss." Keely had eaten ham hocks before. Plenty of times. No part of an animal was ever wasted on the farm. She just hadn't been able to understand the southern pronunciation of a dish her mother had often cooked.

When the waitress shuffled off, Keely pulled a paper napkin out of the metal dispenser, flicked it open and tucked it under the collar of her prim silk blouse. "Well, I don't know about you two gentlemen, but I'm so hungry I could eat an entire *hawg*."

"You know, Ms. LaRoux, you're okay," Spike said. "Most of the clients we travel with wouldn't set foot in a place like this."

Keely glanced at Chuck. He was smiling broadly. "I don't think Ms. LaRoux here is your typical boring executive," he told Spike.

"For sure. She's a lot prettier, for one thing," he agreed.

The food arrived on thick, chipped plates, and it was delicious. The three travelers cleaned their plates by swiping slices of cornbread across them to soak up the gravy. Spike had two pieces of pecan pie for dessert, but Chuck and Keely settled for mugs of strong coffee. They both drank it black, Keely noticed. At least they had one thing in common. Chuck left a twenty-dollar tip on the table for the waitress.

"That's a little extravagant, do you think?" Keely couldn't help but remark.

"Don't worry. I'll only bill your company for my meals. The tips are on me."

"Last of the big spenders," Keely murmured, but she had a certain fondness in her heart for people who tipped well. It was a holdover from her early days in New York City, when she had waitressed on weekends to supplement her secretarial wages in order to pay for Joy's baby-sitter and her own college tuition.

They left the diner and continued on their journey to Duane. Chuck turned on the radio and sang along with the country-western tunes, making up nonsense rhymes when he didn't know the words. His deep baritone was definitely off-key. Keely couldn't carry a tune either and joined in with her flat alto. Zinko moaned from the back seat and begged them to stop, which only encouraged them to raise their voices louder. Finally he gave up trying to sleep over the racket and joined in, too.

Spike had a surprisingly sweet, dulcet voice, and Chuck and Keely stopped singing to listen to him. His melodious tenor soothed Keely, and she leaned back in the plush leather seat as the pleasant scenery glided by. At that moment she couldn't think of a more pleasant place to be than where she was, with Chuck right beside her. She liked the way his large, tanned hands looked on the steering wheel. Strong, competent hands, she thought dreamily, and she wondered how they would feel stroking her body. She sat up straight and banned such a thought from her mind.

They arrived in Duane by midafternoon. Chuck told Keely it was too late to take pictures at the Citation plant; it would be closing by the time he set up his equipment. He suggested that they check into a motel and get a fresh start the next morning, but Keely insisted that they check out the Citation facility immediately. He called her a slave driver but agreed.

The plant manager, William Billings, was cordial enough when he came out to the reception area to greet them. But Keely sensed a reserve in his attitude, almost a reluctance to show them around the small factory. This was his territory, and he made clear, in an indirect way, that he resented any interference in daily routine by a corporate headquarters representative.

Keely had expected Mr. Billings to be more enthusiastic and helpful, but it seemed Citation annual report photos were the least of his concerns. His primary concern was assembly line production, and the last thing he wanted was any disruption. Keely was sympathetic but still insisted that an area of the factory floor be cleared for the next day's shoot. Billings agreed to cooperate. They shook hands goodbye without smiling.

"You think Billings will come through for us?" Chuck asked Keely once they were back in the car.

She was surprised that he doubted it. "Of course he will. He promised."

"I've met his kind before," Chuck said. "They'll yes you to death, but in the end nothing gets done. You've got to be firm with these guys, Keely."

"I believe I was," she replied huffily. "I think I handled Mr. Billings quite well. I certainly don't need you to tell me how to do my job."

"Excuse me, LaRoux. I forgot what a hotshot executive you were." He drove on without offering further advice.

There was only one motel in the Duane area, and it was a small one at that. "We have reservations," Keely told the elderly man behind the desk when they walked into the office. "LaRoux, Dickens and Zinko."

"Sounds like some kind of vaudeville act," he said, giving them the once-over.

Chuck was amused by that. "We are," he said. "Zinko rolls the drums while LaRoux throws knives at Dickens. We're on the road with the act now."

The desk clerk scowled, not sure whether to believe him or not. He handed each of them a key attached to a big plastic tag. "I gave you the three best rooms we have. Right next to the vending machines."

"What time do you start serving dinner?" Keely asked.

"Anytime you want, ma'am. Just get yourself some cola and snacks out of the machines. We don't have a restaurant, and the closest eating place hereabouts is twenty miles down the road. You'll like it if you like fried chicken, because that's all they serve."

Keely sighed. She was bone-tired and had planned on a quick, light salad for dinner, then a hot shower and a good night's rest. It seemed to her that they had been traveling an entire week, rather than only one day. Being in the sometimes irritating but always stimulating company of Chuck Dickens had worn her out. And they were just beginning their business trip together!

She hoped she could get through the next three weeks without doing something she would later regret. The problem was that he still attracted her as strongly as he had the moment she first laid eyes on him in the elevator. Even more so. But the more she felt the pull of this attraction, the harder she pulled back against it. No doubt that was why she was so exhausted now.

She had trouble unlocking the door to her room, and Chuck, standing at his right next door, came to her aid. "The trick is to jiggle the key a bit." He showed her how.

"Thanks." She took back her key but paused before going in. "I didn't mean to snap at you about Mr. Billings, Chuck. I realize you were just trying to give me some advice."

"Which I had no business doing. My job is to take the pictures. I'll let you handle the rest."

"No, I owe you an apology," she persisted. "I've been very short-tempered since I got my promotion. Maybe the pressure and responsibilities are too much for me." She didn't usually admit the possibility of failure to anybody, even herself, but it had just slipped out.

"Listen, Keely, I've dealt with a lot of corporate types in my time, and in my humble opinion, you've got what it takes to succeed. If that's what you really want."

She doubted he had ever had a *humble* opinion about anything, but she was grateful for his encouragement. She smiled up at him, and his incisive gray eyes were like magnets, holding hers. She was deeply drawn to him at that moment, unaware that she was slowly listing toward him, her lips parted expectantly. She caught herself just in time and stepped back, into the open doorway.

"Why don't you invite me in?" he said softly, persuasively.

"You know I won't," she replied, almost sadly.

"Maybe not now, but you will." There was no doubt in his voice or in his glinting eyes. Then his expression changed to one of casual friendliness. "Why don't we all head down to that chicken place for dinner?"

"I think I'll skip it. You and Spike go. I'll get something out of the vending machine."

"You can't make a meal of stale potato chips and cola," he protested.

"I'm really not that hungry, Chuck. We've been traveling all day, and I want to stay put." She couldn't very well tell him that she needed a break from the masculine energy he constantly exuded. It made her feel almost weak.

Spike came out of his room, which was next to Chuck's. He had changed for dinner. Now he was wearing a Donald Duck T-shirt. "Hey, you two, let's go get some fried chicken. I'm starving!"

Keely insisted again that they go without her and felt both relief and disappointment when they drove off. She took a handful of quarters out to the machines and got herself a bag of peanuts, a candy bar and a diet soft drink. There were no chairs in her motel room, so she sat on the bed in front of the television set and watched the evening news as she nibbled on the peanuts. They were so dry that she could barely swallow them. She caught her rather forlorn reflection in the mirror over the cheap Formica dressing table and toasted herself with the can of soda pop. "Here's to you, Keely LaRoux. Isn't business travel glamorous?"

After she called New York and talked with Joy, she took a hot shower. Her intention, at least, was to take a hot shower, but the best she could get was lukewarm. She wrapped a threadbare, scratchy towel around her head and searched through her suitcase for her hair dryer. It didn't elevate her mood to discover she had forgotten to pack it. If she didn't tame her hair with a blow dryer, it tended to be too wavy and wild.

She had forgotten to pack her toothbrush, too, she noted. And her comfy robe and slippers. She suddenly missed these old favorite things almost as much as she missed her daughter. She asked herself what on earth she was doing all alone in a cheap motel room far from home. You're doing your job, she answered. So grow up and stop feeling sorry for yourself.

At least she hadn't forgotten to pack her faded flannel nightgown, and it gave her a little comfort to slip it on. She tried reading the book on corporate management she had brought, but the light in the room was poor and the text was dry and boring. She gave that up and turned on the TV again. The silly situation comedy she tuned into couldn't hold her attention, even though all the actors seemed to be shouting. Without realizing it, she was listening for the sound of Chuck's car returning and nothing else. She must have dozed, because the next thing she heard was a thumping on her door. She jumped up from the bed, blood pounding in her ears.

"It's Dickens Delivery Service," she heard Chuck call.

She rushed to her suitcase to get her robe, then remembered she hadn't taken it. Not that it really mattered. Her flannel nightgown covered her from neck to toe. She opened the door halfway and peered out at him, frowning.

"What do you want?" she asked in a less than civil tone, self-conscious about her appearance. She thought she must look a sight, with her wet hair and shiny, scrubbed face.

"If you want hot thighs and breasts, I can give them to you, lady," he replied.

"Oh, really!" She had thought he would be a little more subtle than that and tried shutting the door in his grinning face.

But his sturdy suede boot acted as a wedge. "Hold on, Keely. That was a joke. I was referring to the chicken I brought you." He showed her the brown paper bag he was carrying. It emitted a tangy aroma that made Keely's mouth water.

She opened the door a little wider and reached out for it. "Thanks, that was very thoughtful." She was suddenly famished.

But he held the bag just out of her reach. "Aren't you going to invite me in to partake in the feast? There are two take-out orders here. One intended for me."

"Chuck, I can't let you in. I'm all ready for bed."

He winked broadly and twirled his mustache. "All the more reason to, my dear."

This time she smiled, despite herself. The aroma of the chicken was very tempting. So was Chuck's wide smile. Until he'd knocked on her door, she hadn't realized how very bored and lonely and hungry she was. What could be the harm of sharing dinner with him?

"I promise I won't make a pass at you," he said, as if reading her mind. "I'd just like a little company, and I bet you would, too."

Still, she hesitated. "Would you mind waiting a minute while I change into something more decent?"

His laughing eyes took in her towel-swathed head and flannel-covered body. "More decent than what? A nun's habit?"

She certainly wasn't going to tell him that she was absolutely naked beneath her flannel gown. "Okay, bring in the food," she acquiesced. "But please, no more double entendres, if you don't mind. You do a very poor imitation of Groucho Marx."

He looked crestfallen. "I thought I was pretty good."

He walked into her room and placed the paper bag on the Formica dressing table. He took out two fragrant, grease-stained cardboard boxes, paper napkins and plates and plastic forks and knives. Last but not least, he pulled out a bottle of wine.

"I don't know where this came from," he said, catching Keely's distrustful look. "The bottle of Tab I bought must have magically changed into Chablis during the trip back here. It's truly amazing."

His expression was as innocent as a little boy's. Except little boys didn't have thick golden beards, Keely reminded herself. Or incipient lines etched around penetrating eyes. She guessed Chuck's age to be around thirty-five, give or take a few years. The beard made it hard to tell. Was he hiding something behind it? she wondered.

"What other tricks do you have up your sleeve, Mr. Dickens?" she asked, nodding toward the wine.

He took off his bush jacket and rolled up the sleeves of his soft blue cotton shirt. His forearms were rock solid and tan. "None. See? I always make it a point to dine with fine wine and good company. It's the only civilized way to eat."

"Sorry, but I didn't pack a corkscrew."

"No problem. I always do, and it's never let me down." He put up his hands, as if to deflect her anger. "That wasn't a double entendre. Honest!" His slow, easy smile slid up his handsome, high-cheekboned face as he pulled a waiter's corkscrew out of the back pocket of his wrinkled chino slacks. "Now, your assignment, if you wish to accept it, Ms. La-Roux, is to find us some fine crystal wineglasses."

She couldn't help it. He made her laugh. "I'm afraid the water glasses in the bathroom will have to do." She went to get them, and when she returned she found Chuck, his boots off, sitting cross-legged in the middle of the bed like a sultan. "Now, wait a minute," she said. "I think this impromptu dinner party is getting a little out of hand, Dickens. I didn't invite you into my bed."

"Well, where else can I sit?" he asked. "There aren't any chairs in this hovel of a motel room. But if you'd prefer, we can rough it on the shag rug. I've seen worse."

But Keely hadn't. The high-pile rug was a strange mustard color and looked as if it harbored all sorts of obscene things better left undiscovered. Rather than let her bare feet touch it, she had been wearing her leather pumps and missing her slippers very much.

"Pretend this bed is an island in the middle of shark-infested waters," Chuck said, no doubt noticing her wrinkled-nosed glance at the rug. "Or better yet, pretend it's a picnic blanket. What could be more innocent than that?"

The last time Keely had been on a picnic was twelve years ago, with Roy LaRoux. And the result of that innocent pleasure had been her daughter, Joy. She thought it best not to mention this to Chuck Dickens.

But Keely had changed a lot in twelve years. For one thing, she wasn't so willing to give her heart away to the first man who sent it thumping. Her girlish romantic fancies had disappeared long ago, along with Roy LaRoux. She sat on the edge of the bed and took a cautious sip of the wine. It was good, and so was the spicy chicken. Chuck kept the conversation impersonal and light, and soon she felt very comfortable with him. He was glib and humorous, a perfect companion. *Dinner* companion, that was.

"This was fun," she said, clearing away the remnants of their shared meal and tossing the bones and paper plates into the brown bag. "How fast the time has passed. It's getting late."

He got up from the bed and stretched his long, wide frame. "I guess that's a hint I should leave."

He had kept his word and been the perfect gentleman all evening. He hadn't so much as even flirted with her, despite the fact that she had never been so vulnerable. Alone. In her nightgown. In bed with him, no less. She watched him put on his boots, impressed by his reserved conduct. And oddly disappointed by it, too, she had to admit as she walked him to the door.

His hand was on the doorknob, but he hesitated before turning it. "I really don't want to go, you know," he said almost casually although there was the glitter of intensity in his eyes as he looked at her.

Every natural instinct within her suddenly urged her to ask him to stay. But she listened to her logical mind instead. "Let's not muddy our working relationship with sex, Chuck."

He shook his head. "A romantic you're not, Keely LaRoux. That's the bluntest rejection I've ever had." But there must have been something about her that continued to capture his interest, because he touched her upturned, freckled nose very gently with his index finger and forced a smile. "Okay. I'll give you a little more time. Don't forget to bolt your door and put on the chain lock, since you insist on sleeping alone." And then he was gone.

She didn't feel rejected, exactly, when he left without persisting further. But she did feel dejected. She glanced at herself in the mirror above the cheap dressing table. The awful motel towel was still wrapped around her head, and the constellation of freckles across her shiny nose stood out like neon dots. Her flannel nightgown, she decided, made her look like a dumpy old maid. No wonder he had taken her refusal so easily! His hesitancy to leave had probably been only his way of being polite. Men like Chuck Dickens no doubt thought it their duty to offer their charming selves to every available woman who crossed their paths, even the less than glamorous ones. Keely went to bed unreasonably angry with him.

But the next morning she awoke to the sound of his off-key baritone coming through the thin walls as he sang in the shower, and for no reason at all her toes curled with pleasure.

Chapter Five

When they arrived at the Citation plant at nine sharp, Mr. Billings's secretary informed them that he had been called out of town suddenly.

"I smell a rat," Chuck whispered to Keely. "I told you Billings was a wimp. Rather than face any problems, he's cut out."

They were directed to the plant foreman, Eddie Littlefield. He had a glass-enclosed office in the middle of the factory floor. Keely introduced herself and Chuck and Spike to him. He remained seated behind his cluttered desk, not moving a muscle. He was a tough-looking man with barbell arms.

"We don't get many tourists from New York City here," he said.

"I'm more than a tourist," Keely told him, making sure she smiled. "Didn't Mr. Billings apprise you of the situation?"

Littlefield rubbed his broad nose, as if it had just been put out of joint. "You mean did he *tell* me why you're here? Sure he did. And I told him that there was no way I was going to hold up production for some pictures."

Chuck groaned. Spike, sensing a delay, left the office to get a snack. Keely continued to smile, but she was taken aback by his attitude. She had assumed that every Citation division would be eager to be included in the annual report. "It's the company president who decides that," she replied calmly. "Not you or I, Mr. Littlefield."

He shifted his mighty bulk, and his chair squeaked. "I never met the man. While he's sitting up there in his fancy New York office, I'm down here making sure we meet production quotas."

"But Billings agreed to our photo session," Keely insisted.

"Did he?" Littlefield folded his hefty arms across his chest.

Keely examined his stubborn face. "Are you telling me that you're not going to clear a section of the floor for us?"

His slow nod was affirmative. "For once you got something right, honey."

"Now wait a minute, *Little*field," Chuck interjected. "I don't like your attitude toward this lady."

"Oh, don't you, mister?" He pushed himself off his chair and rose to lock horns with Dickens. They were exactly the same height.

Although momentarily flattered by Chuck's defense, Keely immediately resented his interference. "Let me handle this," she hissed.

"I don't think you can," he replied.

She flashed him an angry look; then, green eyes still blazing, she turned to the plant foreman. "It seems you're the one who calls the shots around here," she said.

A flicker of pride crossed his rough face. "Just doing my job."

"So am I, Eddie," she reminded him softly. "But it seems I should have cleared things with you instead of Billings yesterday. I should have known better, too. When I worked assembly line, it was the foreman who got things done in the end. Not the guy in the suit and tie upstairs."

He looked her over, noting her corporate attire, and snorted. "You never set foot in a factory before, much less worked the line, missy."

"Sure I did. That's how I got my start at Citation." She gave him her clear, even stare. "So you don't have to tell me about production quotas. I understand the pressure you're under. My brother's a foreman, too, you know. Up at the Vermont division. He doesn't like corporate interference, either."

"Oh, yeah?" He seemed a little less defensive.

"Why don't you give a working gal a break, Eddie, and clear a section of the floor for us?" Her tone was neither threatening nor pleading, only open and sincere. "The sooner we get things started, the sooner we'll be out of your hair."

He considered her a moment, his resentment fading now that she had acknowledged his importance at the plant. "Well, I guess I could help you out. Give me about ten minutes. You and your friend with the beard and short fuse can help yourself to some coffee." With that he left them alone and went out to the factory floor.

"Well, I've got to hand it to you, Keely," Chuck said. "You just won King Kong's heart. Must have been those big green eyes of yours that did it."

Without offering Chuck any, Keely poured herself a cup of coffee before replying. "What did it was good common sense, Dickens. I know how to deal with Citation personnel. That's my job, and you should have let me do it instead of getting mad at Littlefield. What were you going to do? Get into a fist fight with him? That really would have helped the situation."

"Sorry, LaRoux," Chuck said, looking more irritated than apologetic. "You're obviously a woman who doesn't need any man's help. I'll make sure to remember that in the future." But then he smiled. "That bit about working on an assembly line was pretty good, by the way."

"That was no *bit*. I sure as hell did. Not all of us start at the top, you know."

"I worked hard to get where I am, too, Keely. You don't have a patent on it."

He took the paper cup from her hand, sipped some coffee, then handed it back to her. The simple intimacy of the gesture disarmed her despite his rather belligerent tone.

"Want to tell me about it, Chuck?" she asked softly.

"About what? My struggle to the top?"

She nodded, interested and serious. But he only laughed.

"Why dwell on the past? You can't change it. It's the future that interests me. Onward and upward—that's ole Chuck Dickens's motto."

How like him, she thought, to drop some telling detail about himself into the conversation like a bomb, then take refuge behind glibness to defuse it.

"It's a good motto to have," she agreed.

She herself had always believed in a better future, even during the bleakest periods of her life. But right now it was the present she found so compelling. This man. This stranger.

She wasn't about to press him to open up to her, though. Not when she'd already decided to keep up her guard against his power to interest and excite her. Even so, when she sipped her coffee again, her lips touched the cup exactly where his had.

"Here comes King Kong again," Chuck said, turning away from her and gazing out the plate-glass office wall. "Your latest conquest. You don't even need bananas to have him eating out of your hand."

Keely didn't find that terribly amusing. She understood Eddie Littlefield. Which was more than she could say about Chuck Dickens. She gave Eddie a friendly smile when he entered his office, all bustling and officious.

Now that the plant foreman had decided to let them into his territory, the shoot went smoothly, if not as quickly as Keely had thought it would. The procedure was much more complicated than she had expected. It took hours for Spike to unload all the silver cases and set up the equipment under Chuck's exacting directions. Because the factory lighting would turn everything he photographed a sickly green, he had to create his own environment with strobes and reflectors.

The workers on the assembly line, mostly women, seemed to find the process fascinating. Or perhaps it was Chuck they found so fascinating. Keely observed how they would nudge each other and wink whenever he walked by them. Big and blond, exuding a compelling intensity, he was a man whose presence captured women's attention.

And he knew it. While he didn't openly bask in their admiration, he was extremely comfortable with it. He answered their glances with his slow, easy smile as his sharp gray eyes took them in, recording a curve here, a curl there. He was definitely a man who appreciated women of all shapes and sizes. Keely noted this and pitied the poor woman who expected him to remain interested in only her for long. Not one for self-pity, she was determined that that woman wasn't going to be Keely LaRoux.

The Duane plant produced electronically controlled power tools, and Chuck's assignment was to photograph a router. He took his time envisioning interesting shots of this mundane subject, squinting and sighing a lot and pacing and tugging at his beard. Keely understood now why he wore such comfortable, casual clothes. The man never stopped moving, bending and stretching, trying to zero in on the right angle.

"Talk about boring assignments, this one just about tops it, LaRoux," he mumbled irritably, finally acknowledging her existence after ignoring her for an hour or so. "After our little chat at Lawley's Bar, I thought it would be a lot more exciting. But it's turning out to be as dull as dishwater."

Keely cautioned herself not to take this remark personally. "It's your job to make the product exciting," she replied. "That's why we hired you, Mr. Dickens. You have complete artistic freedom. All I request is that you make sure the Citation logo on the router shows in the photograph."

"Okay, okay. You've only mentioned that twenty times already. Once would have been sufficient."

His sharp rejoinder seemed to pierce Keely's tear ducts, making her eyes sting irrationally. She wasn't usually so sensitive. And she, too, tended to be short-tempered when she was working under pressure, as Chuck was now. So what if he had snapped at her? When other men did, it rolled off her like water off a duck's back. But Chuck's little burst of pique had hurt her. Don't be silly, she chided herself, swallowing the tears.

He began waving a light meter in front of her face. "Sit behind the workbench, Keely. I need to soften this picture up with a pretty woman's face. The router alone is just too damn ugly."

"I can't be in the picture," she protested. "How would that look at headquarters? I'm not here to be a model. My job is to supervise the project."

"Don't worry. I'm not trying to undermine your executive status, LaRoux." His voice was tinged with sarcasm. "Once I bracket the subject and get the lighting right, I'm going to select a model off the assembly line. But since those ladies out there are working and all you're doing is hanging around, I figure you've got nothing better to do. Except bug me to show the company label again."

"Well, pardon me for living," she said, immediately regretting that her reply had been around the sophistication level of her daughter Joy's, or even below it. She complied and sat behind the workbench. She disliked the bright lights and Chuck's attention focused so intently upon her face. She was sure her nose was shiny.

"How much longer is this going to take?" she asked with annoyance after more than twenty minutes of flashes popping in her face.

Chuck examined yet another Polaroid snapshot and told Spike to adjust one of the strobe lights a fraction of an inch. "Just a few more, Keely. Didn't anyone ever tell you that patience is a virtue?"

That was the last virtue she ever expected Chuck Dickens to value. He seemed to her a man who was always in a rush. Yet his attention to detail as he worked impressed her. For a man who seemed to expect instant connections with women in his personal life, he certainly showed a lot of forbearance in his work. Then she remembered the time they had spent together the evening before. He hadn't rushed her then, as he had in the elevator when they first met, or at the bar after she had searched him out. No, he hadn't rushed her at all.

"Take your time and get it right," she told him.

"That's exactly what I intend to do with you," he replied.

He took a half dozen more Polaroids and studied each one carefully. The last one seemed to satisfy him, and he placed it in the pocket of his bush jacket. "Okay, Keely, that's it for you. I'll find your replacement on the floor."

Was it always as easy as that for him? she wondered. One woman was as good as another? But of course that wasn't the point, she reminded herself. She was taking this much too personally. She watched him prowl up and down the assembly line looking for a suitable model. He found a young woman with coloring similar to Keely's but not quite as vivid. She was shy, and Chuck had to persuade her to pose. Put at ease by his casual charm, she finally agreed. Keely had guessed she would. Women seemed to have difficulty saying no to him.

Her name was Selma, and Chuck told her it was the most beautiful name he had ever heard. He repeated it softly, drawing it out, and her rather plain, pinched face relaxed a little.

"I never in my life modeled before, Mr. Dickens," she said.

"Call me Chuck," he told her. "And don't worry. There's nothing to it. You sit behind this workbench every day of the week, don't you?"

"Not with some fancy camera poking me in the nose!"

"Forget the camera. Forget me."

Easier said than done, Keely thought, giving Selma an encouraging smile. It went unobserved. The young woman had eyes only for Chuck.

"Lean closer to the power tool, Selma," he coaxed. "No, don't smile. Study it intently, as if it's the most beautiful piece of equipment you ever laid eyes on." He laughed softly. "No, love. Don't look at *me*. Like I said, pretend I don't exist. It's just you and that router. Relax."

She eventually did, but when his Nikon began to click and whir she tensed up again. He took it away from his face and smiled at her. "I bet a pretty girl like you has a boyfriend, Selma," he said.

"There's someone who's made his attentions known," she answered vaguely.

"Then pretend that router is him, and give it your most intimate look. Like you're really interested."

"Can I pretend it's you instead, Chuck?"

"Forget me!" he stressed again. "I want your eyes on that power tool, not on my camera. Pretend this boyfriend of yours has just told you that the fire in your hair makes his blood hot with desire.''

That was a bit too much for Keely. ''You're taking pictures for an annual report, not *Playboy*,'' she muttered.

''I sure wish someone really would say something like that to me,'' Selma said, her greenish-hazel eyes melting as she gazed at Chuck.

''Listen, Selma, why don't you just pretend that the router is simply a router and in five minutes you're getting off work,'' Keely suggested.

That seemed to work. Selma's expression became moderately interested and happy, and Chuck began clicking away, but not before throwing Keely a withering glance. When he finished the roll, Spike handed him his second loaded Nikon, and he kept shooting without breaking pace. Spike, meanwhile, unloaded the first camera, labeled the roll and put it into the canvas bag Chuck always carried with him.

''That wraps it,'' Chuck said when he had finished the second roll. ''Thanks, Selma. I won't take up any more of your time. You did great. I bet you're the prettiest girl in the two Carolinas, unless you have a twin sister.''

She giggled. ''I don't know about that, but I am one of the best cooks around. Want to come by and sample my ribs tonight, Chuck?''

''Oh, honey, my mouth's watering already. But I'm sorry to say we've got to move on. Ms. LaRoux here has me scheduled to shoot pictures in Alabama tomorrow morning.'' He sighed wearily. ''She's a real slave driver.''

Selma gave Keely the kind of look reserved for people who kicked dogs or whipped horses before she flounced off.

''Thanks for making me such a nasty culprit,'' Keely told Chuck.

He took her arm with a less than gentle grip and led her out of Zinko's earshot. ''Don't you ever interrupt one of my shoots again,'' he hissed. His gray eyes were as cold and blank as glass as he looked at her. ''You ruined the whole mood with Selma. I was striving for some kind of special connection between a worker and a machine. Something that could have jumped off the page of your damn annual report. But you destroyed all that by butting in the way you did.''

She twisted her arm from his hold. "I thought you were just coming on to her."

"Well, I wasn't. And even if I had been, that's none of your business either, is it?" Oh, he was angry. The small muscle in his cheek was twitching. "Listen, lady, you already set down the rules very clearly: You do your job, and I'll do mine." His voice was harsh but no louder than a whisper.

"Well, now you know how it feels to have interference," she retorted defensively. "You didn't make my job any easier with Littlefield, either."

"Stalemate," he said. "Does it make you feel any better to have us both wrong?"

"No, it doesn't," she answered truthfully. "I hate it."

"Me, too." He didn't look mad anymore. Just a little regretful. He reached out and skimmed the silky top layers of her flaming hair with his fingertips. Then he withdrew his hand quickly, as if it had been singed.

Zinko, who was busy packing up the equipment, hadn't even noticed their brief tête-à-tête. The three of them shook hands with Eddie Littlefield, who told them, quite sincerely, that he looked forward to seeing them again the following year.

They walked across the parking lot to their car, Zinko, with his extra-long stride, a few yards ahead. Chuck took Keely's hand, and it was such a friendly, casual gesture that she allowed him to hold it.

"Are we friends again?" he asked in a low voice.

"I hope so," she replied emphatically. "I don't like arguing with you, Chuck."

"Oh, yes you do," he countered. "You're as contrary as I am, Keely LaRoux."

She opened her mouth to contradict him, but then closed it. That would only prove his point. "Sometimes I just don't understand you, that's all," she said instead.

"Yeah, well, that makes two of us. I don't understand myself half the time," he quipped.

She gave his hand a squeeze to show she appreciated his honesty. That he'd revealed, even obliquely, any weakness whatsoever made her feel a little closer to him. They caught up to Zinko, who was waiting for them by the big shiny car.

Keely liked being on the road again. She liked sitting beside Chuck as they glided to their next destination. She liked the way he drove—perhaps a little faster than the posted limit, but with such complete competence that she didn't mind the speed at all. At this moment she even liked hearing Zinko's now familiar snoring in back. A growing boy needed his sleep, she thought fondly. She leaned back in the plush seat, and a reassuring coziness enveloped her. She suspected the feeling of security had a lot to do with the fact that Chuck was only touching distance away and would be for the next few hours.

"This car is beginning to seem like my second home," she drawled lazily.

"I suppose it's as good a home as any," Chuck replied. "The roof doesn't leak, and we have stereo and air conditioning. Who could ask for more?"

"Not me at this moment," she agreed, taking to the fanciful idea of it.

"Want to move in on a permanent basis, Keely? I could use a good traveling buddy."

She let out a surprised laugh. "What exactly's expected of a traveling buddy?" she questioned a bit suspiciously.

"She'd have to be able to take the driver's seat once in a while," he said. "More than once in a while actually. The way I see it, it should be fifty-fifty all the way down the road."

She liked that. "I'm an excellent driver," she said. "And more than willing to do my share."

"So far so good. But the ideal traveling companion also has to be damn good at reading road signs along the way to keep me on the right track. Sometimes I tend to go off in too many directions at once and lose my way."

Was this another admission of weakness? Keely wondered. Or was she beginning to take this game a little too seriously? It was so hard for her to tell what Chuck really meant at times, and that frustrated her.

"I've always been careful to stay on the right path," she replied after a moment.

"So I've noticed." His eyes left the road for a moment, and he smiled at her. "But you shouldn't *always* stick to that road map of yours, Keely. Sometimes it's fun to take an adventurous detour."

"Well, you'd know more about that than I do," she answered a tad caustically. She'd seen how women warmed up to him so quickly, and she could well imagine his many adventurous detours. "Personally, I believe in being cautious and making very sure I don't get lost so I don't waste time."

"Waste time!" he repeated in a disbelieving tone. "No, Keely, you mustn't have that attitude. It's a long haul before we get to the end of the road, and it's taking a chance on a detour that could change the whole destination."

He was good at this kind of game, she thought. He was a master at hiding behind words that could either be taken at face value or have deeper connotations. Was he suggesting that she take a chance on a relationship with him? It was a detour she didn't dare risk, and she put up a roadblock.

"I don't think I'd be the best traveling buddy for you, Chuck. I wouldn't be able to keep your interest during those long, boring stretches of highway."

"Oh, I think you would, Keely. Those stretches are boring, but you never are."

She wanted to believe him but couldn't. "No, you seem the type of man who gets distracted too easily by the lush scenery along the way."

He laughed, seeming to appreciate the way she'd picked up on his little game. "Since I've been with you, I haven't noticed that scenery at all, lady."

Her heart picked up a few beats, but her innate common sense brought it back to normal again. He was playing with her. Even his compliment was oblique. He'd never come out and say what he really meant. She had to admit that part of his charm was in being so cleverly evasive, but because she wasn't at all that way, it also irritated her. Where Keely came from, people said what they meant and meant what they said. You always knew where you stood with people in Jasper, Vermont.

But Chuck remained a riddle to her, too elusive to be taken seriously, and she resented his ability to pull her heartstrings. In his roundabout, joking way, he'd just described to her what she would consider a perfect marriage: two people sharing responsibilities as they traveled toward compatible goals and having a pretty exciting time of it along the way.

But of course he wasn't talking about marriage. Or love. Or anything definite at all. He was just passing time and having his fun with her, she concluded. Since Keely LaRoux was nobody's fool, she wasn't about to be the butt of his joke.

"You might as well go back to enjoying the pretty scenery, Mr. Dickens," she told him. "You know as well as I do that once this assignment ends, we won't be traveling buddies anymore."

There was a little catch in her voice when she stated this, but it was so small that she was sure he'd missed it.

He swerved into the passing lane and stepped on the gas before replying. After he'd passed a string of cars and a very large truck he slowed down and turned his eyes to her.

"Fine," he said tersely. "I won't consider you for the position. I have enough *temporary* applicants already."

"I'll just bet you do."

She dared a glance at him. His eyes were straight ahead, on the road again, and his bearded profile was strong but impassive. For a brief instant she was tempted to press her fingertips against his high cheekbone. She longed for the touch of him, some kind of meaningful communication, but she stifled the longing, deciding it would lead to nothing in the end.

"Do you mind if I turn on the radio?" he asked her politely.

"Not at all," she replied in the same stilted tone.

He fiddled with the dials until he found a station to his liking. His preference was apparently hard rock. The jolting music filled the car, and Spike's snores in the back seat added to the racket. The noise level effectively ended further conversation between them for the time being.

* * *

For the next three days Keely, Chuck and Spike traveled by car and plane to the Citation facilities throughout the southeast. Despite transportation delays, frustrating luggage losses and retrievals and less than convenient overnight accommodations, they always made their appointments on time. And they always got their pictures. Keely handled the sometimes tricky company politics. Spike took care of the equipment. And Chuck, intense and untiring, continued to strive for perfection at each shoot.

They became such a smooth-working team that they took one another's contributions for granted. With a common goal, they supported one another without thinking about it. There was a job to be done, and they simply did it. Keely had never experienced such complete satisfaction in her work. Each night, before she drifted into exhausted slumber, she reviewed how they had managed to overcome all the little hitches and big problems during the day, and she would sigh with relief. Her last thought would always be of Chuck. It was more an image than a thought: Chuck with his cameras, clicking away, circling his subject like a big cat ready to pounce.

They ended up in a restaurant in Webster, Georgia, late Thursday evening. The restaurant was attached to a chain motor inn not famous for fancy cuisine. However, at least it was clean and convenient, which was more than Keely could say about the places they'd been forced to eat in the last two evenings. Except for the fried chicken picnic on her bed with Chuck on Monday, they had shared all their meals with Zinko. He was an unlikely but very effective chaperone. It never even seemed to cross his mind that Keely and Chuck might want to be alone.

And why should it? Keely reminded herself. She would have been deeply offended if Spike assumed that she and Chuck were ripe for an affair just because she was a halfway attractive female client. So she had absolutely no cause to fault Spike or, for that matter, his boss. Although Chuck sometimes teased her, often argued with her and occasionally gave her a brief hug or pat on the back after a successful shoot, he never made the slightest attempt to become more intimate.

Keely knew she should take it as a compliment that he respected her as a business associate. And she did. At the same time, however, she wanted him to want her. It was very confusing. By the time of their last dinner together that Thursday, she knew the strain showed on her face. There were shadows under her eyes, and her normally peachy complexion was pale.

Chuck had shadows under his eyes, too. When the waitress came to their table he requested a bottle of wine to toast the end of their first week of travel together. They would be taking a flight from Atlanta back to New York the next morning. The waitress, who had seen better days and no doubt better times, informed him that the restaurant didn't serve wine in bottles, only decanters.

"What kind of wine is it?" Chuck asked, giving her his handsome smile.

She was immune to it. "White or red or pink," she replied, barely moving her lips.

"I mean, what label is it?" Chuck wanted to know.

She sniffed, then drew a finger under her long nose. "Hey, mister, I'm no wine expert. Just tell me the color, and I'll get it for you."

"Fine. A bucket of the white stuff, then. And three straws."

"You're real funny, mister," she said without a hint of a smile. And then she turned her back on him.

"It seems she's impervious to your charm," Keely couldn't help but comment. She had seen him delight too many waitresses, too often, during their trip. And she was also slightly edgy tonight, for some reason.

"Maybe her feet hurt," Spike suggested. Clearly he wasn't used to seeing Chuck Dickens treated so abruptly by any female—except Ms. LaRoux, maybe.

When the wine arrived, Chuck pronounced it undrinkable. Then he pronounced the food inedible. He crumbled his paper napkin into a ball and threw it down. It bounced off the table. He stood up and stomped out of the restaurant.

Keely put down her fork and looked at Spike. "What's bothering Chuck tonight?" The meal was no worse than many others they had shared.

Spike took a big bite of his hamburger. It would take an earthquake, and maybe not even that, for him to break his stride. "I guess all this traveling is getting to him," he said around a mouthful. "I only assist him part of the year, but he's on the road all the time."

"Why does he work so hard, Spike? He certainly makes enough money to take some time off."

Zinko dipped a fat, greasy french fry into ketchup until it was completely coated. "Who knows? It's like he's on this treadmill and can't make himself stop. I don't even think he cares that much about the money anymore. He never has time to enjoy it. And he's always giving people loans they'll never repay. He's a real soft touch for a handout."

Yes, she had sensed that about him already. His expansive nature attracted her as much as his energy and ambition did. He had so many appealing traits. So many irritating ones, too. She poked at the congealed sauce on her dried-out fish. "Chuck was born a traveling man," she said aloud but mostly to herself. "He probably can't settle down."

Spike took a gulp of his soda. "You know why I think he keeps accepting one assignment after another?" he said, thoughtfully munching on an ice cube.

"Tell me." The topic fascinated her.

"He's running away from his real talent. He's always saying he'll do serious art photography when he has more time, but I think he's afraid of failing. Chuck can't stand to fail at *anything*. So instead he makes sure he doesn't have the time and wastes his talent on corporate work and commercial junk like that." Spike swallowed the ice cube. "Oops, sorry, Ms. La-Roux. No offense meant."

"No offense taken," she said. She appreciated learning whatever she could about Chuck. But she didn't allow herself to pump Spike for more details. It had been an unwritten code among the three of them to keep conversations friendly but impersonal. For all the time they had spent together, it was surprising how little they knew about one another's private lives.

As Keely paid for their meal at the cash register, Spike looked into the small lounge adjacent to the restaurant. "There's a piano in there!" he said with the joy of discovering something wondrous.

Keely glanced into the lounge. It was a very ordinary-looking piano, she observed. Nothing to get excited about. And then she noticed that Chuck was seated at the empty bar, shoulders a little hunched, staring into his drink. He looked so alone that her heart expanded with sympathy as she thought of the lonely life he must lead, always traveling, always with strangers. Her immediate inclination was to rush to him, to keep him company. But then she remembered how rudely he had left them at the dinner table awhile ago.

"Good night, Mr. Dickens," she called out coolly.

He slowly turned his head in her direction. "Just the person I was thinking about," he said. But he didn't invite her over.

"Let's go in, Ms. LaRoux," Spike urged. "I'll play the piano for you." He looked as eager as a child at his first recital, and Keely complied, not entirely looking forward to being his audience.

Chuck's light eyes glittered in the shadowy gloom as he watched them approach. "Ah, so you've decided to join me."

"I'm just here to listen to Spike play a tune," she said quickly to set the record straight as Zinko headed for the piano.

"Is he really going to play? That's great." He patted the stool beside him. "Sit here. You're in for a treat."

She was tired, and the beginning of a headache was nagging at her temples. "I'm not really a rock music fan."

He seemed amused. He signaled to the bartender and ordered two stingers. "I hate to drink alone," he said to cut short her protest.

"Then I would have preferred a glass of wine, not one of these sting things." She eyed her glass suspiciously.

"A stinger," he corrected. "Crème de menthe and brandy. Sip it slowly, and it'll soothe away that headache of yours."

"How did you know I had a headache?"

"I can see it in your eyes, Keely. There's a lot I can see in your eyes." He grinned. "Like your desire for me."

She knew he was teasing, but it made her angry nonetheless. She made an effort to stand up, but he stilled her with a light touch on her back. "Listen," he whispered.

Spike had begun to play, very softly at first, but then the sweet music filled the room and Keely's whole being.

"Good Lord, what's he playing?" she asked Chuck.

"Mozart, I believe." Her stunned reaction made him smile. "Not exactly hard rock, is it?"

"How beautiful," she said softly. She was touched by the sight of gawky Spike at the piano, his skinny arms jutting out as his fingers glided across the keys to produce such glorious music.

Keely was enthralled, and when Chuck took her hand in his she didn't notice for a moment. But as his broad thumb stroked her sensitive palm, ripples of pleasure swept through her. She sat very still, in an almost trancelike state, as he slowly brought her hand to his lips. When he kissed the inside of her wrist she could feel the heat of it surge through her veins. He leaned closer, his breath tickling her ear. "Let's go," he whispered. "I'll walk you back to your room."

She stood up obediently, a dreamy smile on her lips, and experienced a mild dizziness. It couldn't have been caused by the drink, which she hadn't touched. So it must have been the heady combination of Mozart and Chuck's caress. She stumbled, caught her balance and laughed awkwardly. The trance, though, was broken.

"No," she said. "Stay here and enjoy the music."

"It's late, Keely. I won't let you cross a dark, lonely parking lot to your room all alone."

She didn't exactly relish that prospect herself. As independent as she wanted to be, she also accepted that her size and sex limited her absolute freedom. The company of this big man would be protection against muggers or worse.

But there was another kind of danger inherent in letting him accompany her to her room. It was the temptation of asking him to stay once they got there.

"You don't have to come with me," she told Chuck. "It would hurt Spike's feelings if we both walked out while he was playing."

"Hell, he won't even notice, Keely. Don't you realize that he's in a world of his own right now?"

They both looked toward Spike, bent over the piano. His eyes were closed, he was smiling broadly and he was indeed oblivious to anything but the music floating off his fingertips.

"He really is," Keely agreed. At that moment Spike appeared to her to be some magical alien from a more advanced planet than theirs.

"Spike doesn't need an audience," Chuck told her. "He's one of the few talented people I know who couldn't care less about applause. Or critics' reviews. Or recognition of any kind." He shook his head. "I truly envy him for that."

Chuck's deep regard for Spike touched Keely. She also heard a deep sadness in his voice and wondered where it came from. Did he want such recognition for himself? She recalled Spike's hamburg-muffled words at dinner. He'd told her Chuck was afraid of failing. But Keely had difficulty believing that this big, bold hunk of a man would ever be afraid of anything.

Yet the melancholy that seemed to hang about him now moved her. "Okay, walk me back to my room. I could use the company," she said, thinking he could use it even more.

When they left the lounge the cold air outside hit them like a slap in the face. Keely shivered, buttoning up her light wool suit jacket.

"I thought Georgia was supposed to be mild in the fall," she said.

Chuck put his arm around her, and it felt like a warm, comforting overcoat. "You can never depend on the weather, Keely. Only love keeps you warm in the end."

"You can never depend on that, either," she said flatly, thinking of Royal LaRoux. But she didn't shrug off Chuck's arm.

They reached her door, and Keely, as usual, struggled with the lock. She had no patience with strange keys in strange doors.

"Allow me," Chuck said. The door unlocked easily for him. "Seems I haven't lost my touch. With locks, that is. But I can't seem to find the right key to your heart, can I, Keely?"

His blatant corniness made her laugh. "Where'd you steal that line? From a Valentine card?"

"Hell, it worked for me in third grade with cute little Penelope Wintergarten. My first love." He thumped his chest and sighed. "She had red hair, too."

"I don't believe you."

"You're right. She was a pony-tailed blonde. She let me kiss her right on the lips."

"Weren't you a precocious little boy!" She tried to imagine him as a boy, but right now he seemed so world-weary and melancholy. And vulnerable, too. Which made her vulnerable. She was tempted to take his face in her hands and kiss away the fatigue and unhappiness in it. Instead she turned away. "Good night, Chuck. Thanks for escorting me back to my room."

"I hate to go back to mine alone," he replied. "These impersonal motel rooms really get to me after awhile." There was a deep sense of longing in his voice, and in his eyes, too, as he gazed at her. "Sometimes I feel life is passing me by because I can't stay put in one place long enough to meet it head-on. You ever feel that way, Keely? That your career has taken over your real life?"

She nodded slowly. "More and more I do, the older I get. When I was younger I used to think there was plenty of time for everything." Even time for love, she added silently, meeting his eyes. "Want to watch the evening news together?" Her invitation slipped out without forethought. "It's too early to go to bed." That slipped out, too.

"I'd like that very much," he said politely, although a spark had sprung into his eyes that was not in keeping with his reserved tone.

"I meant just what I said, no more. We'll watch the news together, and then you'll go," she quickly explained.

"Don't worry, Keely. I'm not going to pounce on you. I haven't yet, have I?"

She couldn't refute that. But once he was inside her room, she experienced a sense of danger. After he turned on the TV and stretched lazily across her bed, a slow smile split his golden beard, and again Keely had the image of him as a lion. A lion playing with his prey.

"Aren't you going to join me, Keely?" he asked, patting the bed.

Chapter Six

She was angry with herself for inviting him in now, and she didn't reply. The dull ache in her head was beginning to throb again. Tension, she told herself. The room seemed stuffy. She took off her jacket and hung it in the doorless closet. The hangers were attached to the rod to prevent theft. But this chain motel was the height of luxury compared to the one in Duane, where they had stayed their first night. For one thing, it had a chair, which Keely chose to sit in. She had to crane her neck to see the television.

"That doesn't look very comfortable," Chuck said. "They design these rooms so that you have no choice but to watch TV in bed."

"I'd prefer to sit here, thank you." Her proper tone almost duplicated that of her high school English teacher's back in Jasper. The one who'd told her how disappointed she was that Keely had chosen to marry the school's football hero rather than take advantage of a college scholarship. Proper Miss Rimsley had not known, of course, that Keely was three months pregnant.

Chuck laughed at her prim reply. "Emily Post says it's perfectly acceptable for two fully clothed adults to watch TV together in the same bed on a business trip. Especially if protocol has already been established on a bed when one party was wearing a godawful flannel nightgown and the other party did not attack her. Or vice versa, of course."

Remembering that he had seen her in that shabby old nightgown, her wet hair wrapped in a towel, made Keely feel more comfortable with him. She left the chair and perched at the foot of the bed, facing the TV but with her back to him.

"Hey, lady, now you're blocking my view," he protested. "Lean back and rest your head against my chest."

It was a sensible suggestion, and she followed it. His wide, solid chest was an extremely comfortable support. She could feel the warmth of his big body through his blue cotton shirt and her own white silk blouse. His chest pressed against the base of her neck with each breath he took, and soon, without realizing it, she was breathing in unison with him.

"Want me to massage away that headache of yours?" he asked in a hushed tone, tenderly touching her temples with his cool fingertips.

She neither accepted nor refused his offer but kept her attention riveted on the newscaster, who was reporting on changing housing values in the Atlanta area. Since Keely had no plans to move to Atlanta, she had little interest in the subject. But she pretended fascination in it as Chuck gently massaged her temples, her forehead, and then let his fingers comb through her thick, short crop of copper hair. Her scalp tingled. In fact, her entire body began to tingle.

He continued to play with her hair, wrapping a glossy lock around his finger, letting it slip away, then selecting another strand to delicately tug and fondle. Keely experienced a soothing pleasure in being petted like this and almost started purring. Her headache evaporated as a relaxing warmth replaced it. Somewhere far away the newscaster droned on, but whatever was happening in the world didn't matter to her right now. All she cared about were the delicious sensations Chuck's gentle ministrations produced within her. She closed her eyes and floated in a sea of bliss.

"I want you very much, Keely," he said, his voice a hoarse whisper.

The rasp of desire in it made her back arch. Her green eyes flew open as she stiffened. He dropped his hand from her head, as from a suddenly balking cat's. But when she didn't move away he began stroking her back, his hand gliding across the smooth silk of her blouse. "I want to see your eyes," he said, pulling her backward until she was lying across the bed with him, face-to-face. His own light gray eyes were luminous.

He began to delicately outline the shape of her full mouth with one fingertip, and her lips parted instinctively. His finger slid across her small, pearly teeth, and she flicked out her tongue to taste his skin. How easy it would be to let herself go, she thought. To let her body blend with his.

"Did you hear what I said?" he murmured. "I want you. Let me make love to you. It'll be wonderful."

Yes, it would all be so perfectly easy, she thought. Here they were, a man and a woman who were physically attracted to each other, alone in an impersonal motel room far from home. But it was exactly the impersonality of it that suddenly struck Keely as wrong. Did he want *her* or would any woman have suited him at this lonely hour? She turned her face away and pushed herself up on her elbows.

"You know, you can't always have what you want, Dickens." She meant to sound abrupt and angry because she was hurt, thinking that this Camera Casanova considered her just another easy conquest. She knew that making love with him would mean much more to her. Too much. When she pushed herself off the bed and stood up, her bones felt like butter. "I think you'd better leave now."

"Okay," he agreed easily, standing up, too. His handsome face was a bland mask. "I'm not going to persist. I only want a woman who wants me as much."

His cool, aloof demeanor contrasted sharply with her own deep agitation. "This is all a game to you, isn't it?" she accused, regretting her own participation in it. "Win some, lose some, right?"

His eyes were as cold as a winter sky now. "Maybe we're both losers tonight, Keely."

He bowed quite majestically and departed, closing the door very softly behind him. Keely's hand was shaking as she connected the chain lock. That had been way too close a call, she told herself. And then she realized that she and Chuck hadn't even kissed.

Chuck didn't accompany Keely and Spike to the airport the next morning. "He decided to take an earlier flight back," Spike told her casually, as if it was no big deal.

Their own flight to New York was rather rough because of rainstorms, and when the plane made its bumpy landing Keely longed to have Chuck beside her, holding her hand. She and Spike parted at LaGuardia, and she took a taxi into the city. The streets were shiny with rain, and a cold dampness pervaded the cab, seeping into her bones. Horns blared, traffic snarled, and when they got caught in gridlock, tears of exasperation sprang to Keely's eyes.

She rarely cried, and this flood of emotion surprised her. She had planned to go directly to the office and at least check all the mail and messages that had been piling up on her desk during the week. But it was already midafternoon, she was exhausted and she missed her daughter. She decided to go home instead. She suddenly wished she could *really* go home, back to the peace of Vermont, far from this jangle of traffic and pressures.

The one thing Keely was determined to do that weekend was erase all thoughts of work from her mind and devote her attention to Joy. She told her daughter they could do whatever she liked, and Joy immediately suggested shopping at Bloomingdale's on Saturday.

Keely disliked shopping, but since it was Joy's favorite pastime, she complied. And when Joy found a purple suede jacket she did not think herself capable of living without, Keely agreed to buy it for her. Joy hugged her and told her that she was the best mother in the WORLD, but the compliment rang empty in Keely's ears. She didn't want her daughter's approval just because she had a Bloomingdale's charge card. Yet she admitted to herself that she was trying to appease Joy for her having been away all week. But how could a purple suede jacket make up for a mother's absence? she asked herself.

They rode down the escalator, and Joy gave out a little shriek of delight. "Look, Mom!" she commanded, pointing at an elongated silver mannequin costumed in a peach silk-and-lace teddy. "Isn't it beautiful? Please let's buy it."

Joy's taste had certainly gone way beyond her age, and Keely decided it was time to draw the line. "You have absolutely no business even considering something like that for yourself, Joy."

"I meant for YOU, Mother. It's about time you bought some pretty underwear. All yours is so plain and boring."

Keely did not think it necessary for Joy to inform everyone on the escalator that her mother wore plain, sensible underwear. She gave Joy a little pinch on the arm to silence her, but it was such a mild one that Joy ignored it. "Let's go take a closer look at it," she insisted. "Come on, Mom."

Joy hopped off the escalator and headed in the direction of the mannequin. Keely followed to humor her. She had little interest in such an elegant but useless piece of frippery. And when she peeked at the price tag, she had even less. She let out a whistle. "This little nothing costs more than I used to make in a week as a secretary!"

"Well, you're not a secretary anymore," Joy pointed out.

"And I don't own the company, either. No, Joy, as pretty as this teddy is, I'd never spend that much money on myself. On something no one but me would ever see, no less."

Taking Joy's arm, she turned from the mannequin without looking back. The only thing she purchased for herself that day was a heavy casserole dish imported from Finland, which she thought self-indulgent enough. Keely had a weakness for fine cookware, if not fine lingerie.

Keely made veal marengo in her new casserole late Sunday afternoon. It was a double recipe, enough to feed twelve. Although she planned dinner only for Joy and herself, she'd freeze the rest. Since she had helped her mother feed four hungry, growing boys and farm hands, too, it was partly habit to cook in large quantities. And she enjoyed doing it. She was at peace in her tiny kitchen. All the dicing and slicing, stirring and blending took her mind off work problems. It almost took her mind off Chuck Dickens, too.

Still, his blond, bearded image drifted in and out of her mind as she worked. She nicked her finger slicing onions. She burned the butter while browning the veal cubes. She poured red wine instead of white into the stock and almost forgot to add the bouquet garni. She did forget to stir paprika into the tomato puree. It was all his fault. Not only had he been invading her dreams for the past few nights, but now he was invading the sanctuary of her galley kitchen. She felt cramped enough in it already without disturbing thoughts of him poking and pulling at her. Without even being there, he was crowding her.

She missed him. She hated to admit it to herself, but she did. Although she had been in his company for only a week, life now seemed dull without him. He made her laugh, he made her furious, he made her spark with desire by a simple look or a light touch. He made her feel alive.

She kept reminding herself that he had come into her life on a temporary basis only. In a few weeks he would be out of it just as abruptly, off to his next assignment. His next woman, too. She had no doubts about that.

She had absolutely no regrets about refusing to make love with him their last night together. Well, maybe a small twinge of regret now and then, like every five minutes or so. He had said it would be wonderful, and it probably would have been. Not probably, she corrected herself. It really would have been wonderful.

More the reason to be thankful they hadn't made love, she decided. At least now, when they parted company for good, he wouldn't be taking her heart with him. All she wanted to do was get through the next few weeks without falling in love with him.

Keely didn't notice that her light red sauce had begun to boil until the bubbles started exploding. She quickly reduced the heat to a gentle simmer, then slammed a lid over the casserole dish. No more thoughts about Chuck Dickens, she admonished herself, wiping her hands on her chef's apron.

The trouble was, she had nothing to occupy her mind while the sauce simmered for an hour and a half. Joy was visiting a school friend who lived in the same building, supposedly to do homework. But Keely had seen her slip three record albums into her book bag, and she was sure the two preteens were practicing dance steps instead.

Keely had hoped to spend every precious minute of the weekend with Joy, and she felt a little abandoned now. To fill the time she decided to make two apple flans and got to work mixing dough. She would give one of the pies to Mrs. Alphonso. And most of the veal marengo, too. Although Keely paid her well for looking after Joy when she traveled or worked late, she also shared most of her culinary creations with her. Keely liked to imagine Joy and Mrs. Alphonso enjoying the food she had cooked when she couldn't be with them. It made her feel less distant.

By six Keely had one tart cooling on the counter and another baking in the small oven. A spinach salad was waiting to be tossed with olive oil and tarragon vinegar. She had set up a card table in the living room and covered it with a lilac cloth, Joy's favorite color next to deep purple. A blooming African violet and two tall white candles in pewter holders decorated the table. She was looking forward to a cozy meal with her daughter.

But Joy called a few minutes later and begged to be allowed to have dinner with her friend, instead. The entire family, it seemed, was involved in a game of Monopoly, and if she left, she would ruin it for everyone.

"But I made us such a nice dinner," Keely protested.

"Aw, Mom, PLEASE. We're sending out for pizza, and I'm having so much fun."

After being assured that Joy had done her homework and would come home no later than eight, Keely gave her permission. She wasn't going to force Joy to enjoy a meal with her. Enjoyment couldn't be forced. But she did feel more than a little hurt when she hung up the phone. It seemed Joy wanted her mother home more but did not necessarily want to be there with her when she was.

Keely returned to the kitchen to finish the sauce. She strained it into a saucepan, then thickened it with a flour and butter paste until it was smooth and heavy. Her heart wasn't in it anymore, though. It lightened considerably when she heard a knock on the door. She was sure it was Joy, who never remembered her key. She must have heard the disappointment in Keely's voice and decided to share dinner with her poor, lonesome mom after all.

"I'm coming, sweetie," Keely called as she hurried across the room to the door. She flung it open, a wide, welcoming smile on her face. But instead of coming face-to-face with her daughter, she was face-to-chest with Chuck Dickens.

"I'm not by any chance the sweetie you were expecting?"

"Of course not. Why would I be expecting you, anyway?" The shock of seeing him there brought out her natural bluntness.

He shifted uncomfortably. "Sorry. I really should have called first. I just stopped by to drop these off." He handed her two shiny yellow boxes.

"You brought me a gift?" Her astonishment increased.

"Uh, not exactly. They're slides. The lab developed some of the film I shot last week, and I figured you'd want to see the results as soon as possible. The rest will be ready on Tuesday or Wednesday, but this will give you an idea of the technique I'm using on this project. You wanted dynamic images of the products, and I think I more than succeeded, if I do say so myself."

Yes, he would say so himself. One thing she could never accuse Chuck Dickens of was false modesty. "I can't wait to take a look," she said. She went into the living room, sat on the sofa and opened one of the boxes. Then she glanced over her shoulder to see Chuck still hovering at the threshold. "Aren't you coming in?" she asked a little curtly.

"Well, now that you've invited me to, I will," he replied.

Sheer nervousness had made her forget her good manners, and she realized she'd been treating him like a delivery boy. "Please sit down," she said more cordially. "I really appreciate this. It was thoughtful of you to bring me the slides on a Sunday evening."

He shrugged. "It was no big deal. I happened to be in the area anyway. I'm headed for Lawley's Bar." He didn't sit down. "I really can't stay."

She had taken a slide from the box and lifted it to the reading lamp to examine. She noticed her hand was shaking and quickly brought the slide down, hoping Chuck hadn't noticed, too.

"Well, I can't see anything like this. I'll use the projector at work tomorrow morning." She stood up again, racking her mind for something more to say to him. "Lucky you took an earlier flight back Friday. You probably missed the rainstorms. Did Spike mention how bumpy our flight was?"

"I should apologize about that, Keely."

"Why? You're not responsible for the weather." Her tone was light. She wasn't going to let him know how disappointed she'd been that he had left Atlanta without her.

"But I am responsible for my own immature actions. I went out of my way to avoid seeing you that morning because I was still damn mad that you had turned me down the night before. So I packed my bag and left in a huff."

For some reason, that pleased her. At the time he had acted as if it meant nothing to him. "You left in a huff, not a plane?"

He smiled a little sheepishly. "That's right. Not the most comfortable way to travel."

He looked around the room, and Keely had the urgent desire to start straightening things out. Scattered sections of the Sunday newspaper were strewn across the sofa and coffee table. She controlled the urge, though.

"Would you care for a drink?" she offered politely and then remembered that she had nothing but a bottle of wine in the cupboard.

"Oh, no," he refused quickly. "I really have to go. Like I said, I'm on my way to Lawley's."

No doubt on his way to meet the pretty waitress there, Keely thought. He was dressed with more care than Keely had ever seen him before. His gray flannel trousers were perfectly pressed, and his camel-hair blazer and red turtleneck sweater brought out the golden highlights in his hair and beard. His hair had been clipped and his beard trimmed, she noted.

She resented the fact that he looked so good when she looked so awful. She was wearing a faded blue rugby shirt, baggy gray sweatpants, a white chef's apron with spatters of tomato sauce decorating it, and her ratty pink fuzzy slippers, which she should have thrown out ages ago but couldn't bear to part with. She hadn't passed a comb through her thick hair all afternoon or powdered her nose. It was the second time he had caught her looking her worst, she thought with exasperation.

"Well, I'm sure you have better things to do, Chuck." Her tone was a little too bright, almost brittle, as she freed him to get on with his life.

"It's pretty obvious that you do." He gestured toward the linen-covered card table set for two. "That *sweetie* you're expecting is one hell of a lucky guy. Dinner smells delicious. Sorry I intruded on your romantic evening."

For an instant Keely was tempted to go along with Chuck's false assumption. The tinge of jealousy in his voice gave her smiling satisfaction. But she had never indulged in little games with men. Especially a man who was beginning to take over her thoughts and maybe her heart.

"Do I look as if I'm dressed for a romantic evening?" she asked, lifting up one fuzzy-slippered foot.

"You look absolutely adorable," he stated without smiling. "I'm sure he'll think so, too. I wish you'd mentioned that you have someone special in your life when we were traveling together last week, Keely. I guess it was stupid of me to assume you didn't, but you didn't say a word. Maybe it would have made your rejection of me easier to take if you had."

She was more than a little surprised by the dejection in his expression. Maybe he wasn't such a Camera Casanova after all, but a man whose feelings ran as deeply as hers. "That some-one special in my life isn't a boyfriend, Chuck," she told him softly. "It's my daughter, Joy, I was expecting when you knocked."

"You have a child?" He stepped back, as if pushed off balance.

"Well, she doesn't like to think of herself as that. She's eleven years old, going on forty."

He slowly shook his head in wonderment. "It's amazing. We just spent a week together, and I don't know you at all, do I, Keely? I assumed you were married to your career."

"I think you assumed a little too much about me from the very beginning," she replied.

"And is there a Mr. LaRoux, too?"

"Not anymore," she answered abruptly, turning away from his intense gaze. When he looked at her like that she had the feeling he was recording every nuance of expression with his camera eyes.

He blinked, and it was like a shutter snapping. "Okay. I get the picture. You don't want to talk about your personal life with me. Good night, Keely. Have a pleasant dinner with your daughter." He moved toward the door.

She couldn't control her desire to halt him. "She's not coming back for dinner, Chuck. She made other plans at the last minute. And I have all this veal marengo just waiting to be eaten."

He paused, his hand on the doorknob. "Is that an invitation to stay for dinner, Ms. LaRoux?"

She shrugged to appear nonchalant, although every fiber in her body was tugged in his direction.

"Unless you have a date to keep at Lawley's Bar," she said in a good imitation of casualness.

"No one's waiting for me there, if that's what you mean," he said. "They serve fish and chips every Sunday night. But veal marengo sounds a lot better."

But it wasn't her veal marengo that concerned Keely at the moment. That wasn't the issue at all. "What about that pretty waitress you seemed so interested in when I searched you out at Lawley's?'' she asked him. ''Surely she'll be disappointed if you don't show up tonight.''

Chuck tugged at his beard, lost in thought for a moment. Then his light eyes flickered understanding. ''Oh, you must mean Cindy! Yes, she is very pretty, come to think of it. But I doubt she's waiting with bated breath for me tonight. She's devoted to her husband and new baby. Every time she serves me a beer, she mentions that baby and gets a big tip out of me.''

He laughed, and Keely joined him, relieved to hear about Cindy's husband and baby.

''Then you might as well have dinner with me, since you're here anyway,'' she said, not quite the gracious hostess but with a welcoming smile on her face.

Chuck let go of the doorknob and took a few steps back into her living room. ''Sounds good to me,'' he said. ''And I'll accept that drink you offered earlier, when I thought for sure I was intruding. Scotch on the rocks would be nice.''

For the first time in all her years in New York Keely regretted not having a fully stocked bar. ''Would you settle for a glass of rather good Pinot Chardonnay instead?'' she asked him.

''Keely, I'd settle for anything with you,'' he replied.

He followed her into the kitchen and took over the task of opening the wine. He stayed to watch her as she added the finishing touches to the meal.

At first his presence made her nervous, but she was so intent on getting the dinner ready that she almost but not quite forgot about his male frame looming in the doorway.

When all was ready she turned to him and asked him to light the candles on the card table. She took that moment to disappear into her bedroom and check out how she looked. The image in her dresser mirror didn't please her. She was shocked to see a streak of flour across her nose and rubbed it away quickly. Just as quickly she tore off her stained apron and sweats and kicked off her awful fuzzy slippers. She changed into an aquamarine silk caftan she'd bought on sale more than a year ago.

It was the easiest thing she could slip into, she assured herself. It required no slip or bra or pantyhose. In fact, the only thing beneath it was her bikini panties. She quickly ran a comb through her hair and tossed her head from side to side to fluff it up a bit.

When she returned to the living room Chuck looked her over carefully. "The color of that dress contrasts well with your hair and accents your eyes," he said with the cool objectivity of an artist appraising a subject.

"Thank you," she said, not quite sure it was meant as a compliment.

It wasn't. "But it doesn't show off your figure at all," he added. "None of the clothes you wear do."

"Use your imagination," she suggested dryly.

"What do you think I've been doing all week?"

She ignored the question but couldn't be offended. She had imagined him naked more than once, too. They sat down to dinner, and she watched intently as he took the first bite of the veal dish she had spent much of the afternoon preparing in her effort to keep from dwelling on him. Now here he was in the flesh, eating the meal, as if she had conjured him up with all her stewing and simmering.

"I've never tasted anything so wonderful," he pronounced, and there was true admiration in his often critical eyes. "I never pictured you at a stove, Keely. I thought of you as being much more at home behind a big, important executive desk."

His approval warmed her. "Oh, I've been cooking since I was a kid. I thought I was Vermont's answer to Julia Child. I had big dreams then. I was going to open a gourmet restaurant. I like cooking for people. I always have."

Safe in her own territory, Keely was more comfortable with Chuck than she ever had been. She felt the inclination to open up to him, to tell him all her foolish dreams. And to listen to his dreams, too. But their talk throughout dinner remained light. He made her laugh with a few silly jokes, some of them more off-color than she would normally approve. But he had such a pleasant, easy way about him that she couldn't help roaring with delight at the punch lines.

"I love to watch your face when you laugh," he said. "And I love the sound of it. It gurgles up from the base of your throat and sort of sends a shiver through me."

Keely immediately stopped in the middle of a chortle, catching the look of desire in his intent, suddenly serious face. That made *her* shiver. He grasped her hand and brought it to his lips.

"Dinner was superb, but dessert could be even better," he murmured, his hot breath on her fingertips. Then he began to nibble her forefinger, making it clear what he expected for dessert.

A delightful image sprang into Keely's mind—*Crème La-Roux*. Her naked body encased in sweet whipped cream and Chuck slowly licking it off. Now *that* would be a recipe for her private cookbook. But then Keely's sense of smell got the better of her vivid imagination.

"Something's burning!" she cried, snatching away her hand.

"Yeah. Me," Chuck replied hoarsely.

Keely leaped up and ran into the kitchen. When she yanked open the oven door, smoke engulfed her. She held her breath and dived into the cloud, just barely remembering to protect her hands with potholders. She withdrew a charred apple flan, placed it on a counter tile and threw open the little window above the sink. Then she thrashed the air to herd out the heavy smoke.

"Dammit, I've been burning things all day thinking about you, Dickens," she accused without thinking.

She practically yelled this right into Chuck's ear; he had followed her and was standing beside her. Seeing that the emergency had been solved, he captured her flailing arms and gently folded them against his broad chest as carefully as if they were delicate bird wings.

"Have you been thinking about me all day, too?" he asked, his low, deep voice a contrast to her shrill, high one. "I can't get you out of my mind, Keely. That's why I came tonight. I couldn't stay away. I had such a deep craving for you, Keely. Just the sight of you."

His fervent confession surprised her, and as he lowered his mouth to her half-open one, she made no protest. He began their first kiss slowly, tasting the outer edges of her lips with teasing flicks of his tongue. The sable-soft touch of his beard against her face made her shiver with delight, and a surge of desire rushed through her. She lifted her arms to his neck and plunged her fingers into the thick golden hair that curled slightly at the base of it.

He was quick to answer her silent demand as she pressed her body against his. His kiss became deeper, and he took in the sweetness she offered. The passion she had kept reined in for too long now leaped out, unrestrained, and she stood on tiptoe to press against him with even more intimacy. It gave her unabashed satisfaction to feel his strong, hard need for her through the thin silk of her caftan.

He slid his hands down her body to discover she was wearing very little beneath that caftan. His moan of pleasure at this discovery vibrated through her. As he explored the contours of her rounded hips through the filmy layers of her dress and panties, each stroke stoked the fire within her. She answered by digging her fingers into the tight, lean muscles of his buttocks as their bodies melded together.

The air was filled with the sweet, sharp aroma of the burned flan, and Keely had difficulty breathing. She had the odd but delicious sensation that she was melting into Chuck and that at any moment now her legs would buckle and she would sink down to the floor, pulling him down with her.

But then she thought of her daughter and the clear possibility of the child walking in and finding her mother in the embrace of a total stranger. The thought cooled her ardor considerably, but it still took a great deal of willpower for Keely to tear her mouth from Chuck's.

"Please let me go," she managed to say, just finding her voice. "Joy could come home at any moment."

"Who?" As he gazed down at her, he seemed dazed. His usually sharp eyes were dulled by passion. And rather than let her go, he merely tightened his hold on her hips.

"My daughter, Joy," Keely said with more conviction, pushing against Chuck's hard chest. "I expect her home soon."

He released her with such abruptness that she almost lost her balance and fell backward. "Of course," he said. "Your daughter." He turned away and pretended great interest in the copper molds displayed on the wall above the stove. "How very convenient," he muttered under his breath.

"Chuck," she whispered, wanting to rest her flaming cheek against his stiff back but not daring to. "I'm sorry."

"Are you?" His voice was tight with disappointment, and he didn't turn around. "I wonder."

"About what?" Her tone sharpened. His controlled but obvious anger put her on the defensive.

He faced her now, point-blank, his silver eyes like bullets. "I wonder if this daughter of yours actually exists, Keely. Or is she just some convenient excuse you use when things get a little out of hand? I think you're a tease, Ms. LaRoux. I think you get a kick out of driving me crazy."

His accusation was sharper than a slap across the face, and for a moment she was speechless. But then words bubbled out of her, spattering hot.

"How dare you accuse me of that? My daughter is *not* some convenient excuse. She's the most important person in my life, and I don't give a damn if you believe she exists or not. Oh, she's real enough, all right. A lot more real than what you have to offer me."

"What exactly do you think I'm offering you, Keely?" His gaze softened, but his expression remained stiff.

"Passion!" she spit out, as if she disdained rather than longed for it. "For a night. Or a week, maybe, if you didn't find the conquest too boring."

He rubbed his eyes with his long, artistic fingers and let his shoulders slump. "Hell, it's been a long night, and you've worn me out," he finally said. "I give up, Keely."

These were hardly words to comfort her. "Then why don't you leave," she suggested in a hollow voice.

The kitchen clock ticked loudly, filling the silence before he spoke again. "Because I can't," he told her. "Not without a cup of coffee, at least. I won't be able to sleep tonight anyway."

She wasn't angry anymore. She felt as exhausted as he looked, yet she couldn't bear to have him leave just yet, either.

"Yes," she agreed. "We'll have a cup of coffee. Would you like a piece of pie, too?"

He threw a wary glance at the charred flan on the counter. The sliced apples Keely had so carefully arranged in pinwheel fashion were now black and shriveled. It was not a very appetizing sight. "Sure," he replied gamely, although his expression showed he would prefer to eat toads.

Her heart rose on a brief current of delight as she concluded that he must love her just a little if he insisted on staying, knowing full well that there would be no further intimacies between them. And even more proof than that, he was willing to choke down a piece of charred pie to please her!

She whisked off the cotton towel covering the perfect tart she had baked earlier. "I meant a piece of this one, of course." They both gazed at the golden creation, she with a certain degree of pride, he with a small smile of relief.

He offered to make the coffee while she glazed the top of the pie with melted red currant jelly. The galley kitchen was so small that they kept bumping into each other, and each time their bodies grazed a thrill vibrated through Keely's very bones. She hadn't quite recovered from their kiss, and she was clumsy now, constantly dropping utensils that clattered to the floor. Chuck would immediately pick them up. They bumped heads retrieving a dropped fork at the same time and almost knocked each other out.

They laughed, but then Chuck got serious. "Before your daughter comes home, I want you to tell me about her father, Keely," he insisted, very slowly and carefully pouring boiling water into the freshly ground coffee beans nestled in the paper filter.

Keely said nothing. Royal LaRoux was the last person she wanted to talk about right now. Or ever. She had slammed the door on her past years ago. Or at least she hoped she had. Her mouth firmly shut, she continued to glaze the apples circling the tart with more concentration than the simple task required.

Chuck was not put off by her silence. "I want to know if he's someone you still care about," he persisted. "Please let's get that straight before we go on."

There was a plea in his voice that Keely couldn't ignore. Nor could she ignore the fact that he hadn't given up on her after all. Most men would have been out the door long ago, but he was staying. At least long enough to hear her story, that was.

Chapter Seven

She didn't respond right away. She delayed the moment of truth by getting a carton of cream from the refrigerator and pouring the silky liquid into a small white pitcher decorated with pink cornflowers. It had been her mother's pitcher, one of the very few pretty things she had ever owned.

"How silly of me," she said. "We both drink coffee black, don't we?"

"Do you still care about him?" Chuck repeated.

"Royal LaRoux died in a motorcycle accident over six years ago, Chuck." Hoping that would be the end of the discussion, she carried the two plates of apple tart into the living room and placed them on the glass table in front of the white sofa.

Chuck sat down beside her on the sofa. "You must have married very young. You don't seem old enough to have an eleven-year-old child."

"Maybe I wasn't old enough when I had her, but I'm certainly old enough now. I'm thirty!"

"You make that sound like you're over the hill. Which makes me feel like I've gone 'round the bend. I'm five years older than you, Keely."

She was relieved that the topic of conversation had changed. "I don't think any woman would ever accuse you of being past your prime, Chuck. You seem to have your way with all of them."

He frowned. "I don't want my way with *all* of them. Or anyone except you." He placed his hand on her knee. She thought he was going to kiss her again. He didn't. He wanted to talk, but not about himself. "How did you meet your husband?"

So they were back to that again. She met Chuck's interested, intelligent eyes and suddenly felt like telling him the whole story.

"Roy and I were high school sweethearts." How trite that sounded, she thought. But at the time she had loved the boy beyond all reason. "I got pregnant at the end of our senior year. I was going to have the baby and give it up for adoption, but Roy wanted to get married. He never thought much beyond the present moment, and at the time he thought it would be fun to have a wife and baby to come home to. But two months in a little trailer with a crying baby was about all he could stand. The winters in Vermont can be very long and trying. He took off for California."

She related all this in a conversational tone, as if chatting about the weather, and then passed Chuck a plate. "Please try my *tarte aux pommes*," she said, her voice artificially gay, her French accent almost perfect.

Chuck broke into the crust with his fork and took a small bite. "Very good," he said politely, but she could tell he wasn't paying much attention to the taste. "You must have hated him for that," he said softly.

She shook her head. "No, not for that. I adored my little baby, and it was really thanks to Roy I had kept her. I even forgave him for taking off and not sharing the responsibilities. It almost destroyed me at the time, but I would have gotten over it eventually."

She picked up her own dessert, stared down at it for a moment and then put it back on the table very carefully. "The trouble was, Roy kept coming back. He kept coming back to me and then leaving me again. And again and again." She heard the shrill rise of her voice and stood up abruptly. "I forgot to bring in the coffee."

Chuck grabbed her hand and pulled her back down. "Wait. Tell me one thing. Why did you put up with it?"

"Why do you think?" She flicked back a strand of her copper hair impatiently. "I loved him, of course. Every time he came back I welcomed him with open arms. And every time he walked out I told myself it was over between us. But for all the pain he caused me, I felt committed to him. He was Joy's father, after all. And my first love."

She swallowed hard. Now that she had started, she couldn't stop. All the emotions she had buried for so long were erupting to the surface. "At times I really did think I'd go crazy. One of the reasons I moved to New York was to put an end to that cycle, his coming and going. But he managed to find me. I couldn't turn him out. He had no money, no place to stay. What was I going to do, let him sleep on a bench in Central Park? Royal was so helpless, really."

The wayward strand of hair had drifted across her eyes again, but Keely scarcely noticed. Chuck gently brushed it back. He also brushed away a tear that had slipped from her eye. His own eyes were filled with tenderness. "He made your life hell, didn't he, Keely?"

"Not always," she replied. "Roy could be very sweet, and he was very kind to Joy whenever he was around. She doesn't remember much about him, of course. He could never stay put for more than a month or so. The last time he told me goodbye, he said he was heading for Florida." She shrugged. "But I guess he changed his mind. The state police in South Dakota eventually notified me that he'd been killed there when his motorcycle crashed into a truck."

"I'm so sorry," Chuck whispered, taking her hand.

She interpreted his compassion as pity, and she couldn't stand that from him. She pulled her hand back. "You needn't feel sorry for me, Chuck. I learned a good lesson in life very young: you can never depend on anybody but yourself. And once I realized that, I did just fine on my own.''

"Are you alone because you're still mourning him?'' Chuck watched her face carefully.

She shook her head slowly, heavily. "No, I mourned the loss of Roy long before he died. A little of my love for him died each time he left me until there was none left in the end.'' She lifted her head and looked at Chuck. Her emerald eyes were hard. "I'll never allow myself to go through that pain again.''

"Pain and love are not synonymous, Keely,'' Chuck told her very quietly.

She took in his strong, angular features, so different from Roy's. His build and coloring were similar, though. Was that why she had experienced such a strong, immediate attraction to Chuck? Like Roy, he was also a rolling stone, with the excuse of his photography assignments to keep him traveling constantly. Was he a more mature, successful version of Royal LaRoux?

As a girl she had loved blindly, letting passion rule her, but she'd never forgive herself if she let it happen a second time. She no longer had youth and inexperience as an excuse. And now she had her daughter's welfare to consider. Joy's future was of primary importance, and she had worked too long and too hard for her security to become distracted now. She had to concentrate on her career. Nothing could get in the way of that. Especially not this handsome, magnetic man sitting beside her. Their kiss had proven to her that he had the power to take her over, body and soul. She could not allow that to happen.

She got up swiftly. "It's getting late. Perhaps you should go now, Chuck.''

If he was surprised by her sudden dismissal, he didn't show it. He casually glanced at his watch. "But it's not quite eight. I'd hoped to meet your daughter before I went.''

"I don't think that's really a good idea,'' she replied sternly. "Joy isn't used to finding strange men in our apartment. Preteen girls have romantic imaginations, and she may read more into our relationship than there is. It's best you leave before she returns.''

"What *is* our relationship, Keely?'' Chuck asked abruptly, standing up, too.

Keely had no idea how to answer that question, and, fortunately, she didn't have to. At that moment Joy burst through the door. The first thought that sprang into Keely's mind was that her daughter could have entered just as suddenly while she and Chuck were passionately kissing in the kitchen. The very thought of it made Keely greet the girl with a false, guilty smile.

"Joy, you're back!'' she said, stating the obvious. "I'd like you to meet a business associate of mine. Mr. Charles Dickens.''

"How's your pal Oliver Twist doing these days, Mr. Dickens?'' Joy asked, tossing an impish look at the bearded stranger standing beside her mother.

"Don't be a wise guy, sweetie,'' Keely reprimanded, nervously recalling her own crack about his name when they first met.

But Chuck laughed this time. "Your daughter is just demonstrating that she's well-read, Keely.'' He extended his hand to the girl. "How do you do, Miss LaRoux? I've been looking forward to meeting you this evening.''

Joy shook his hand and beamed, pleased at being treated with such formal adult courtesy. There was no doubt about it, Keely noted, Chuck had a way of putting people at ease. Everybody seemed to like him immediately. She had noticed how people warmed up to him during their week of travel. Which made it all the more puzzling to her that they had clashed so strongly during their first encounter. Everything about him had rubbed her the wrong way, and she had bristled. It was as if she had sensed he would become a danger in her carefully constructed world.

"Mr. Dickens is a photographer, and he dropped by to give me some slides,'' she explained to her daughter, feeling a need to make an excuse for his presence.

Joy's eyes skimmed the living room, taking in the card table in the corner, with its flowers and snuffed-out candles.

"And then he stayed for dinner, I guess," she said, pleased with her detective work. She grinned at Chuck.

"I say! Excellent deduction, Mr. Holmes," he replied in a broad English accent.

Joy took a deep bow. "Why, thank you, Dr. Watson."

They laughed together. After a slight hesitation, Keely joined in, realizing there was no reason to be tense. Joy seemed to think that her mother's inviting a man to stay for dinner was perfectly natural.

She was glad now that Joy had arrived in time to meet Chuck. She very much wanted her to like him. He stayed, as if perfectly willing to give Joy the chance to look him over.

He didn't try to ingratiate himself, though. Perhaps because of this, they hit it off splendidly. Chuck's sense of humor appealed to Joy, who had the same tendency to be a bit teasing and arch. And they had no trouble finding topics of conversation. Keely was at a loss when Joy began rhapsodizing about her latest celebrity crush, a pop singer whose trademark was diamond rings on his TOES. But Chuck knew all about him, apparently. He had taken the picture for this teen idol's latest album cover. Needless to say, this impressed Joy enormously.

"You actually KNOW him, Mr. Dickens!" she shrieked. "What's he REALLY like?"

Chuck thought a moment, taking the question seriously. "I don't know him well at all, Joy. But he isn't like the image he projects to the public. Like most of us, he puts on a good front. But he's really pretty shy and insecure. Again, like most of us." He threw a quick glance at Keely.

His look was so pointed that she wondered if he was really talking about himself. Or her. Or maybe both of them. They both tended to hide behind their professional personas rather than reveal their true selves. Tonight was the first time Keely had let down her guard completely with Chuck. His response had been warm and reassuring. But part of her still remained wary of such openness. It left her too vulnerable.

Accepting a second cup of coffee, he stayed on awhile longer. But after glancing at his watch he refused a third. He said he had an early shoot the next day and got up to leave. Keely walked him to the door.

"I'll see you the day after tomorrow," he said lightly. But then he took up her hand and lowered his voice. "We can take up where we left off." His luminous gray eyes were filled with all kinds of promises.

She shook his hand formally, sensing Joy in the background, all eyes and ears. It gave her an excuse not to respond to his remark. She wasn't quite sure where they'd left off or how much further she wanted to take it. But it was obvious from the gleam in his eye that he expected the next step to be an affair. It would be a giant step for her though, one she couldn't take so easily.

She told him good-night softly, and when she turned back to the living room Joy was waiting, an expectant smile on her face.

"Well, I'd better see to those dishes," Keely said, hoping to avoid a discussion about Chuck with her daughter.

But Joy followed her into the kitchen and leaned against the counter, observing her mother closely. And it wasn't the way Keely washed dishes that fascinated her.

"Mr. Dickens is a nice man, Mom," she said. "I hope you invite him back real soon."

Keely directed her attention to scrubbing the bottom of the burned pie plate with a scouring pad. She'd picked up the eager note of hope in Joy's voice. One of her chief reasons for avoiding introducing her daughter to the men she casually dated was that she knew how much Joy longed for a dependable father figure and how quickly she would assume that any man in her mother's life could become exactly that.

"Yes, Mr. Dickens *is* nice, Joy," she admitted to herself as much as to her daughter. "But when we complete our business together, we'll probably never see each other again." Her heart squeezed tight as she stated this, but she was careful to keep her face natural and relaxed, aware that Joy was staring at her.

"He isn't married, is he, Mom?"

It was a guileless question but also very much to the point. It demonstrated to Keely that Joy, raised in New York, was much more sophisticated than she had ever been at that age.

"No, sweetie," she replied. "According to Spike Zinko, his assistant, Mr. Dickens doesn't think much of marriage. He's not the sort of man to settle down."

"Oh." Joy's disappointment hung heavy in the air as she polished a wineglass. Then she perked up. "Well, maybe he's never met the right person before. I mean, he never met YOU before, Mom."

Despite herself, Keely couldn't help but smile at that. She gave her daughter a peck on the cheek and told her it was time to get ready for bed. Left alone, she tried to quell the little burst of hope Joy's naive remark had spawned in her heart. She reminded herself that Chuck Dickens had managed just fine before meeting her and would no doubt continue on his merry way after they parted.

Back at the Citation office Monday morning, Keely was relieved to find that efficient Edith Hamilton had typed out a succinct report of the week's happenings for her and handled much of the everyday department business on her own. Keely had learned years ago, when she herself was a secretary, how invaluable a good one could be to an executive. The experience had given her the ability to fully appreciate her own.

The rest of the staff, too, she was pleased to discover, were following through on the projects she had assigned them before leaving last week. All except Peter Plack. When she called him into her office, he was more defiant than defensive.

"I simply haven't had a chance to get to all that work you dumped on me before you took off, Keely. While you were out gallivanting I had to make sure things ran smoothly around here."

Keely ignored his breezy description of her business trip. "I don't remember putting you in charge, Pete. I suggest you concentrate on doing your own job rather than trying to do mine. I didn't ask you to do any more than anyone else on the staff. And nobody else seems to have any problems."

"Who said I did, *Mizzz* LaRoux?"

She sighed with frustration. There was no getting through to the man. He would always be an enemy in her camp, but he was too sly to give her a clear-cut reason for firing him. Not that she wanted to fire him. As much as Keely disliked Plack, she wasn't vindictive. She truly hoped they could work out their personality conflict and get on with business.

"I'll tell you what, Pete," she said, making a slight compromise. "I'll forget your report was due today if you have it on my desk by Thursday, when I return from Providence."

He didn't appear the least bit thankful for the reprieve. "Oh, taking off again?" he asked snidely. "You're becoming quite the little jet-setter since your promotion."

"Accompanying the photographer was Mr. Wellfleet's idea, not mine," she quickly pointed out. The fact that Chuck Dickens's company was becoming extremely enjoyable to her made Keely defensive. "And Citation divisions aren't exactly located in spots the jet set would find glamorous."

"Even so," Plack persisted, "you must feel pretty important when you visit those hick towns. How do those backwater bozos like taking orders from a female?"

His condescending tone offended Keely, not only personally, but because of his attitude toward people and places he knew nothing about. She thought of gruff Ed Littlefield at the Duane plant. He had given her a hard time, but at least he'd been honest about it and they'd managed to work things out. She would choose to work with Littlefield any day over sneaky, snide Plack, with his smooth, phony smile.

"The people I've met are hardly bozos," she told him. "Speaking of which, I won't keep you any longer, Pete. I know you have a lot of work to do before Thursday."

Plack opened his mouth to make a quick retort but apparently thought better of it and left without another word.

Keely's morning brightened up considerably when she set up the projector in her office and viewed the slides Chuck had given her the night before. They were excellent. The images were right on target, and she was sure Wellfleet would be pleased. She exhaled with relief. Chuck's talent and perception had given her one less thing to worry about.

But aside from the annual report-photography, she had plenty of other worries. Clay Johnson had left many overdue projects behind when he retired, and it was now up to her to see that they got done. She felt like a juggler caught a little off balance with too many balls in the air. She was confident she could have everything under control in a few months or so, if only she had some time at her desk. It didn't seem fair to her that Wellfleet had insisted she accompany the photographer to all the shoot locations. It was almost as if he was setting her up to fail at this crucial time in her new position.

To make matters worse, not only was she obliged to travel with Dickens, but she was becoming more and more infatuated with him. If it was the wrong time to travel, it was most definitely the wrong time to fall in love. She simply didn't have *time* for such an overpowering emotion. But when she thought about seeing Chuck again the next day, her insides quivered with anticipation. It made it rather difficult to concentrate on the work at hand. But she persevered.

Always diligent, she decided to work through lunch hour. By late afternoon, the hunger pangs she had ignored for hours abated, only to be replaced by a headache. It was time to take a break, she had to admit, and she decided to go for a brisk walk.

When Keely left the building, she breathed in the cool October air. The sun was low but bright, reflecting its golden glory in the blank windows of the tall gray buildings lining the avenue. Her feet carried her uptown, and without really thinking about it, she took a right turn and headed a few blocks east, only to find herself in front of Bloomingdale's.

Perhaps this was where she had subconsciously directed herself, because she walked right through the revolving door and took the escalator to the lingerie department. She had no need to browse but cornered a saleswoman and pointed to the peach silk teddy on the silver mannequin.

"Size thirty-four, C, please" was all she said. She didn't even wince when she signed the charge slip, although for Keely it was an extravagant purchase.

That night, packing for her trip to Providence, she included the silky little piece of frippery in her practical carry-on suitcase. She had not quite admitted to herself that she intended to have an affair with Chuck Dickens. That would have been too calculating. And her heated, indecisive frame of mind was hardly that. She simply tucked the teddy into her suitcase without allowing herself to ask why. After all, it didn't take up that much room, did it?

Chuck was waiting for Keely Tuesday morning when she arrived early, as usual, at the airport. He grinned broadly as he watched her approach, and when she reached him he bent down to kiss her cheek.

"What a lovely woman you are, Ms. LaRoux," he pronounced, taking her suitcase from her.

And taking her breath away, too. The very sight of him was immensely pleasing to her. Only a day separated their last encounter, but during that time she had sorely missed his every feature. Even his traveling clothes now delighted her. She had developed a fondness for his beat-up canvas bush jacket, unpressed chinos and duck boots with their ridged rubber soles.

She could not imagine Chuck sitting behind a desk in a proper business suit. He was a mover. A doer. She could well imagine him heading down the Amazon at a moment's notice if the assignment and the fee were right. Still, there was a certain inherent elegance about him that came across no matter what he was wearing.

He was taking her in with the same appreciation, as if they hadn't seen each other for years rather than hours. She was wearing a soft gold cashmere sweater beneath her staid suit jacket, and she knew her ivory, lightly freckled complexion glowed against the color. Her eyes were glowing, too; she couldn't help it.

"You look almost as happy to see me as I am to see you," Chuck said. "I wish we were flying off to some magical tropical island together instead of to Providence. Of course, that, too, could be a very romantic spot if you wanted it to be, Keely."

She tore her eyes away from his piercing gray gaze. "We'd better concentrate on business while we're there," she advised herself as much as him. "The shots you took down south last week were fantastic, by the way."

He looked almost annoyed, or at least impatient with her compliment. "Of course they were. That's what you're paying me for, isn't it? I'm as much of a professional as you are, Ms. LaRoux."

Yes, he was definitely annoyed with her, she decided. But his mood passed quickly, and he was his usual, easygoing self when Zinko joined them and they boarded the plane.

The Citation facility was located less than twenty miles from the Providence airport, and the general manager greeted them enthusiastically. Unlike some, he valued having products from his division featured in the company's annual report. He even arranged a catered lunch for them in the conference room. Spike, especially, enjoyed the royal treatment they received. Not only was there plenty of food, but Ms. Proctor, the pretty young woman catering the luncheon, made sure Spike's plate was never empty. He asked her first name and beamed when she told him it was Angel.

If a sure way to Zinko's heart was through his stomach, then Angel Proctor had already won it. But she found an even more direct path by suggesting he attend a chamber orchestra recital with her that evening. She, too, was a great fan of Mozart. The fact that she had long brown hair and a tall, thin figure made the route to Spike's heart all the more smooth and easy.

"I think I'm in love," Spike told Chuck and Keely as they toured the plant to find suitable locations for pictures.

"Are you?" Chuck arched a blond eyebrow. "Love at first sight can be risky, pal."

Keely winced at his sardonic tone.

Spike, though, was oblivious. "Angel is the answer to my prayers. I'm going to take her out to dinner before the recital. I hope you two don't mind."

"Of course we don't mind," Chuck assured his assistant. "We'll somehow manage without you, won't we, Ms. La-Roux?" He smiled at Keely, showing his strong white teeth.

"You have a nice evening," she replied, wondering what kind of evening she and Chuck were going to have alone. Her stomach tightened with apprehension.

Edith had booked them into the elegant Biltmore Plaza, and the large, luxurious hotel was quite a change from the modest motels they had stayed in the week before. As Keely was unpacking in her well-appointed room, there was a knock on her door. She caught her breath and shoved the peach silk teddy back into her suitcase. She opened the door to Chuck. His tall, broad frame filled the doorway.

"It's too early for dinner," she told him. "It's not even four o'clock yet."

"Well, I know a very pleasant way to kill a few hours together, Keely," he drawled.

She stiffened. She had not expected him to come on to her so directly, so suddenly. She needed a little more time. "Oh, do you?" she managed to say.

"Yep. A stroll through the city. I'll show you the sights."

His unexpected suggestion made her experience both relief and disappointment. But mostly relief. The idea of touring a new city with Chuck appealed to her. It would be a chance to spend more time with him in neutral territory. She had not yet resolved the conflict between her desire for him and her wariness about becoming involved. As he looked down at her, his smile soft, he seemed to understand this. She grabbed her jacket and purse, and they left her room.

Chuck knew Providence well, as he did most cities. Taking Keely by the hand, he led her up Benefit Street's Mile of History to admire the beautifully restored brick and columned homes. One of the houses turned out to be a museum featuring antique furnishings. Chuck seemed mildly bored as they roamed through rooms of early American furniture, Paul Revere silver, Chinese porcelain, Oriental rugs and English pottery.

"I'm surprised you're not more interested in these beautiful things, Chuck," Keely said, fascinated by this wealth of domestic history.

"I grew up surrounded by antiques," Chuck replied, totally unimpressed. "Both my grandfather and father were avid collectors."

"Oh, really? Well, my grandfather and father were big collectors, too—of debts," she couldn't help but remark dryly. "You were fortunate to be raised in such elegance."

"My brother and I didn't think so. We were always being warned not to touch this, not to bump that. It wasn't exactly a house two little boys could feel at home in."

Keely could understand that. Her four brothers were never reprimanded for bumping into furniture or tracking in dirt. Of course, the furniture was cheap, and the floor was covered with linoleum, not antique Persian carpets. "We come from different worlds," she said, thinking how little they had in common.

But for two people with little in common they found plenty to talk and laugh about after they left the museum and continued their stroll. Until she came to New York, Keely had never left Vermont, and she was an enthusiastic sightseer. She viewed everything with a fresh eye, and it all was of interest to her. Chuck suddenly bent down and grazed the top of her head with a kiss.

"What was that for?" she asked, warmed by his spontaneous gesture of affection.

"For being such good company," he replied. "One day I'll take you to Europe. Ever been there?"

He might as well have asked if she'd been to the moon. But she didn't take his offer seriously. She assumed it was an offhand remark, as spontaneous as his kiss. "Let's tour Providence before we start on Europe," she answered lightly.

"Are you sure you're not getting tired?"

"My dear Mr. Dickens, I bet I could outwalk you any day."

But the city's hilly streets finally got the better of her, and when Chuck noticed her brisk stride slowing, he immediately suggested they stop for a drink at a convenient bistro.

He ordered cider laced with vodka for both of them. He was always ordering drinks for her without asking what she wanted, and she was always leaving them untouched. But this time she picked up the heavy mug and took a deep sip. It was delicious.

"I had fun this afternoon," she said. "You're good company, too."

He leaned forward and took her hand. The warmth of his touch blended with the warmth caused by the drink. "We have the whole evening ahead of us, Keely. What do you want to do now?" His husky voice and glinting eyes made it obvious to her what *he* wanted.

"I don't know what I want to do!" she blurted out, as confused as a child.

He examined her flustered, heated face for a moment, then leaned back, releasing her hand. "Like I said, we have the whole evening ahead. Let's just sit here awhile and talk."

She wondered why she had ever thought him impatient or rude. Hadn't he been the very image of kind consideration all afternoon? But no matter how calm and polite he remained on the outside, Keely sensed the force of his desire lurking just beneath the surface.

She raised the mug to her lips again and studied his face over it. There was a coiled, restless energy in his taut, high cheekbones and sharp gray eyes. This was the face of a man who would not wait too long for any woman, she concluded. And although he had not said or done a single obvious thing to make her uncomfortable, she felt pressured.

And very warm. She took off her suit jacket and draped it over the back of the chair. "Why don't we have dinner here instead of back at the hotel," she suggested. "All that walking has made me famished. And this drink is going to my head."

"That's fine with me," he agreed easily. "I'm hungry, too. You seem to stimulate my appetite, Keely." He lowered his gaze to her full breasts encased in the clinging knit of her cashmere sweater and smiled his approval. She felt warmer than ever.

When the waiter took their order he lit the candle stuck in a wine bottle on their small table. The flickering glow of it accented the hollows beneath Chuck's strong cheekbones, shadowed by his thick blond beard.

They had both ordered the small restaurant's specialty, onion soup, and it arrived in steaming stoneware bowls. Each bowl was lidded by a thick crust of melted cheese, and the awkwardness of bringing stringy loops of the cheese to their mouths made them both start laughing. Other diners began throwing looks in their direction.

"Shh!" Keely softly cautioned Chuck, stifling her own giggles. "People are staring at us for acting so silly."

"No, I think they're just admiring you, Keely. The way the candlelight shimmers off your red hair lights up the whole room."

His compliment sent ripples of pleasure through her. She smiled tenderly and reached toward him to brush away a thread of cheese caught in his beard. And then she continued to softly stroke it until he caught her hand and pressed it to his lips.

"Don't keep driving me crazy," he begged in an urgent tone. "Tell me we'll spend tonight together."

She was not surprised by his request. They had both been leading up to this moment all day. Perhaps since the moment they had first laid eyes on each other. But still she tensed, pulling back her hand and curling it into a fist in her lap. "I'm afraid, Chuck," she admitted in a barely audible voice.

"Of what?" A flicker of exasperation crossed his lean face, but then he smiled gently. "I would never hurt you, darling."

She truly believed he would never intentionally hurt her, but she also knew him to be a man who lived for the moment, not the future. Her fear was not of making love with him, but of giving her heart to him completely. He would take it away with him when he left her, and she was sure he would leave her eventually. Chuck Dickens was a traveling man. That was his way of life.

"I don't want to become emotionally involved with you," she told him, her throat tightening.

"But I thought you were. Or didn't that kiss we shared Sunday mean anything to you?"

"You know it did!" She took a deep breath to steady herself. "But it was a mistake. I can see that more clearly than ever now. And I *have* to see things clearly if I'm going to succeed in my new position. I have to concentrate on that."

"Oh, I see." The muscles around his vivid gray eyes tensed. "Well, that's a very practical, cold-blooded approach to emotions, Ms. LaRoux. You'll go far in your career—I've no doubt about it. But they say it's lonely at the top."

"It's lonely at the bottom, too," she said flatly, his sarcasm scraping her nerves. "I know all about that firsthand. What good did emotions do me when my husband walked out? They sure didn't help pay the rent!"

"You can't stay bitter for the rest of your life, Keely."

"Oh, I'm not bitter. Just smarter. I learned that love can be like a sickness. But now I'm completely immune."

He nodded slowly. "Yes, maybe you are. And the one thing I wish right now is that we had never met."

Neither of them touched their soup again. Or said a word. The waiter approached and asked if they were finished.

"Oh, we're quite finished, aren't we, Ms. LaRoux?" Chuck's reply was so harsh that it surprised even the waiter, who hurriedly cleared the table and gave him the check.

It was dark when they left the cozy little restaurant, and a heavy mist had moved in, chilling Keely to the bone. She tried not to shiver as they walked back to the hotel, but Chuck took off his jacket and draped it over her shoulders.

"That really isn't necessary," she said, dismayed rather than pleased by his kind gesture in the face of his obvious anger and disappointment with her.

"The hell it isn't," he replied gruffly. "I know a cold woman when I see one."

His remark drifted in the mist, making Keely wonder if she really was as coldhearted as he now assumed she was. Maybe the cool front she put up in business was no longer a front. As a girl she had been spontaneous, even impetuous with her emotions, but that had cost her dearly, and she could no longer afford to make mistakes of the heart.

They crossed Kennedy Plaza and entered the Biltmore. The lobby was cheery and bright in contrast to Keely's bleak mood. They took an empty elevator up to their rooms on the sixth floor. Keely remembered the first time she had ever seen Chuck, when he had practically smashed his way through the elevator door.

"We must stop meeting this way," she said.

It was a feeble joke, meant to break the tension between them, and it fell flat. Chuck ignored it. He ignored her, too, as the elevator carried them up. He kept his storm-gray eyes straight ahead, toward the doors. When they slid open he gestured for her to exit first.

"Good night," he said abruptly when they stepped into the hall. "I'll see you tomorrow morning."

With that he turned away and headed for his room, down the long hall from hers. Keely remained immobile, almost stunned, as she watched him walk away from her, his broad back rigid beneath his wrinkled blue shirt. Desire for him swept over her with such force that she thought she would faint. Her head drooped, and the geometric pattern of the thick carpet beneath her feet swirled before her eyes. If she actually did pass out, the thump of her body dropping to the floor would surely get his attention and bring him back to her.

But of course she didn't do any such thing. She simply breathed deeply to steady herself. When she raised her head, she saw that Chuck was coming back to her anyway. So he'd decided to give her one more chance. Well, she was ready to take it this time, despite all her sensible misgivings. She wasn't going to hesitate for an instant when he asked her. She would reply with a clear, resounding *yes*.

But his request was not what she hoped it would be. "Could I have my jacket back, please?" he asked without a hint of a smile on his stern face.

Keely hadn't even realized the garment was still draped around her shoulders. She shrugged it off and handed it to him, immediately missing the fresh, soapy scent of him that infused the soft, worn fabric.

"Thanks for the loan," she managed to say.

"You're welcome," he answered politely. She had noticed that he had a tendency to become more and more polite, the more upset he was. "Well, good night again."

This time, when he turned, she grabbed his arm, her fingers digging into his hard muscles. "Chuck, wait! Don't go away again." Her firm grip was no match for his strength, but it stopped him in his tracks. "I have to say something."

"You've said plenty already." His face was pale and weary with disappointment.

Oh, how she wanted to kiss him. And the power of knowing she could bring pleasure to his face again coursed through her. In the subtle turn of events in their game of love, she had now become the seducer. If he had given up the chase, then she would take it up. It didn't matter anymore that it was a dangerous, foolish pursuit more than likely to end in heartbreak for her. She could not bear to end the excitement of what they had already started.

"I want you to spend the night with me, Chuck," she said. Her green eyes glinted with daring and desire as she whispered this, sure that it would please him.

But it didn't seem to please him at all. In fact, he frowned. "I don't understand you, Keely. Less than half an hour ago, at the restaurant, you made it very clear to me that we would never become lovers. It would interfere with your career."

She gave a self-conscious laugh. "Well, I changed my mind." Her throaty voice was low and sexy.

"You changed your mind," he repeated in a hollow voice. And then he raised it. "Well, that's just find and dandy, La-Roux. You seem to think that you can string me along like a yo-yo. Up and down. Yes and no. You're warm, then you're cold, then you're warm again. Listen, I don't like to have my feelings toyed with like that. No, thank you, Lady."

His angry response took her completely aback. He was acting as if she had just insulted him rather than agreed to what he so obviously wanted. The fact that she had rejected his advances until now gave him no right to act so indignant. Or did it? Did this big, powerful male have feelings as subtle and intricate and complicated as her own? She was beginning to realize that he did.

"Chuck, I never meant to be coy," she told him. "I'm just confused, that's all."

Her confusion must have shown on her face, which burned with hurt in the glare of his unexpected rejection. His own face showed a sudden softening as he took in her discomfiture.

"Oh, Keely," he sighed. "I just don't know where I stand with you. Why must you make it all so complicated? Either you want me or you don't."

Was it as simple as that? Perhaps, in the end, it was, she thought. She lifted her chin and met his eyes. "I do want you," she replied. "I have from the very beginning. And I want you right now, Chuck."

He responded with a quick intake of his breath, then swiftly picked her up and carried her to her room. Keely leaned her head against his solid chest, enjoying the sensation of being gently cradled in his arms like a priceless work of art.

Chapter Eight

When Keely awoke she had no idea what time it was. The room was dark except for the light coming through the half-open bathroom door. Chuck was sleeping beside her.

In the dim light she saw the outline of her suit jacket neatly arranged over the back of the desk chair. Her skirt was folded on the seat. Chuck had been careful not to get them wrinkled as he undressed her. He had been a very considerate lover in every way.

He had made her feel that everything about her was special, even the simple ordinary nylon slip he had stripped off her. How she had wished she'd been wearing the silk peach teddy instead, but Chuck had made the full slip seem like the most sensual garment possible as he slowly peeled it from her body. He had kissed each inch of flesh he revealed, and the touch of his sable beard had made every nerve beneath Keely's skin throb.

Her memory was much more hazy about the exact details of everything that happened after that. An eruption of sweet sensations had blended together as his lovemaking progressed, and she had overcome her initial awkward shyness as he stroked, fondled and kissed away her inhibitions. She smiled now and blushed a little as she took in the tangle of his clothes and her underthings strewn across the carpet by the bed.

A rush of remembered pleasure heated her naked body. Chuck had proven to be an experienced, uninhibited lover, bringing her long-denied passion to a peak. He had reached deeply into the very center of her sexuality, where no man had ever touched her before. Keely had matured both physically and emotionally since the years of her unhappy, erratic marriage. Chuck had made it possible for her to glory in her femaleness. She had given of herself freely and taken back all he could give her until they had lost their separate identities and become fused as one.

He stirred slightly in his sleep now, and Keely held her breath, hoping he wouldn't awaken quite yet. She needed a little time to compose herself before facing him again as her own separate self. In many ways he was still a stranger to her. Although they had shared profound intimacies, they remained two individuals without commitments to each other.

Keely was sharply aware of this as she carefully turned to study his sleeping profile. Who was this man, really? What were his dreams, his hopes, his aspirations? Perhaps he didn't even have any. Perhaps he thought his life was perfect as it was, without ties or any obligations beyond his demanding profession. He had made wonderful love to her, but he had never told her he loved her. And she had no right to expect that, she reprimanded herself. All he had offered her was passion, and she had accepted it with her eyes wide open. But now her eyes blurred with tears as she gazed at him. The worst had happened, as she'd known it would. She had fallen deeply and completely in love with him.

Well, so be it. She had no choice but to resign herself to what she had always known would happen if she let it. And she had, of her own free will. No, that wasn't quite right. Her emotions had gotten the better of her will the moment she first saw him and was so forcefully attracted to him. Her only salvation at that time would have been to avoid seeing him again. But that had proven to be impossible. In the end, the strain of traveling with him had been too much for her willpower, strong as it was. Finally releasing the pent-up desire for him had been thrilling. Wonderful. But now what, Keely LaRoux? she asked herself.

Of course there was no immediate answer to that question. The future with Chuck was unpredictable, and all she could be sure of was that he was with her right now, at this sweet moment. She would have liked to dawdle in the snug cocoon of their shared warmth forever, but there was still a real world outside the bedroom door, with its schedules, demands and duties. Even in love, Keely was not the sort of person to forget that. Not knowing what time it was began to nag at her. It could still be evening or already morning. They had an early shoot scheduled at the Citation facility.

Ever so carefully, she stretched over Chuck's sleeping body to reach for her watch on the night table next to him. The covers slipped away from her as she leaned across him, and Chuck opened his eyes at that moment. He was greeted by the sight of her lush breasts dangling before him. He laughed softly, gently cupping one globe in his palm.

"Good morning, darling," he whispered. "Or is it morning yet?"

"That's what I'm trying to find out," she said, but as he raised his head from the pillow to kiss her breast she was stilled in the motion of picking up her watch.

He pulled her down to lie beside him again. "Let's pretend for a little while that time has stood still," he suggested in a mellow voice as he pressed her body against his long, hard one, his hand strong and insistent against the hollow of her back.

A fresh wave of desire swelled within her. "Yes, a little while longer," she acquiesced.

They made love a second time, even more slowly than the first. As they caressed each other with a new, tender knowledge of the other's pleasure, gray light filtered into the room. Morning had crept in.

They were late getting down to the lobby to meet Spike for the shoot. They had showered together to save time—or at least that's the reason they gave each other. But the shared shower had taken much longer than two separate ones would have.

"I just called your room to find out where you were," Zinko told Chuck as they approached him.

"Sorry we're late," Chuck replied coolly. "Actually I stopped by Ms. LaRoux's room to go over some details, and we got involved in the discussion."

This excuse, vague as it was, satisfied Spike. It became clear that he was too involved in his own affairs to be even the least bit curious if they were having one. For the rest of the day all he talked about was his dinner and concert date with Angel the night before. He was totally infatuated with the young caterer.

"I'm going to ask her to marry me," he announced as the three of them drove to the airport after the photography shoot.

"Whoa! Slow down, boy," Chuck enjoined. "Don't do something you'll regret later, Spike."

His adamant advice to his assistant rang in Keely's ears. She pretended great interest in the scenery whizzing past the front windshield as Chuck drove them down the highway.

Spike sat up straighter in the back seat. "Why would I regret it, Chuck? I love Angel!"

"But you just met her, Spike." Chuck's tone was exasperated. "Okay, you have a strong attraction. You think you're the first two people in the world who ever experienced *that*?" He made it sound like an everyday occurrence, at least to Keely's ears. "But how can you be sure you love her, Spike? Or for that matter, if she loves you?"

"That's something you can tell right off," Spike insisted.

Chuck shook his leonine head. "No, it isn't. Love is much more complicated than that. Don't go rushing into this blindly or you may get hurt, pal." Chuck took his eyes from the rearview mirror, where he'd been observing Zinko's face, and turned to Keely beside him. "Isn't that right, Keely? The boy could get hurt."

Was Chuck trying to warn her that *she* could get hurt falling in love with him? she wondered. Well, she already knew that. His advice to Zinko only reinforced her belief that Chuck thought little of lifetime commitments. It made little difference that whenever they broached the subject of love, it was usually she, not he, who tinged the conversation with caustic circumspection and bitter memories.

"It's Spike's business, not mine" was all she said now through a tight throat. She was determined to keep her growing love for Chuck a secret from him. She feared it would jeopardize their relationship. If they even had a relationship. For all she knew, Chuck had wanted her for one night only. His passion for her had been so exuberant and exhaustive, he could have used it all up. That this could be possible made Keely ache with despair, but she tried to hide her anxiety.

Chuck gave her a long look before returning his eyes to the road.

"That's right, Ms. LaRoux," Zinko said from the back seat. "It's my business. I'm not going to let Chuck dampen my spirits. I don't care if he thinks love at first sight is stupid."

"I didn't say it was stupid, Spike," Chuck said, swinging the car out to the passing lane and accelerating. "Just dangerous."

"Hey, man, what's dangerous right now is your driving," Zinko said.

"Yes, Chuck, please slow down," Keely cautioned, her foot automatically pressing down on an imaginary brake pedal.

He did immediately. "Whatever you say, Ms. LaRoux."

Chuck and Keely said their goodbyes at New York's LaGuardia Airport. She was going back to Manhattan. He was heading for Chicago on a photography assignment for another client. Zinko was arranging the transfer of their equipment to the next flight.

"Well, I think the Providence shoot was successful, don't you?" Keely said to him before they parted. She kept her voice cool and forced a smile.

"I hope it was," he replied seriously, gazing down at her. "I'm not talking about the shoot, Keely. I hope our time together meant as much to you as it did to me."

She nodded. The lump in her throat left her unable to speak. They had not been alone together since they left her room that morning, and she wanted so much to cling to him now, to never let him go. But she did not allow herself to lose control in this bustling terminal as people jostled past them, hurrying to catch planes.

"I'll call you when I get back from Chicago," Chuck said. "If you want me to, that is." His usually incisive gray eyes were clouded, as if with doubt.

"Yes, please call me," she said, trying to keep the urgency out of her voice. "You could even call me from Chicago tonight," she suggested lightly.

He smiled weakly. "If I don't get in too late I will." He sighed. "Oh, Keely, I hate saying goodbye to you."

"Well, it's not exactly goodbye forever, is it?" Her voice squeezed out in a high pitch. She lowered it. "I mean, you're not finished with the Citation project. We've got California and Vermont ahead of us."

"And maybe a lot more than that," he said. "What I meant to say is that I hate saying goodbye to you in this damn terminal. It's too impersonal. I've been going crazy all day wanting to touch you again, darling. As much as I like Zinko, I felt a very strong inclination to push him out of the car or the plane during our trip back to New York."

Keely's laugh came out strained. "You, too?"

They should never have mentioned him, because Zinko appeared then like an unwanted genie. "Hey, Chuck, the baggage is all loaded. We'd better get moving to be on the same plane with it."

Keely and Chuck tore their eyes from each other and looked at him blankly, as if he had no place in their private world. Spike shuffled his large sneakered feet. "Our flight takes off in a few minutes, Chuck."

"Right." Chuck grabbed Keely's hand and shook it formally in front of Spike. "See you soon, Ms. LaRoux." His thumb massaged the base of her palm for a brief, intimate moment before he released it.

As Keely watched Chuck walk away from her she stood as still as a statue, scarcely noticing when people brushed against her and muttered impatient apologies. She stared at his broad back until he disappeared in the crowd. Then she took a cab to the Citation building.

Edith gave her a worried look when she walked into the office with her small suitcase. "I'm so glad you're back, Keely. I have an important message for you."

Keely's shoulders slumped. Now what? She hoped Wellfleet didn't want to see her. She had so much work to catch up on. Every time she traveled away from the office, she fell behind on daily administrative duties. It was no easy matter to direct a staff on various projects while supervising photography shoots on the road. She was beginning to resent the fact that she hadn't even had a chance to replace herself in the managerial position she had vacated when she was promoted. Interviews took time, and that's what she had precious little of now.

"Unless it's a message from Wellfleet, it'll have to wait, Edith," she insisted. "The first thing I have to do is call my daughter. She must be home from school by now. I hope I can get out of the office at a reasonable time tonight and spend a long evening with her."

Edith bit her thin bottom lip and looked even more worried. "Now, don't get upset, Keely," she began hesitantly. "But this message concerns your daughter."

Keely paled as cold fingers of apprehension ran up her spine. "Has something happened to Joy?"

"She became very ill at school, I'm afraid. Mrs. Alphonso picked her up there and took her to your family doctor after trying to reach you here. The doctor diagnosed a severe case of influenza. Mrs. Alphonso called back a short while ago to say they were back home and Joy was in bed. The poor thing is going to be all right, but she's been crying for her mother."

Unreasonable guilt washed over Keely, as if her absence had been the cause of Joy's illness. "I must go home to her immediately," she said, picking up her suitcase again. She said goodbye to Edith and hurried out, all thoughts of work eclipsed by her worry for her daughter.

Keely stayed home for the remainder of the week, nursing Joy. By Friday the girl's high fever was down and her muscle pains and nausea had subsided. But she was still weak and looked very pallid and fragile against the fresh pink sheets, Keely noted, bringing her a bowl of homemade chicken soup.

Joy wanly shook her head. "I can't eat anything, Mom."

"Just a few bites, sweetie," Keely urged. "A mother's chicken soup is magic, you know." She placed the bowl on the dresser, fluffed up Joy's pillows and pulled up a chair beside the bed. "Come on, I'll feed you."

"You don't have to BABY me," Joy protested, but Keely could tell she liked all the special attention she was getting.

She dipped a spoon into the nourishing liquid and brought it to Joy's lips. "Open wide," she cajoled, smiling down at her child, and Joy complied.

They had been so close these past few days, both of them relishing this private, undisturbed time together. Keely regretted that it had taken an illness for them to have this special time. As Joy regained her strength, she had begun to open up to her mother, sharing her youthful fears and hopes after months of being uncommunicative.

She told her mother how much she disliked school, finding her classmates snobbish and aloof. Her interest in clothes was being replaced by a new passion for animals. When Keely promised her that they would go shopping after she got well, Joy requested a trip to the Bronx Zoo instead. If she could have anything in the world, she said, it would be a dog.

Keely would have bought her one immediately had pets been allowed in their apartment building. It seemed the things her daughter wanted most were the very things Keely was unable to give her. Especially more of her time. As soon as Joy was well enough, Keely would have to go back to work, have to start traveling again.

And at the same time that Keely was finding such pleasure and satisfaction in her daughter's company, she was missing Chuck. Thoughts of him were always in the back of her mind.

He had called her from Chicago the night before and expressed concern when she told him of Joy's illness. Other than that, their conversation had been almost impersonal, a little stilted. It was as if their shared night of passion now made them shy with each other. Neither of them referred to it over the phone. Keely's reason was that Joy was within earshot. She could not guess his. Still, when concluding the conversation, he had called her darling, and the caress of his tone lingered in her ear.

No, she could not get him out of her mind. She even felt his presence in the room this very moment as she picked up a book and began reading to Joy. The book she had chosen was *David Copperfield*—because it was on Joy's school reading list, not because the author was Charles Dickens. But it did give her pleasure to see the name on the cover. The scent of freesia in the room also made her think of Chuck. He had sent a delicate bouquet to wish Joy a quick recovery that morning, and the thoughtfulness of his gesture was etched in Keely's heart.

Keely read to her daughter for almost an hour, and the sound of her mother's voice soothed the girl. Keely sensed that she was just about to doze when the phone rang, disturbing their peace.

Joy moaned. "It's probably your office, Mom. Why can't they leave us alone?"

Keely received three or four calls a day from one member of her staff or another when questions arose or decisions had to be made. Joy resented these calls, although Keely had insisted she be kept abreast of departmental developments while she stayed home to nurse her daughter. She was trying very hard to be both a responsible mother and a responsible executive. Now she closed the book and stroked Joy's forehead, thankful it felt cool to her touch. Her temperature had been normal all day.

"I have to answer that, Joy. It may be important." It may be Chuck, she couldn't help but hope. "I'll come back and read to you some more as soon as I can."

She went to the living room and picked up the phone. It was Edith. "Mr. Wellfleet was looking for you this morning," she informed Keely. "He wanted you to put out a press release for him about some honorary degree he just received. Not exactly front page news, but he made it clear that he was irritated by your absence."

A frown creased Keely's brow. "Did you tell him my daughter was ill?"

"Yes, of course. But I must say, dear, he was not especially understanding. He asked Peter Plack to handle it for him."

Keely didn't like that one bit. "I'm sure Pete took full advantage of the situation," she said through clenched teeth.

"Of course he did," Edith stated flatly. "Whenever you're away, he moves into your territory with the speed of a hyena. He's been coming in early, staying late and rubbing shoulders with Mr. Wellfleet whenever he can. Anyway, the president would like to meet with you first thing Monday morning. Do you think Joy will be recovered by then?"

"Most likely. She's much better today, and I'll make sure she takes it easy all weekend. She may even go back to school Monday. If not, Mrs. Alphonso will keep her company. I know it's important for me to make that meeting with Wellfleet."

Keely thanked Edith, said goodbye and returned to Joy's bedroom. If she was worried about the situation at the office, she didn't let it show on her face. But Joy guessed their quiet time together was coming to an end.

"It's almost worth being sick to have you home with me, Mom," she said. "At least I get all your attention then."

"Oh, sweetie, don't say things like that," Keely told her softly, stroking her daughter's long red hair.

Chuck called later that day, back from Chicago. He wanted to get together with Keely over the weekend, but as much as she longed to see him, she had to refuse. She couldn't possibly leave Joy for her own selfish pleasure. Chuck offered to drop by the apartment, but Keely didn't think that was a good idea. Joy needed peace and quiet. Chuck made an effort to hide the disappointment in his voice and acted understanding. Keely pressed her lips against the receiver in a silent kiss before she hung up the phone.

He didn't call again during the weekend. Although Keely had no reason to expect him to, she still hoped he would. As busy as she was, she was always half listening for the phone to ring.

And she was plenty busy. Joy was well enough by Saturday morning to be bored and restless. Keely did her best to entertain her and at the same time make sure she didn't overtire and have a setback.

When Joy went to bed she stayed up late writing a detailed report updating her department projects. She wanted to be fully prepared for her meeting with Wellfleet. It was important for her to demonstrate to him that she was on top of things even though she'd been out of the office all week. She was learning what a precarious position staying on top of things could be. It was all she could do to keep her balance.

Not that she couldn't handle her new position if given the chance. But Wellfleet seemed to expect so much more of her than he had of her predecessor, Clay Johnson. Johnson had never been expected to travel like Keely was. And he'd never had to work her long hours, mainly because he'd had *her* on his staff and she'd taken over many of his neglected responsibilities. Yet he'd been making more money as a director than Wellfleet had offered her to take over. That searing fact certainly didn't soften Keely's growing resentment and disillusionment.

The fact that Chuck hadn't called didn't help her mood much, either. By Sunday evening Keely and the silent telephone had developed an antagonistic relationship. Inanimate object though it was, it seemed to be deliberately refusing to ring just to spite her.

Then it occurred to her that she was spiting herself. If she longed to hear Chuck's voice so badly, all she had to do was pick up the phone and call him. She wasn't some insecure teenager, after all. She was a mature, liberated female executive. But she was also a woman in love, and love could do funny things to one's self-assurance. What if her call annoyed Chuck? Interrupted him during something important? Worse yet, what if a female answered his phone? The very idea of that sent a rush of outrage through Keely's entire body.

She reminded herself that Chuck had made no declarations of love or faithfulness to her before or after their passionate night together. He was a free man. Always had been and always would be. She'd accepted that unstated condition from the start. This acceptance of his freewheeling life-style had been the biggest hurdle she'd had to overcome in their deepening relationship. And apparently she hadn't quite overcome it. It wrenched her heart to think their love affair could end at any time.

In the end Keely's craving to make contact with Chuck grew stronger than her rankling doubts, and she resolved to call him. However, the decision made her even more aware of how tenuous their relationship was. She didn't know his home number or where, in fact, he lived. She guessed Manhattan rather than any other borough, but she couldn't find his name listed in the telephone book. Then she remembered his studio receptionist telling her that he had an unpublished number.

She let the heavy telephone directory slide from her lap and thud to the floor. She stared into space for a long while. It stunned her to realize she didn't even have his private number. Yet she had entrusted her heart to this man. She finally went to bed at midnight, exhausted from waiting so tensely for the call that never came.

Armstrong Wellfleet did not smile when Keely walked into his office Monday morning. "I expect you to be around when I need you, Keely," he said as a greeting.

"I'm sorry I wasn't here to get out that press release, sir, but it couldn't be helped. You see, my daughter was ill, and—"

"Yes, yes, your secretary told me," he interrupted, waving away such a paltry excuse. "Luckily Peter Plack was available to handle it for me. He's a good man, Plack. Very devoted to his job."

Keely bit the inside of her lip to keep from disputing the president's absurd appraisal of her least productive staff member. It would sound like sour grapes right now. And it was always unwise to disagree with the president.

He had not asked her to sit down, but she did anyway, rather than stand before his desk like some errant schoolgirl. She waited, though, for him to speak again. During her few brief meetings with him since her promotion, she had learned to let him initiate, direct and conclude all conversations.

"Care to discuss any problems, Keely?" he began.

It was a question that immediately put her on the defensive. The assumption behind it was that she was having difficulties with her new position. In fact she was, because of her tight traveling schedule during such a busy time, her problem with Plack and her need for a manager as capable and hardworking as she had been when Johnson was director of communications. She sensed, though, that this was not the time to air those complaints. She would have to prove herself to Wellfleet before voicing problems that he could interpret as excuses for her own shortcomings. She would have to make a great success of a very important project. And that project was the company's annual report. He had told her himself, less than a month ago, that it was to be her top priority.

"No problems to speak of," she responded with a brave smile. "Everything is under control, sir."

He looked dubious. "I'd like a detailed report of what's been happening in your department this month as soon as you can put it together."

"You've got it," she replied, handing him the folder she had brought to the meeting in anticipation of his request. Seeing Wellfleet's expression change from doubt to reluctant approval made the long weekend hours Keely had devoted to writing up the report well worth it.

But then his approval faded. "Seems you outguessed me, Keely."

She knew instantly that she had made a stupid mistake by handing over the report like that. There was absolutely no advantage in showing herself to be one jump ahead of her boss. She should have waited and sent it up to him, through her secretary, the following day. Then he would have thought she was reacting to his orders, not acting before he had even given them. She had inadvertently blocked a power play, and that was bad corporate politics. Damn these strategy games. All she wanted was to do a good job and be rewarded for it.

Wellfleet tossed aside her report and scowled at Keely. She doubted he'd even bother to read it now. "How's the photography for the annual report coming along?" he asked.

She recited all the Citation facilities she and Chuck had already covered and told him their next shoot was scheduled for the following week. It would be at Citation's new and important electronics division in Salinas, California.

"Go there this week instead," Wellfleet ordered.

It seemed like such an arbitrary order that Keely couldn't keep herself from objecting to it. "But I've been away so much lately, sir. I really think my staff could benefit from my supervision this week."

"But you just told me there weren't any problems in your department," he snapped back. He showed his teeth in what could have been a smile, and Keely was reminded of a bulldog from her childhood who always bared its teeth like that.

"Well, yes, I did. But I find it difficult directing my staff when I'm never here." The complaint had escaped her despite her better judgment.

"Don't worry about that, Keely. You're fortunate to have Peter Plack as one of your managers. He can take over if problems arise during your absence."

Keely had no choice but to ignore the fact that Wellfleet was playing Plack against her so deliberately. Perhaps he thought it would motivate her to work even harder. "Of course I'll supervise the Salinas shoot this week if that's what you want, Mr. Wellfleet," she said. "But may I point out that the annual report won't be printed until February? I don't understand the rush."

"Oh, I have my reasons." Wellfleet studied Keely a moment, as if deciding whether or not to let her in on them. He leaned forward and lowered his voice. "Those pictures you and Dickens get won't only be used for the annual. They're going to be sent out to the media to announce the X25."

"The X25?" Keely had no idea what that was.

The president enlightened her. "That's the code name for a revolutionary home computer system Citation's developed. Production isn't slated until next year, but the prototype is ready to be photographed right now. As soon as possible."

Keely still didn't understand the urgency. She knew she should simply accept the assignment without further questions, but she felt she had the right to know more. "Why announce a product that won't be available for another year?"

Wellfleet tapped his pudgy fingers impatiently against the sleek surface of his desk. Clearly he wasn't used to explaining his orders to his employees. But then he leaned back in his leather throne and smiled benevolently. "I'll tell you why, Keely, since you insist on knowing. You see, UltraTech has developed a similar system. I know this from an inside source there. They plan to announce theirs in the spring, but we're going to beat them to the punch. The publicity will make our stock go up even before we start production." Wellfleet looked quite proud of himself. "Needless to say, this is strictly confidential, Keely. Can Dickens be trusted?"

"Absolutely," Keely said. From a professional standpoint, she had complete faith in him. It was her heart she didn't trust with Chuck.

"Then fly out to Salinas with him tonight. Tomorrow morning at the latest," Wellfleet instructed.

"I only hope he's available on such short notice, sir. He may have other commitments."

"If he has, he can damn well cancel them." Wellfleet's tone was abrupt. "It's your job to handle Dickens, Keely."

She almost laughed at that. She doubted that anybody, man or woman, could "handle" Chuck. Perhaps that was why she found him so irresistible. He appealed to the wild, spontaneous part of her nature that she had long since tamed to fit into the corporate organization. Or maybe she hadn't quite tamed it. Her passion for Chuck was bringing out her own natural desire for independence, her inclination to rebel when restrained. Each time she met with the dictatorial Wellfleet, she had a stronger and stronger urge to tell him off. She didn't like the man. She didn't like his high-handed manner of dealing with her. She didn't approve of his using information from a spy at UltraTech. She didn't like the way he kept hinting that Plack was waiting in the wings if she didn't follow his script exactly. But she wasn't going to lose her temper and throw away everything she had worked so hard to achieve these past ten years at Citation. It wasn't only her job that was at stake, but also her daughter's security and future.

"I'll do my best, Mr. Wellfleet," she said. It was all she could say.

The president's thick eyebrows met in a frown, demonstrating his doubt that her best was good enough. He said nothing but nodded, dismissing her.

Keely hurried back to her department, her head spinning. She had to get in touch with Chuck as soon as possible and convince him to accompany her to California. She asked her secretary to call his studio, and if he wasn't in, to track him down.

Edith smiled calmly, unperturbed by the urgency in her boss's voice. "I don't have to track him down, Keely. Mr. Dickens is waiting in your office for you."

His presence was unexpected, but Keely didn't question it as relief coursed through her. When she entered her office she saw him standing by the window. "Chuck," she cried. "Thank goodness you're here. I really need you. Tonight, if possible."

He turned to her, a little surprised by her blatant admission. His laugh was deep and pleased. "I'm yours for the asking, Keely," he said. "Why don't you close the door and show me just how much you need me?"

She did close the door but eluded Chuck's arms when he crossed the room and reached for her. She had thought her office spacious, but his tall, majestic frame seemed to make it shrink. If she let him hold her now, she would forget all about the urgent business at hand.

"What I meant is that I need you to fly to Salinas with me tonight to take product pictures," she hurriedly explained, a little breathless. "I just met with the president, and he insists we go as soon as possible."

The glee in Chuck's face quickly diminished. "Oh, does he? Well, when he says jump, *you* may ask how high, Keely, but I don't have to."

"You needn't sound so superior, Chuck," she shot back. "Citation is paying you very well for your services."

"But I'm still my own boss," Chuck insisted. "And no self-important corporate executive is going to tell me what to do."

Keely wasn't sure if the self-important executive he'd so scornfully alluded to was herself or Wellfleet. But it was obvious that they had gotten off on the wrong foot, which always seemed to be the case when they discussed business. She wanted to work with Chuck, not against him, but the battle lines were drawn once again. She walked behind her desk, a defensive barrier.

"Chuck, don't refuse this assignment until you hear me out," she said, careful not to sound too pleading. "Sit down and let me explain it to you."

Impatience skidded across his strong features, but he folded his long, big-boned frame into the chair she indicated. More than her desk separated them now, Keely knew. The passionate intimacy they had shared less than a week ago seemed more a dream than a reality, and she longed for some sign of warmth or reassurance from him. She wanted it so badly that it didn't occur to her that he could be waiting for the same from her. She was too involved in trying to hide the eruption of sensations his nearness caused within her.

His virility was almost tangible, enhanced by the faded, tight jeans he was wearing. His wide shoulders and broad chest were encased in a rib-knit gray sweater. The color accented but couldn't come close to matching his eyes, which were a lighter, more luminous gray. Sometimes the color of Chuck's eyes reminded Keely of fine silver in the glow of candlelight. Right now they reminded her of morning frost on a Vermont field.

It was his cold stare that made her keep her cool. Picking up her gold Cross pen and twirling it between numb fingertips, she explained the X25 project to him—as much as she knew about it, anyway.

"When Citation announces this new system, your photographs of it will be published in all the industry magazines," she concluded. "General magazines and newspapers, too, no doubt. It's big news. You'll get photo credits, of course. Think of all the publicity you'll reap from one location shoot. A shoot you've already agreed to, by the way."

Chuck did not appear impressed by her sales pitch. "I agreed to take on the assignment next week. That was the arrangement. Believe it or not, I have a private life, too."

A private life she knew nothing about, she reminded herself. It gnawed at her. She had given her love to a man who was still, in many ways, a stranger to her.

"If I could delay this trip, I would," she told him. "The last thing I want to do is leave my daughter and fly across the continent tonight."

His expression became more sympathetic. "I hope she's feeling better, Keely."

He seemed genuinely concerned, and Keely appreciated that. "Oh, much better. She really could have gone to school today, but I had her stay home one more day. No doubt she and Mrs. Alphonso are making a holiday of it, sipping hot chocolate and playing card games." The cozy scene Keely had evoked made her wish to be part of it. She should be the one handing Joy a cup of cocoa right now. How she had wanted to stay home with her daughter this morning instead of leaving for the office.

"It can't be easy being a working mother," Chuck said, seeing the yearning in her face.

"I wish Joy and I had more time together," she admitted. "Thanks for sending her those flowers, Chuck. That was very kind and unexpected."

"You don't expect me to be kind, Keely?" His tone was light, but his look was more serious.

"That's not what I meant at all," she said quickly. For some reason they were communicating like beings from different galaxies. And yet they had been one with each other. Their bodies had communicated so perfectly. But their minds could not connect now.

Keely suddenly needed the safety of their mutual business. "Let's get back to this assignment, Chuck. It will only take a few days of your time. Especially if we fly out there tonight."

He groaned. "If I spend any more time in planes, I'm going to grow wings. Hell, I haven't even had a chance to unpack my suitcase since I returned from Chicago."

Keely's green eyes narrowed. "Then you must have been pretty busy all weekend."

A slow smile eased up Chuck's lips. Perhaps he had glimpsed a brief spark of jealousy in Keely's eyes before she hid them with her thick brush of auburn lashes. "I managed to enjoy myself despite the fact that we couldn't get together," he readily admitted.

"I'm sure you did," she uttered between clenched teeth. The logical conclusion was that he had spent the weekend with another woman. She paled at the thought.

Chuck's teasing smile became more tender. "I spent the weekend with relatives on Long Island, Keely."

Her tension eased somewhat. "You never mentioned you had family nearby."

"I don't have much time to spend with them actually," he said with a hint of regret. Although Keely gave him an expectant look, hoping he'd tell her all about these relatives, he immediately directed the conversation back to her. "God, I missed looking at that pixie face of yours." His low, deep voice matched the sheer pleasure his eyes held as he took her in.

His relatives on Long Island dimmed in importance. His warmhearted regard for her filled her heart with reassurance. "I missed you, too," she replied a little above a whisper. "Terribly."

He reached across the desk and took her hand. "Maybe we should have started off by at least saying that to each other."

She made no effort to remove her hand from the warm, snug cocoon of his. She wanted it to remain there forever. "Yes, we should have," she agreed. "But I was so upset after my meeting with Wellfleet. His impossible demands infuriate me at times. Especially after a sleepless night." She hadn't meant to mention that to Chuck, but now that she had, she went on. "I wanted you to call me so badly last night, Chuck."

Her confession seemed to please yet puzzle him. "Somehow I can't imagine Keely LaRoux pining away by a telephone. You're much too efficient and direct. Why didn't you just call me?"

"You never bothered to give me your private phone number, that's why." There was a bit of a sting in her voice now. And a bit of hurt, too.

He frowned, looking truly puzzled now. "Didn't Trudy give it to you?"

"Who's Trudy?"

"My receptionist. I'm sure I gave her specific instructions to give it to you last week or so." He rubbed his eyes, and when he took his hand away from them they looked even more tired. "Or maybe I didn't. Traveling so much, I don't remember what I say from one day to the next."

Keely fingered her Cross pen and waited. Forget this Trudy. Forget how much he traveled. Was he going to tell her his unlisted number or not? Keely wondered.

He still had hold of her other hand, the one that wasn't gripping her expensive pen so tightly. He brought it to his lips and kissed it. Then he took out his own felt-tipped pen and wrote his number on her sensitive palm.

"I wish that were a tattoo," he said. "But it'll wear off soon enough."

"No, it won't," she replied. Every numeral he'd imprinted was now etched in her heart.

He kissed her hand again, the palm and then the back of it for good measure. "You mean a lot to me, Keely," he said.

But that didn't mean much to her. A lot? What was that? Was that love? If only he would tell her he loved her, she would pour out her own full heart to him. But she kept her feelings dammed up within her, afraid of washing him away with the mighty flow of them.

No, she couldn't show him how much she cared. Not yet. She didn't want him to think she was binding him in any way. And so she forced a casual laugh. "Then why pass up this chance to travel out to the west coast with me?" she asked lightly.

He released her hand so suddenly that it almost dropped to the desk. "Back to that, are we?" His gray eyes narrowed. "Back on track with business. That always comes first with you, doesn't it, Ms. LaRoux?"

Once again she'd said the wrong thing to him at the wrong moment. She sighed inwardly. She wasn't very good at this new game of mixing love with business. Or politics with work. Or any of the subtle games other people played so easily. Deep down she would always be that simple farm girl who played it straight. Chuck, though, was more complicated. More sophisticated. How she wished she understood him better. Now he was angry with her, and her frustration lit her own short fuse.

"I have a job to do," she said evenly, but the color rising to her face gave away her temper. "And you're not making it any easier for me by being stubborn about this."

"Me? Stubborn?" He jabbed his own broad chest with his index finger. "Lady, you invented the word. The answer is no, Keely. I'm not traveling any more this week. I'm tired. I need a break. And I have other, more personal work to do, dammit." He stood up and loomed over her, casting his big shadow over her desk.

He did look tired, she noted. The tan skin across his high cheekbones was drawn, and his eyes reflected the strain of constant travel and deadlines. If she had been his wife, she would have advised, even begged, him to stay home and rest for a few days. But she was *not* his wife, of course, and even imagining herself as such for a flickering second was sheer foolishness on her part. It was against her best interests to worry about Chuck Dickens's need to relax when, in fact, she needed him to work for her.

"Then you leave me no choice," she said dryly. "I'll have to find another photographer to replace you on this shoot."

His handsome features hardened into a mask. "You think I'm that easy to replace, Ms. LaRoux?"

"As I said, you leave me no choice, Mr. Dickens." She was bluffing and tried to keep her expression blank, too. But her breath came short and shallow, making her chest heave beneath the armor of her gray tweed business jacket. She had played her last card, hoping Chuck's ego would not allow him to let another photographer interfere with a project he had taken on.

She had not considered that his ego would not allow him to give in to her demand, though. "Have a good trip, Keely" was all he said before he turned to go.

She shot up from her chair, ready to run after him and stop him from leaving. She did have one other card to play if she chose to. She could plead with him to go on this trip as a personal favor to her. They had become, after all, more than just business associates.

But she couldn't bring herself to use their new relationship to get him to change his mind. She had given herself to him freely, without ulterior motives, and she would not tarnish the shining memory of their intimacy by bringing it up now. Her success at Citation meant a lot to her, and this photography shoot was crucial, but what she felt for Chuck was more complicated and ran much deeper.

Now he was walking out of her office, and maybe her life. She let him go without another word.

Edith came in a few minutes later to find Keely still standing behind her desk, staring at nothing. "He's a good-looking man," she commented in her clipped voice. When Keely did not respond, she went on. "I was referring to Mr. Dickens."

"What he is is a stubborn ox!" Keely exploded, anger sweeping past all the other emotions she felt for him. "Where does he get off, refusing an important assignment because it inconveniences him? He expects to be courted, like he's King of the Jungle or something."

"Well, he does look more like a lion than an ox," Edith said wryly.

Keely was not amused. "Please get me the file on all the photographers Citation has used in the past, Edith. Someone's got to take those Salinas shots this week. I can't let Wellfleet down the way Dickens just let me down."

If Edith noticed that Keely's eyes were bright with contained tears, she didn't mention it. "I'll get on it right away." She paused in the doorway. "I almost forgot. On his way out Mr. Dickens told me he'd left something on your desk for you. He didn't want you to miss it." She hurried off to find the file.

Keely's desk was piled high with messages and paperwork she'd wanted desperately to clear away during the week. But she immediately spotted a cream-colored envelope atop the clutter. It was addressed to her in what she assumed to be Chuck's handwriting. She'd never seen his handwriting. There was so much about him she didn't know. But this bold scribble, strong and artistic, reminded her of him.

She turned over the envelope and slid a fingernail under the flap, thinking it looked rather like a wedding invitation. For a horrible moment Keely allowed herself to imagine that it actually was one. Maybe Chuck couldn't travel to California with her because he was too busy getting married. He'd claimed personal reasons, after all. She caught herself getting carried away with crazy thoughts and gave herself a mental kick in the pants. She took out the card inside and read it quickly. In fact it was an invitation. She read it again. It was an invitation to a gallery exhibition. The date was the following Saturday. The artist featured was Charles Dickens. *Please be there, darling* he'd scrawled on the bottom with his felt-tipped pen. *It would mean so much to me.*

She hadn't realized he was a serious art photographer. Then she recalled her conversation with Spike Zinko that night in Georgia. His words echoed vaguely in her mind. Something about Chuck's running away from his real talent. Something to do with more serious work than commercial photography and Chuck's fear of failing at it. Keely sank back in her deep leather chair and thought long and hard, turning the invitation to Chuck's show over and over in her hands.

Now she understood that he would be tied up all week getting ready for it. Well, he could have explained that to her. But she hadn't asked for explanations, had she? She'd only demanded that he accompany her on this urgent business trip. She hadn't even bothered to inquire why he had paid such an unexpected visit to her office. Despite her rapid heartbeat at the sight of him, she'd put Citation business first, over her own emotions.

She'd got into the habit of doing that through the years. Citation first, her private life second. Why, even her own daughter had taken second place many times while Keely told herself it was all for Joy's good in the long run. It was a habit, she suddenly realized, that could leave her very lonely in the end. Her success at Citation gave her cold comfort. A fancy office and a fat paycheck couldn't keep her as warm at night as loving arms could.

But then she reminded herself that her job at Citation *had* kept her and her daughter warm at night. Her salary paid for the rent, the heat, the food on the table and Joy's education.

She looked down again at the invitation Chuck had left her. It was frayed at the corners now from her nervous fingering of it. She reread the last line he'd written. *It would mean so much to me.*

The words blurred in front of her eyes. She deeply regretted treating him so abruptly. If only she'd known about his upcoming gallery show, she would have been understanding when he refused the assignment. But then little demons of doubt began to crawl into her mind. Maybe she would have placed Citation business first anyway. In a rush of remorse she remembered all those times she'd let Joy down because her work obligations came first.

Which they had to! she reminded herself emphatically. If she couldn't be present at school events Joy thought so important, that was only because she was her daughter's sole support and was looking out for her future. A chaotic mixture of guilt, love for Joy and love for Chuck began to swirl in her head just as Edith entered her office.

"Keely, I brought that file you asked for," her secretary said, her clear, no-nonsense voice bringing Keely back to the world of Citation.

"Okay. Fine. Thank you, Edith."

"Are you all right?" Edith gave her boss a close, motherly examination. "You look pale and flushed at the same time. You must have a fever."

Keely was sure Edith would pull out a thermometer at any moment. "I'm perfectly fine," she insisted. She opened the file and pretended to study it intently. But when she looked up, Edith was still hovering over her.

"Looks to me like you could at least use a cup of coffee," she prescribed. "I'll make a fresh pot."

"That really isn't necessary, Edith."

"No bother. Happy to do it. I won't be away from my desk for long." She left, intent on her mission of mercy. Edith believed good coffee was like a balm to the soul.

The moment she left, Keely dialed Chuck's home number but only got a recorded message for her effort. She glanced at her watch. Over an hour of musing had evaporated since he'd left her office. Time enough for him to be back at his studio. She dialed that number next. The bored receptionist answered.

"Is he in?" Keely asked peremptorily.

"Yes, but he can't be disturbed." The reply was equally peremptory.

Keely sweetened her tone. "Would you please tell him it's Ms. LaRoux? I'm sure he'll want to speak to me." But she wasn't sure at all.

"Okay. Hold on."

"You're all heart, Trudy," Keely muttered, but she'd already been put on hold. She waited in that limbo for what seemed to be forever, nervously biting her lip.

His deep voice finally filled her ear. "You never take no for an answer, do you?" he said without preamble.

"Chuck, I didn't call about the trip. I got your invitation and can understand why you can't leave New York this week. I'd love to come. I'm sorry if I sounded too demanding before."

"Oh." Her apology seemed to have caught him off guard.

"I'm really happy for you," she went on. "Your own gallery show! Why didn't you ever mention it to me?"

"It wasn't that important."

Despite his brusque reply, she sensed it was. "I just wish you hadn't kept it a secret."

"What secret? I gave you an invitation, didn't I?" He let out a laugh that rang false. "It'll probably be a total bomb anyway. I'm crazy to do it. I should have refused. I'm just setting myself up for the critics."

She couldn't believe this was the great egotist Chuck Dickens talking. "I'm sure it'll be a great success," she soothed although she had little knowledge of art photography and gallery exhibitions. "And don't worry about this Citation assignment. I can find another photographer to replace you. No big deal."

"No big deal?" he boomed, not in the least soothed. "You think I'm that easy to replace, lady?" All the self-assurance and bravado was back in his voice. "Who have you decided to use?"

She looked down at the thick file Edith had brought her. "Well, no one yet. Any suggestions?"

"The best I could recommend still wouldn't be half as good as me. And I thought our agreement was that I took all the pictures for the annual report. It's supposed to be *my* book."

"You know this can't wait, Chuck. Wellfleet insists. If you won't come with me, I have no choice but to use another photographer."

There was a long pause at the other end of the line. "Okay, Keely. You win," he finally said.

"What?"

"You win. You talked me into it. I'll fly out to California with you tomorrow morning."

She couldn't believe what she was hearing. She hadn't intended to talk him into anything. "But what about your show?"

"Oh, hell, if I'm not ready now, I'll never be. Besides, I find the idea of having you all to myself for a few days very appealing. Especially since our trip to Providence was such a big success. Do you think about that as often as I do, darling?"

She found herself blushing. "It's crossed my mind," she admitted in perhaps the biggest understatement of her life.

"I know exactly where I want to make love to you again."

"Do you?" Keely's toes curled in her sensible black leather pumps as she remembered the pleasure of his touch.

"You'll love it. A lovely inn on Monterey Peninsula. The perfect setting to make every inch of your lush little body sing with pleasure, Keely LaRoux."

Her blush heated up. This conversation had certainly taken a turn for the better. "Don't forget this is a business trip," she managed to caution.

He laughed at that. "We'll take our pleasure when we can. It took every ounce of my self-control not to ravish you in your office this morning."

Keely crossed her legs, wriggled out of a shoe and let it dangle off her toes. The shoe swung back and forth as he whispered in her ear and her excitement mounted. If he had been whispering to her in person right now, she would have ravished *him*.

"I'll leave the room reservations up to you then," she said in a less than steady voice. "Edith will book us on the first morning flight out."

"Have you ever made love in the state of California before, Keely?"

"What a question. I've never even been there." She didn't add that her experience with love affairs was as limited as her travel until Chuck Dickens had come into the picture.

"Let's set a goal to make love in every one of the fifty states," he suggested.

If this was as close as he'd come to defining a future with her, then she'd have to be satisfied. "I like having goals, Chuck," she replied as blithely as she could.

He laughed again, a deep, throaty chortle. "You don't know how I long for you, darling," he said before hanging up.

Keely gently replaced the receiver in its cradle and smiled softly to herself.

"Something has certainly pleased you, Red."

The shoe dropped off her foot. Peter Plack was looming in her doorway, a leer on his narrow face.

"Isn't Chuck the name of the photographer you've been traveling around with?" he asked, putting as much insinuation as he could into his tone.

Keely replayed her side of the telephone conversation in her mind, praying that Plack hadn't overheard anything he could use against her. If he knew she and Chuck were having an affair, he *would* find a way to use it against her—she was sure of that. She didn't think she had said anything incriminating, though.

"Yes, he is," she replied as calmly as possible. "We were arranging the next shoot."

"Oh? Where's that going to be?"

"California," she said curtly.

"Ah, the Salinas plant, no doubt. What products are you going to be photographing there?"

Keely remembered Wellfleet's admonition that the X25 project was confidential and became wary of Plack's sudden interest in her plans. "Why do you want to know, Pete?"

His face sharpened. "Top secret stuff, huh? Well, you don't have to tell me, Keely. I have other ways of finding out what I want to know."

"You'd be better off concentrating on your own job instead of mine, Plack."

"The way I see it, you're still on trial as director, love. If you don't make the grade, I'm next in line for the position."

"Oh, is that your game plan?" Keely smiled coldly. "Sorry to disappoint you, but I'm not going to fail. Under my direction, this annual report is going to be the best the company's ever produced. And except for you, my staff is doing good work. I intend to succeed and win Wellfleet's confidence. So watch your step, Pete, because you're the one on trial here. If you don't shape up, I don't want you in my department."

Muscles tense, she waited for Plack to challenge her, but his only response was to leave, slamming the door behind him. She was going to be forced to fire him eventually, she knew. But now would be the wrong time. First she would have to convince the president that he was insubordinate and a detriment to her department. That would take some doing. Plack had been with the company a long time and knew exactly how much he could get away with. She would have to build a strong case against him, and that would take awhile.

Contemplating this gave her no pleasure, and her thoughts drifted. A small, soft smile curved her full lips. She would be with Chuck tomorrow. He had come through for her. The warmth of gratitude and love flowed through her.

Chapter Nine

Chuck had been right. He had chosen the perfect romantic setting for them—a charming Victorian seaside inn on Monterey Peninsula, less than twenty miles from Salinas. A sweet ocean breeze wafted through the windows on the top floor turret room, billowing the white ruffled curtains. The low afternoon sun streamed in, making the delicate roses on the wallpaper glow. The king-size bed was canopied with swags of white silk. What more could a couple who had yearned to be together for days want?

To be on speaking terms, for one thing, Keely decided.

Arms folded across his broad chest, Chuck was gazing out the window toward the water. His expression did not reflect any pleasure in the view. A small muscle twitched at the crest of his high cheekbone. Except for this, his face was immobile.

Keely ignored him ignoring her and called home to tell her daughter and Mrs. Alphonso where she could be reached. She called Edith, too, to give her the number of the inn. Then, with more energy than the task required, she began to unpack her suitcase.

Rattling hangers and slamming dresser drawers did not get Chuck's attention. Crossing the large room on her way to the closet, she practically tripped over his worn canvas travel bag. She gave it a kick.

"Ouch! Was that really meant for me?" Chuck asked, still not turning around.

Not one to hold her tongue for very long, Keely forgot they weren't on speaking terms and responded. "You bet, Dickens. And I'd appreciate your removing that ratty old bag and yourself from this room."

"This room is registered under my name, not yours, La-Roux," he countered. "If you don't intend on sharing it with me, then you'd better pack up again. I'm not budging."

She put her hands on her hips. "Neither am I!"

Chuck was looking at her now, and his face eased into a smile. "Let's face it, Keely. Neither of us is going anywhere. We're sharing this bed tonight. You know it as well as I do."

Of course she did, but she wasn't going to let on. "I'm still very angry with you, Chuck."

He unfolded his arms and spread them wide. "Come here, darling. Our time together is too precious to be wasted on anger."

As if her feet had a mind of their own, they brought her closer and closer to him, until she was near enough for his arms to capture and encircle her. She was a willing captive and pressed her cheek against his chest. She breathed in his delicious essence.

"You're right," she mumbled, her lips grazing the third button of his soft blue shirt.

Their quarrel had started in the New York airport terminal when Chuck told Keely that Spike Zinko wouldn't be accompanying them to California because he was busy practicing for a piano recital. Chuck had arranged for a substitute assistant from San Francisco. This worried Keely. The shoot was too important to use an unproven assistant, one Chuck had never worked with before. Chuck's attitude seemed too cavalier to her. She told him he should have insisted that Spike come with them.

Chuck hadn't appreciated her rebuke. The assistant he chose to use was his business, not hers. He also told her that other people's lives did not revolve around Citation the way hers did. The recital was important to Spike. Chuck could understand that even if Keely couldn't.

Keely had not argued further, but all during the five-hour flight to the west coast she worried. And when she met the assistant, waiting for them in front of the Salinas facility, she was all the more anxious. The young woman hardly fit Keely's image of a capable, reliable photography assistant. She was wearing cutoff jeans and a halter top that showed off her glossy tan. Her long golden hair was braided and wrapped around her head like a crown. She was a California dream girl, and her name was Moonbeam Smith.

Before they were allowed to enter the facility's inner sanctum, they had to get security clearance. Then they received coded badges. Keely pinned hers to the lapel of her beige, lightweight wool suit jacket. Chuck attached his to the pocket of his oxford shirt. Moonbeam stuck hers on the back of her tight, cutoff jeans, right above her left buttock. Chuck found this highly amusing, and Keely found his reaction highly irritating.

The head engineer, an intense young man, gave them a tour of the plant. Chuck chose the settings he would use to photograph the X25 system. Moonbeam came up with some suggestions about backlighting that Chuck readily agreed to, although he usually abhorred such interference with his own creativity on a site.

Keely gnawed at the inside of her lip and observed the proceedings with narrowed eyes. When all the arrangements were completed, everybody shook hands and set a time to meet again the next morning. Moonbeam gave them a bright smile right out of a toothpaste ad and drove away in a pastel-pink convertible. This left Keely and Chuck free to argue about her as they walked to their own rented car.

"I don't trust her," Keely told Chuck.

"You mean you don't like her."

"That, too. It's her eyes I don't like. They kept wavering when she talked to me, just like Peter Plack's do."

"Who's Peter Plack? Your dentist?"

"He's a manager at Citation who's after my job. This Moonbeam is after something, too." Chuck, maybe? Keely refrained from adding that.

"My agent recommended her, Keely. She worked with a photographer he represents on the West Coast and did a fine job. She seems perfectly qualified to me. Her suggestions about backlighting were good ones."

"Ha!" Keely choked out. "Perhaps you're too inclined to go along with anything she'd suggest to you, Dickens."

"Do I detect a hint of jealousy, Ms. LaRoux?" His smile was rather smug as he opened the car door for her.

"That's ridiculous," she said, getting in. But she was the one who felt ridiculous. Did she resent the young woman simply because she was so gorgeous?

She reminded herself that she'd taken exception to Spike when she first met him. She'd unfairly judged him on his rather goofy appearance. But he'd turned out to be as hard a worker as she was and talented to boot. Still, those shifty eyes of Moonbeam's continued to bother her.

Chuck got in and started the car. "Don't be so uptight about this shoot," he advised her.

"Falling right into the California lingo, aren't you?" she replied caustically. "Don't you be so *laid-back* about it. It's important to me."

"That's all that's important to you, isn't it, Keely? Your damn career!"

That hurt. He should have known her well enough by now to understand what really mattered to her. Didn't he realize she needed the security of her Citation job for Joy's sake? And couldn't he sense how much she cared for him? But the stubborn, proud streak in her prevented her from defending herself. Instead, wounded, she attacked him.

"What about you, Dickens? What do you care about besides taking on as many assignments as you can? And charging as high a fee as you can get away with? Do you call living out of a suitcase a worthwhile way to spend your entire life? You're nothing but a . . ." She groped for the right description. "Nothing but a high-paid gypsy!"

"Maybe that used to be true," he conceded. "But I want more from life now."

He left it at that, driving on in silence. This maddened her more than his accusation had. Talk to me! she wanted to scream. She glanced at his set, closed face. She could have strangled him, but then they'd have a car accident. Besides, she loved him too much to strangle him. And she resented him for making her love him. It made her feel weak, out of control, and she hated the feeling.

"We'll never understand each other," she finally said very softly, more to herself than to him.

"Maybe not." There wasn't much hope in his voice.

"We should never have started an affair." She held her breath, waiting for him to refute her.

"I'm sorry if that's the way you feel" was all he said.

There was no further conversation between them until Chuck parked the car in front of a gabled and turreted inn painted sunshine-yellow.

"Isn't this romantic?" he asked sarcastically, almost bitterly.

Keely was completely enchanted with the fanciful edifice but hid this with a shrug. "It'll do. But it seems more suited for a vacation than a business trip."

"Don't worry, Madame Executive. We won't mix pleasure with business if you don't want to."

With that he got out of the car, took their two bags from the trunk and marched up the front steps. Keely had two choices. She could sit in the car fuming for the rest of the day and all night, or she could follow him. She chose the latter.

Now here she was in a delightful, airy room with rose-patterned wallpaper, her cheek pressed against Chuck's broad, solid chest. It was exactly where she truly wanted to be.

"Why, Chuck?" she asked. "Why has this trip soured on us from the moment we left New York?" His shirt button tickled her lips as she spoke.

"I'll be damned if I know." He sighed and stroked her back. "Maybe our expectations were too high. I wanted you all to myself, but Citation business was all you seemed to care about."

"Zinko's absence upset me."

He laughed, and she could feel the deep vibration of it in her ear. "You're not trying to make me jealous, are you?"

"You know what I mean. No matter how much you resent it, Chuck, this shoot *is* important. You know that as well as I do. But we can't seem to see eye to eye about it."

His hands slid from her back down past her waist and cupped the fullness of her buttocks. "Eye to eye contact isn't the kind I have in mind right now," he murmured into her hair.

Desire for him began to lap at her. "Let's promise each other never to argue again," she urged.

He kneaded her buttocks through the light wool of her skirt. "Why make promises we're sure to break, darling? Let's face it, we're going to be arguing with each other for the rest of our lives. That's the way we are."

His dire prediction didn't depress Keely. In fact, it made her heart soar. For the rest of their lives?

"We have to talk," she said.

"Isn't that what we're doing?" He pressed his long, hard body against hers.

"No, what we're doing is warming up for something else."

"I like warming up. Don't you?" He bent down to slide his hot lips across her neck, and the brush of his thick golden beard stimulated every inch of her.

"Yes," she hissed softly. Conversation didn't seem the most important form of communication at that moment. She tilted up her head, offering her lips for a kiss.

He accepted the offer. His mouth pressed against her waiting, half-opened one, and he sucked in the sweetness of her luscious bottom lip. But after enjoying the taste of her for a long moment, he gently pushed her away from him.

"Okay," he said. "Let's talk."

"What?" She blinked glazed emerald eyes and had trouble maintaining her balance outside the warmth of his arms.

"You're right. We should talk." He took her hand and led her to the bed. He sat down on the edge of it and pulled her into his lap.

She felt like a little girl sitting across his knees. Her feet didn't quite reach the floor. As independent and self-sufficient as she was, she rather enjoyed the sensation of being cuddled for the moment. He held her close and stroked her gently. Her arms, her legs, her back, her face.

"Now, what do you want to talk about exactly?" he asked.

"Us," she said vaguely. "Our feelings."

"I'm not so good at that," he confessed.

"I'm not very good at it, either," she admitted. "Maybe we need an interpreter."

"We didn't in Providence," he reminded her. "And I don't think we do right now. We both know what we want." He paused long enough to kiss her again. "We want each other."

"Is that all it is, Chuck? A physical attraction?"

He pressed her head against the ledge of his shoulder—to avoid her questioning eyes? Keely wondered. "Keely, all I know for sure is that I've never wanted a woman as much as I want you now."

"*Now* sounds so temporary." Her voice came out thick.

"My whole life is temporary! You were right when you said I was nothing but a roaming gypsy. I don't even know how to turn on the stove in my apartment. And the only person in my neighborhood I have a relationship with is the dry cleaner down the street. I'm a nomad, Keely. But I'm getting fed up with my life-style. I want to change it. Yet I don't know how to exactly."

You could fall in love and marry a good woman, she thought. But at the same time she doubted if that woman was she. Perhaps it was too late for her to be a wife again. Since Royal, her life had taken a definite, unswerving path. She had her daughter and her career. And she enjoyed her hard-won independence that went even beyond Citation.

"And what about you, Keely?" he asked. "Are you happy devoting your life to a corporation?"

She stiffened in his lap. "You make it sound as if I shouldn't be."

He rubbed her back to calm her. "It was a simple question, darling."

"I heard the disdain in your voice."

"No, you misread me. I just want to know."

She relaxed again and readjusted her face against his shoulder. How she loved the clean, soapy smell of him. "It hurt me when you accused me of caring only about my career," she told him. "I had no choice in the matter. It was either advance or go under. I looked around and asked myself why I should settle for minimum wage when I was just as smart as all those salaried executives in their fancy wing-tipped shoes. The only thing they had that I lacked was a college education. So I went to night school. I went for it all, dammit. And after a lot of hard work, I'm just beginning to get it."

"You're tough, Keely. That's the first thing I liked about you," he said. She didn't feel especially tough, though, sitting in his lap. "But you haven't answered my question. Are you happy?"

"I should be, shouldn't I?" she hedged. "Who knows? In another ten years or so I could be a vice president at Citation."

There wasn't much enthusiasm in her voice, though, as she envisioned ten more endless years working for Armstrong Wellfleet. Ten years of long hours and office politics and travel and pressure. In ten years Joy would be an adult, and all the precious times they could have shared would be gone forever.

"If that's what you want, I'm sure you'll succeed," Chuck told her. "But how do you think I might fit into your scheme of things?"

His question made her heart skip a beat. She raised her head to look him in the eye. "Do you want to?"

"Maybe. Maybe we've got something here that will last."

"That's what I've been thinking. Almost constantly." That was as close as she dared come to telling him she loved him.

"It's been on my mind a lot, too," he replied.

That was hardly a lifetime commitment, she thought. Or even a twenty-four hour one. But she smiled bravely. They really were very much alike, she decided. They both played it close to the vest.

"This talk is getting us nowhere, Chuck."

"You took the words right out of my mouth, lady. And I could think of better things to do with our mouths."

So could she. "But nothing's been resolved," she pointed out.

He playfully bounced her on his knee. "This wasn't a summit meeting, Keely, only an initial discussion. Why don't we just table it for now?"

His hand encircled the back of her neck, and he pulled her face down to his. As vague as his words were, there was nothing elusive about his kiss. His tongue possessively explored the recesses of her mouth as she melted into his lap.

He fondled her with abandon now, as if every private part of her was his for the touching. Which it was. His hand slid over her clothed breasts and stomach, then dived under her very proper skirt to caress her nylon-sheathed thighs. His long, artistic fingers stroked her softly molded contours as her own hand unbuttoned his shirt and roamed the expanse of his broad bare chest.

"If we keep this up, we'll miss the show," he murmured into her ear. "The sun will be setting into the Pacific soon."

It was a sight Keely had never seen before, but she decided she could live without seeing it a little longer.

"You're my sun," she whispered back, clutching him to her.

His face lit up with pleasure. "Oh, Keely, you really can be so sweet at times. I want to make every inch of you throb for me. To make you want me like you've never wanted a man before."

Her green eyes flashed. "Is that a boast?"

"No, my darling. It's a promise."

He pushed her down into the softness of the bed and slowly stripped off her business clothes. He stopped when he reached the final thin layer of very unbusinesslike silk and lace. She'd worn her expensive peach teddy.

He let out a whistle of appreciation. "This is nice," he said. "I'll allow you to keep it on a little longer."

Standing over the bed looking down at her, he appeared even taller than he was, a giant of a man in complete control.

He was still fully clothed as he studied her, so wantonly displayed across the bed. A pink blush stole over her as his sharp camera eyes took her in. She began to pull up a sheet to cover herself from his intense scrutiny, but he yanked it away.

"Don't hide from me, Keely."

He reached for her thin cover of silk, and she was sure he would rip off her teddy with one mighty pull. But he slid it off her quite gently before tossing it aside. And then, still standing above her, he made love to her with his eyes. He said nothing, but the avid approval in his glittering gray gaze made her bask in his admiration. He *was* like the sun, warming her to her very core. She ached to be touched by more than his eyes.

"You undress, too," she urged him.

He complied and soon stood naked and proud before her. She adored him. His powerful masculine beauty excited her beyond measure, and she opened her arms to him.

"Come," she said. "Come to bed with me."

Instead, he sat at the edge of it and with one fingertip delicately traced her pert nose, full lips and stubborn chin.

"I love the contrast of your fiery hair against your creamy skin," he said. "And the sprinkle of freckles along your body. Like stardust. I've memorized each and every one of them."

She smiled up at him. "That's quite a feat." She placed a hand against his chest and slid her palm along the rough texture of his golden mat of hair, enjoying the springy texture of it beneath her stroke. "You're amazing, Mr. Dickens."

"Am I?" He captured her roaming, tantalizing hand and kissed the pulsing vein in her wrist. "Well, for my next amazing feat I'm going to take you to the highest peak of pleasure I can."

Her laugh was low and heavy with anticipation. "I hope you intend to come there with me."

"Oh, yes. But it's going to be a long, slow trip, Ms. La-Roux. I'm going to stop along the way and enjoy every bit of the scenery. You just let me be the guide."

With only a fingertip touch again, he traced the outline of each full breast, then circled one golden-pink halo. Her nipple became a taut, aching point of desire, begging to be kissed. "Makes my mouth water," he said, lowering his lips to it. His tongue savored its texture and taste, and she pressed his face deeper into the lush pillow of her breast, almost crying out.

He directed his attention to her other breast, savoring it just as slowly and thoroughly. His hungry yet gentle mouth sucked and nibbled her to distraction, and she nearly whimpered in delicious helplessness.

He stopped then and cupped the heavy globes in his palms. "My ripe, golden peach," he said, pressing her throbbing breasts together and then running his tongue down the narrow path of cleavage.

She could not remain passive a moment longer and began her own pleasure-giving exploration of his muscled body. She attempted to pull him down to lie on top of her, but despite his obvious and ready arousal, he pulled away. "We've got all the time in the world," he told her. "Lie back and relax, Keely. I'm the tour guide, remember?" A small, commanding smile edged his lips.

He began to massage her all over with strong, expert hands until her muscles were jelly. He kneaded the soft, silky flesh of her belly, and she felt a melting deep within her. His hand roamed to the heated, auburn crest of her femininity, and he tangled his fingers in the bright, springy hair. He gently tugged at her private pelt, coaxing a sweet flow of desire from her. She did indeed feel as ripe and juicy as a sun-warmed peach.

"Take me," she whispered, reaching up for him again and pressing her fingers into his broad, hard back.

"I will in good time, believe me." His silvery gray eyes smoldered like hot ice, and his grin was devilish. He grabbed her arms and pulled them away from him. Then he encircled her delicate wrists in the vise of one hand and arched her arms over her head. "You're at my mercy now, Ms. LaRoux."

She had been from the very beginning, but now, pinioned, she felt completely defenseless in her nakedness. Tears of desire and frustration sprang to her eyes. "What do you intend to do? Torture me?"

"No, just play with you a little while longer," he said lazily, teasingly, displaying his flashing white teeth.

She struggled a moment, twisting and arching her back, but she knew she had no choice but to submit to further tantalizing foreplay from this lion of a man.

His mouth began to skim over her entire body, and his beard bristled against her flesh, singeing it. Every nerve ending in her body became electrified, and she whimpered softly, overcome. He showed no mercy but muffled her cry with a deep kiss. His free hand continued to explore her pliant body, leaving no inch untouched. He explored her thoroughly and completely, and when she began to writhe, seeking release from this buildup of throbbing excitement, he at last relented. Still keeping a grip on her wrists, he stopped his sweet torture and gazed down at her.

Her bright red hair was tousled against the white pillow, and strands of it clung to her damp forehead. Her bright, tearful eyes were wide with pleasure, and her lips were swollen from his kisses. Her chest was heaving, and her body glowed with a hot flush. Chuck's face registered satisfaction.

"Stop looking at me," she begged, squeezing her eyes shut under his penetrating gaze. No man had ever seen her like this before, so hot and pulsing with desire.

"I can't stop looking," he said. "You have never been more beautiful, Keely LaRoux." His voice cracked with emotion.

He released her wrists and covered her overheated body with his. She spread her legs beneath the weight of him, and he entered her swiftly, deeply and with such force that she cried out. Not in pain but in relief. He had made her more than ready to receive his driving, relentless thrusts, and she answered each one with contractions of pleasure.

The red sun sent its last bright rays through the windows of their room, casting a rosy glow over their sweat-glistened bodies. They reached the peak of ecstasy together, just as Chuck had promised. Neither of them noticed or cared when the sun sank into the Pacific.

Keely awoke to a ringing phone early the next morning. Not opening her eyes, she turned toward Chuck, intent on nudging him to answer it. But her eyes flashed open when she discovered that his side of the bed was cold and empty. She called into the bathroom but got no response. The phone kept ringing. Keely had no choice but to answer it, in case there was an emergency at home. Maybe it was even Chuck. Where *was* he?

"Hello," she said groggily, her low voice even more husky from sleep.

"Obviously I've caught you in bed, Red. I do apologize."

Keely stiffened when she heard Peter Plack's insinuating voice. She came instantly awake. "What do you want, Plack?"

"Well, that's a fine how-do-you-do after all the trouble I went through tracking you down, Keely. Since your secretary is always so uncooperative, I was forced to rifle through her desk for a phone number before she came in this morning. The one I dialed was noted on her calendar. Funny, though. You're not registered in that inn. Only Chuck Dickens is. Luckily, I told the desk clerk to buzz the room anyway. And there you are. In the flesh, so to speak."

"I repeat, what do you *want*, Plack?" Her tone was cold, but her face was hot. She had been caught—that much was certain.

"You know, you really are something, Red," Plack replied in a false, awed voice. "To think that you're willing to save Citation a few extra bucks by bunking with your traveling companion. I really should tell Wellfleet about this. He'd be impressed by how cost conscious you are."

Keely gripped the phone in rage. "Listen, Plack, if you think you can blackmail me, forget it. Tell Wellfleet what you want, and be damned with you." She certainly wasn't going to beg him not to; she had too much pride for that.

"*Blackmail* is such a harsh word," Plack said, his voice less smug. "I only called to tell you that everything is fine back here in New York."

Keely impatiently snatched up her watch from the nightstand. "You called to tell me that at five in the morning? Cut the bull, Plack. You're nothing but a sneaky spy."

He clucked his tongue. "My, didn't you wake up in a bad mood? It happens to be eight in the morning here. I came to work early to keep an eye on things for you. Mind if I use your office while you're away? It's so much bigger than mine." He laughed with bitterness.

"Stay out of my office, Plack. You have no business there. I thought I made it clear to you that you're not in charge while I'm traveling. Since you came in earlier than usual, catch up on your own work. I expect to see some results when I return. That's a warning, Pete."

He hooted. "Oh, you talk tough, Red, for a woman caught in your position. Which I assume is lying down. Give my regards to Dickens. He may become a legend at Citation as the man who finally bedded Keely LaRoux."

Keely slammed the phone down hard, wishing it could have been over Plack's head. Then she covered her ears with cold hands. She could hear the rush of blood in them and could almost hear the nasty gossip Peter would soon be spreading about her. He would tell everybody in the corporate offices that Ms. LaRoux was having a little on-the-road fling. And the worst part was that for once the gossip was true! It would hardly matter to anyone that she was in love.

Keely had become used to gossip about herself since she had joined Citation. There was something about her that stimulated it—her blazing red hair and full figure, no doubt. But also her steady rise to the top and the admiration from her superiors. Each time she got promoted there was talk about her boss being infatuated with her.

Ironically, that had never once been the case. Her last boss, Clay Johnson, for instance, saw her as nothing but a hard worker who freed his time for four-day weekends of sailing. Wellfleet had never so much as given a signal of more than a business interest in her. Sure, executives at Citation admired her; she made their work easier for them. Keely had never used her looks to influence any of them. But now, if Plack blabbed, she would be forever tainted. If it was established that she was sleeping with the photographer she was traveling with, then anyone so inclined to would assume she had slept her way to the top.

She had made a mistake. She saw that very clearly now. She should have kept her relationship with Chuck strictly business until he had completed the Citation assignment. Why hadn't she then, dammit? Deep in her heart she knew the answer and hated to admit it to herself. More than passion had driven her to indiscretion. An element of fear had motivated her, too.

The truth was that she had been afraid of losing Chuck forever if she kept him at bay too long. Once their project was completed, he would go his way and set his sights on another woman. It hurt to acknowledge it. It demonstrated, all too clearly to her, that she had little faith in Chuck's lasting love for her.

She could not have asked for a more avid lover, to be sure. But he had never promised her anything beyond sexual fulfillment. He had granted her that and taken his fill of her, too, all through the night. Taken her so completely and with such gusto that she had lost herself to him totally, over and over again. Even now, in the light of early morning, she was still dazed. It amazed her that any man could make her lose herself like that.

Lose herself to what, though? Love? Or lust? What more did he want from her than what he had already received? Nothing more, perhaps. The word *love* had never crossed his lips, and she'd held back from confessing her feelings for him. She didn't want him to think she was trying to tie him to her in any way. He would balk at that, she knew. He was a man without ties or allegiances. He was a pirate, a gypsy, an adventurer. No matter how he complained about it, Chuck Dickens was a traveling man by nature.

She should know him for the kind of man he was. She had been married to one. Royal LaRoux had lacked Chuck's talent, success and style. Frankly, Chuck's sexual expertise and power, too. But like Chuck he had been a roamer, a man incapable of making a lasting commitment or settling down. At eighteen Keely had been too inexperienced and naive to recognize this, but she had no excuse now, at thirty. Was she doomed to be forever attracted to men like that? Men who would eventually leave her? She had never considered herself self-destructive before, but now she wondered what had led her down this twisting path once again. A path that would lead to pain.

Chuck entered the room, a wide grin of satisfaction on his face, not realizing that he had walked smack-dab into the thick gloom of Keely's doubts. He was carrying a tray of food. "Room service, madam," he announced.

"I'm not hungry." Her voice came out very small. She sat propped up by pillows, the sheet drawn up to her chin.

If Chuck noticed a change in her, he pretended he didn't. "Not hungry! Good grief, woman, you should be famished." He laughed. "I know I am." He set the tray down carefully on the nightstand beside the bed.

If only she had awakened to him instead of the ringing phone. How happy she would have been to see him enter the room with his offering. There was a small vase of daisies on the tray, a glass bowl of fruit, a basket of muffins, a silver pot of coffee and two flowered mugs. Chuck was dressed in faded jeans and a royal-blue sweatshirt. His thick hair was still wet from the shower he had taken while she had slept.

He poured a mug of hot coffee and, without asking her if she wanted any, handed it to her. When she reached out to accept it, the sheet slipped down, exposing the tops of her breasts, and with her free hand she hurriedly covered them with the sheet again. She blushed at her belated modesty. Hadn't he seen and touched and kissed every intimate inch of her?

The gesture made him laugh again. "Careful, the coffee's hot," he warned solicitously. He watched her take a sip and waited a long moment as she remained silent. "Okay, Keely, out with it," he demanded. "What the hell's wrong? When I left you ten minutes ago you were smiling in your sleep. What possibly could have happened since then?"

"I'll tell you what happened." She placed the mug back on the tray. "The phone rang."

"And you answered it?"

"I had to, since you weren't here," she accused, ignoring his thoughtful reason for leaving. "For all I knew, it could have been a call concerning my daughter. But it wasn't. It was Peter Plack."

"Ah, your dentist."

She didn't appreciate his levity. "He's not my dentist, dammit! The man is a manager on my staff. I told you about him, Chuck." Her voice was harsh.

The taut area around Chuck's gray eyes tightened as he heard her anger. "Yes, of course. I remember." He stood by the side of the bed, observing her. "The guy who wants a shot at your job, right?"

She nodded impatiently. "And now he's got the ammunition. It was a mistake for you to register us both in one room under your name." She almost added that it was a mistake that they had ever started this affair. She cleared her throat. "So now he knows I spent the night with you."

"So?" Chuck turned aside and poured himself some coffee. "What's the big deal? We're two consenting adults, aren't we?"

His uncaring insouciance was almost too much for her to bear right now. Maybe what they had shared was no big deal to him, but it meant a lot, almost everything, to her. "Listen, Dickens, Citation is a very conservative company, and the last thing an executive—especially a female executive—needs is the reputation that she sleeps around."

"But you don't, do you, Keely?" He took a deep sip from his mug and winced. After warning her, he had burned his own tongue.

She almost hoped it would blister. "You actually think I do?"

"No, of course not. I'm sorry, darling. That was a stupid question. And it was stupid of me not to reserve separate rooms for us. I forgot all about this corporate protocol crap, and I apologize. I never meant to embarrass you."

His apology, rough as it was, came close to disarming her but didn't quite. "Well, you did. I almost died. He said awful, snide things to me, Chuck, and I had no defense whatsoever."

"Yes, that must have been awful for you, Ms. LaRoux." There was no longer the slightest hint of self-deprecation in his voice. "God knows it must have been worse than death to be associated so intimately with me." Holding the warm cup close to his chest, he walked away and gazed out the curve of windows across the room.

It was obvious that she had hurt his feelings, but she simply couldn't muster up any sympathy at this moment. She was too fraught with her own dilemma. "Your ego is getting in the way of my point, Dickens," she grumbled to his back. "Can't you understand how it will undermine my credibility at Citation when Plack starts gossiping about me?"

"Always her job first," he muttered. But then he turned to her, a disarming smile on his face. "There's only one solution to the problem, Keely. I'll simply have to marry you to quell such vicious gossip."

Her mouth dropped open. Then it snapped shut again. She'd be a fool to take him seriously. And he'd almost made her one for a heart-jumping moment. How dare he tease her about something so serious? Especially at this particular moment.

"You don't seem exactly enchanted with my suggestion," he said as she silently glared at him.

"At times I find your sense of humor a little annoying, Dickens." More like heart-wrenching, she thought to herself.

"Pardon me for *annoying* you, Ms. LaRoux." He lowered his glittering eyes and studied the contents of his cup for a moment. Had she seen a flash of hurt in his eyes?

When he looked back up at her, his expression was unreadable. "Don't worry about this Plack. If he's as cunning as you say, he'll hold back before spreading dumb gossip about you. He'll see what you're willing to do for him first."

"Nothing," she vowed vehemently, the sheet over her breasts rising with her agitated breathing. "That little rat will gain nothing from this."

Chuck smiled tightly. "Like I said before, you're one tough cookie. I wonder why that appeals to me so much. Maybe you can tell me what I see in you, Keely."

"Yourself?"

That made him laugh. "Maybe. But I thought you said we had nothing in common."

"That was before we made love," she replied honestly. "We certainly had enough in common last night."

That seemed to please him. "We sure as hell did, didn't we?" He came to the bed and sat down on the edge of it. He plucked up a peach from the bowl and offered it to her with a teasing smile.

She shook her head. "No, thanks. Plack's call took away my appetite."

"Forget that, will you? Don't let it ruin our time together. I'm not going to."

"But don't you understand that—"

He silenced her by gently pressing the peach to her lips. "Eat," he ordered. "We're not going to talk about it anymore."

She bit into the fruit, and the juice trickled down the edge of her mouth. He flicked open a checkered napkin that was folded on the tray and dabbed her lips.

"Good?" he asked.

"Delicious."

"That's how you taste to me," he murmured.

Then he buttered a blueberry muffin and fed that to her, too, breaking off bite-size pieces and popping them into her mouth. When she'd finished the muffin she licked the butter off his fingers. She wondered why he pampered her so if he thought she was so tough. Then she proceeded to feed him.

She took a shower after their breakfast, and when she returned to the bedroom, wearing nothing but Chuck's blue shirt, he announced that they were going on a hike.

"You're going to see one of the most beautiful areas of California this morning, Keely. Or maybe even the world. It's called Point Lobos State Reserve."

"But, Chuck," she protested, wrapping his big shirt more closely around her body, loving the feel of it against her bare skin, "I can't go hiking around some nature reserve in my business clothes. I didn't pack anything else."

"I figured as much. So I brought clothes for you." A self-congratulatory smirk on his face, he went to his traveling bag, opened it and pulled out pumpkin-colored sweatpants, a matching top and a pair of sneakers. He threw them onto the bed. "Put them on, Keely. I'm sure they'll fit perfectly. If there's one thing I know how to judge, it's a woman's size."

At the same time that she was touched by his gesture, she couldn't help but worry about his claimed expertise in women's shapes and sizes. How many women had he enjoyed and then left before her? How many more *after* her was more to the point.

Overcome by another bout of modesty, she went back to the bathroom to try on the clothes. As he had assured her, everything fit perfectly. Even the shoes. He did have a good eye, she admitted grudgingly. He was even right about color. She had always been told that redheads shouldn't wear orange, but the shade of pumpkin he had selected made her ivory complexion and copper hair absolutely glow. She stood before the bathroom mirror and studied her reflection for a long moment. Her lips were slightly swollen from Chuck's many long, deep kisses. There were shadows under her eyes from so little sleep. Even so, she recognized that she had never looked better.

"Stop admiring yourself, and let's get a move on," Chuck called through the closed door. "You missed the sunset, but I won't let you miss the sunrise, too, Keely. We have a few glorious hours to explore Point Lobos before we have to get to work."

They drove to the reserve and followed the Cypress Grove Trail. The air was fragrant with wood mint and sagebrush, and Keely lost herself in the beauty that surrounded them. Nagging worries floated out of her mind. They had come early enough to have the reserve all to themselves, and Keely felt as if they were the only two human beings existing in a strange and wondrous paradise. A brush rabbit hopped across the trail in front of them, startling her, then disappeared in the coarse wild ryegrass. Chuck smiled down at Keely, who had automatically clung to him. He called her his little bunny and kissed the top of her head. She adored his corny sweetness.

The sun was just rising when the trail led them to a stand of cypress growing above the high granite cliffs. The backdrop of the vivid pink sky made the trees' twisted branches, distorted by sea winds, all the more dramatic. Rust-colored birds with strange black hoods fluttered about. Chuck told Keely they were juncos. Between the trees Keely could see a spectacular view of deep green-blue waves crashing against elaborate rock formations.

"Oh, Chuck, how marvelous! Why don't you take a picture?" Chuck had brought along one of his Nikons but as yet had not used it.

"I really don't think the world needs another picture of cypress trees on Monterey Peninsula. Unless, that is, Keely LaRoux is in it. Go perch on a limb, darling, and pretend you're a junco."

She complied, a little self-conscious about posing for a professional photographer. She was aware that Chuck occasionally did fashion work, and she didn't think she could stand up to a comparison with tall, exquisite young models. So rather than even try to look good, Keely mugged for his camera, and he kept snapping each ridiculous pose and face she made. A natural athlete, and at one time a tomboy, she managed to balance on the low limb with one foot, the other leg flung high, at the same time looking cross-eyed into the camera.

"Beautiful, beautiful," he kept saying, encouraging her silliness. And she did feel extremely silly and light-headed. Maybe she was high on the mint- and sea-scented air. Maybe it was a release from tension. Or maybe, just maybe, she was drunk on the pleasure of being alone with Chuck in this earthly paradise.

"And now I'll pose nude for you," she joked.

He lowered his camera. His eyes were twinkling. "I dare you, LaRoux. I even double-dare you to do it."

She shook her head, laughing. "No way. What if someone comes by?"

"Impossible. There were no other cars in the parking lot when we arrived. So do it, Keely LaRoux. Strip for me. Or are you all talk and no action?"

He was just teasing, she knew, but her blood was high and the devil was in her. "You don't think I'd dare, do you?"

"No, I don't. Even with a name like yours, you're too uptight and conservative, Lady Corporate Director," he goaded.

That did it. She jumped off the twisted limb and shucked her orange knit sweatsuit, socks and shoes. Hesitating in her madness for only an instant, she unhooked the front clasp of her simple white bra, tossed it aside and slipped off her panties. "There!" she declared, spreading her arms wide. His camera was already clicking and whirring.

"Lean against the tree," he directed. "And don't make a face! No, don't give me an artificial smile, either. Just look into the lens, Keely, and think about how we made love all last night." *Click, click.* "Yes, that's right. Keep that expression. Are you remembering what I am? Oh, you're luscious. You really are. And the sky matches your skin tones! Oh, this is great. It really is. That's right. Move like that. Press your body against the limb." *Click, click, click.* "Now toss your head to the side. I want some strands of red hair against your cheek. Lick your lips, and look into the camera sideways. That's right!" The camera kept clicking. Keely didn't hear it. She was lost in the sound of Chuck's voice, urging her on. Her lips were parted; her green eyes were glazed with love. "Yes!" he cried. "That's the look I want to capture forever."

And then it was over. There was no more film left in the camera. "Well, that wraps it up," Chuck said.

Keely suddenly felt very foolhardy to have bared everything, even her soul, to his camera like that. She lowered her eyes and saw that her nipples were hard with excitement. She dressed hurriedly, embarrassed by her own brazen sensuality.

"You were marvelous," Chuck said, taking her into his arms. She stiffened and pushed him away, although a moment ago she would have let him take her completely. The fact that her wantonness had been captured on film made her almost dizzy with regret.

"Okay, I took your dare. Now let me have that roll of film, Chuck." She extended her trembling hand. "I want to throw it into the ocean."

He took her hand and kissed it. "Oh, no. That wasn't the deal, darling. The pictures I took of you will be a wonderful memento of our time here. Think of the happy memories they'll conjure up thirty years from now."

She gave a harsh laugh. "You won't even remember my name thirty years from now. Stop teasing, and give me the film."

His face went rigid, as if she had slapped him. "You really don't trust me, do you, Keely? And I thought that at last you did. While you were posing for me, I really thought you did."

"I got carried away, that's all." That was the problem. She was always letting herself get carried away with him.

"What do you think I'm going to do, Keely? Send prints of you in the buff to Citation's board of directors?"

"No. Of course not." She wished he would stop staring at her like that, as if she'd insulted him deeply.

"You still don't trust me," he repeated. His face remained as still as a stone, but pain flickered in his gray eyes. "When is it going to sink into that thick skull of yours that I love you, Keely?"

She could distinctly hear sea lions barking on the distant rocks but wasn't sure she'd heard him correctly. "You love me?"

"Yes, dammit!" he roared.

"You don't have to shout!" she shouted back. Her heart was pounding so hard that she could hardly breathe.

"How else can I get you to listen to me? And stop looking so surprised. I think I've made my feelings pretty obvious from the very beginning."

"But you haven't!" she protested. "You made it clear that you wanted me, but you never once mentioned love, Chuck."

"What is this? A debate?" He turned away from her and looked out at the crashing waves.

She reached out, almost timidly, and touched his arm. "How I wish I understood you better," she said. "Are we even speaking the same language when we talk about love?"

He didn't turn back to her or reply right away. The sound of the wind, the waves, the birds filled the heavy silence.

When he finally did turn around there was confusion in his face. "It was a simple declaration from my heart, Keely. Why make it so complicated?"

"Because it is," she insisted. "We're not two naive kids with simple emotions. The problem is that you're beginning to affect my whole life, Chuck. And I don't know what will come of it."

But he didn't seem to think that was a problem at all. "It's the present that matters," he told her. "It's this very moment that's important. So admit it, darling. Admit you love me, too."

"I do," she whispered with a mixture of pain and relief.

"I knew it!" he cried, encircling her small waist with his large hands and lifting her high off the ground. "I saw it through my camera lens."

She looked down at his delighted face and knew her own reflected the joy in it. For one soaring instant she had never been so happy. Perhaps he was right. It was the moment that mattered, not the future.

But when he put her down, his attention was suddenly distracted. Her eyes followed his sharp gray gaze, directed toward the ocean. She could see nothing in the distance except for a vague spray of water vapor in the air.

"That's a gray whale spouting at the surface, Keely. This must be our lucky day. It's a rare sight. Maybe we should wish on it, like on a shooting star."

"I know what my wish is," she said immediately.

He pressed his finger to her lips. "Don't say it. If you do, it won't come true."

Then he covered her waiting mouth with his. Her wish that they would never have to part remained unspoken.

Chapter Ten

They took a flight back to New York that evening. The plane was half-empty, and they had the luxury of three seats across all to themselves.

"Almost as good as first class," Chuck said, stretching out his long, powerful frame. "Which is the way I usually travel, by the way, darling."

"Humph. You don't get there any faster that way, do you?" Keely leafed through the airline magazine.

Chuck smiled and pushed back a strand of her glossy hair. "You're such a frugal Vermont Yankee, aren't you?"

A polite way of saying she was cheap, Keely thought. But she readily agreed with his assessment. "Where I grew up, we had to pinch pennies. It's a hard habit to break. But I don't suppose you'd know anything about that. You were born rich. And now you make more money than you have time to spend."

"There are other kinds of poverty, you know."

She put down the magazine and turned to him. "Tell me what you mean, Chuck."

He folded his arms across his chest like a shield of armor. "I'm not going to bore you or myself with stories about my deprived childhood, Keely."

"But I want to know." She sensed his life lacked a certain richness despite the fact that the fates had blessed him with wealth, talent and good looks.

He let out a deep sigh. "You always mention how poor you were, Keely, but I bet there was plenty of love around."

"Yes, that's all we had plenty of." The image of her mother's kind, sweet face lit up her mind.

"And that's what we never had enough of in my family. My father was a very cold, severe man. He never took much interest in me or my brother. Or my mother, for that matter. I don't know why she stuck it out with him. I took off as soon as I could. I've made a habit of taking off and not looking back. It saves a lot of prolonged misery in the end."

A deep foreboding loomed over her. "Taking off is another habit that can be hard to break," she said. "You sound so cynical at times, Chuck."

"I am about certain things," he easily agreed. "You have to look out for yourself in this world, Keely. No one else will."

Was that meant as a warning? she wondered. Was he telling her to guard her heart against him even now, after he'd declared his love?

"How exactly should I look out for myself?" she asked him.

"You're too damn devoted to that company you work for," he told her. "Don't you realize that Citation is just another ruthless conglomerate?"

"It's given me the only security I've ever had in life."

He laughed at that. "If you stopped being of value to them, they'd show you the door fast enough."

"Thanks for the comforting words." She looked out the window and saw nothing but blackness.

He reached for her hand and gave it a squeeze. "I didn't mean to upset you. I'm just trying to tell you that it's smarter to take what you can and then move on."

That upset her even more. "Is that what you do, Chuck? Is that why they call you a pirate?"

He shrugged. "I charge the most I can get away with for my talent. But I always produce. For instance, those shots I took of the X25 this afternoon are going to be sensational."

"You sound pretty confident, considering the film hasn't even been developed," she remarked dryly. At the same time she admired such confidence.

"It's already been developed right here," he told her, tapping an index finger against his high forehead. "In the mind's eye. I know exactly what the results will look like even before I snap the shutter. The camera is simply a tool I use to record an inner vision."

He had never talked to her so personally about his work before. She realized that he cared more about it than he usually let on. But then he laughed, as if he had said something stupid.

"Not that I have inner visions about computer systems," he quickly amended. "Or any of the damn products I take pictures of. But in any case, the shoot went well today. You have to admit that Moonbeam worked out, too. Not like having my trusty assistant Zinko by my side, of course, but she managed to set up the equipment and keep my cameras loaded."

"She did a good job," Keely replied only a trifle reluctantly. "I may have initially misjudged her."

Moonbeam had arrived at the Salinas plant right on time, dressed for work in a denim, multi-pocketed jumpsuit that hid her tanned, curvy figure from head to toe. And although Keely thought she had touched and brushed against Chuck more often than necessary, she had been impressed by the young woman's stamina, efficiency and know-how. Keely always gave credit to people who acted professionally, but that still didn't mean she *liked* Moonbeam. Chuck hadn't shown the least bit of attraction toward her, so it wasn't jealousy. It was something else that Keely couldn't pin down. A vague, instinctive apprehension.

Chuck reached under his seat for his camera bag and opened it. "I got so involved with the shoot that I didn't keep track of how many rolls of film I went through," he said, counting the silver canisters in which the exposed film was stored. "Ten," he announced. "I'll send them out to be processed tomorrow."

"Do it first thing, Chuck," Keely urged. "Wellfleet wants to see the slides and choose prints as soon as possible."

"Okay, okay," he replied irritably. "Can't keep the great man waiting, can we?"

Keely stroked the thick, slightly curly hair at his temple to calm him. "I really do appreciate that you came out with me on such short notice. You could have been working on your gallery show. Thank you."

"I'm glad you *do* appreciate it, lady," he said gruffly, but he tilted his head toward her stroking fingers and pressed his ear against her soft palm.

She cupped it gently. "I hate pressuring you," she said. "But I'm under so much pressure myself lately. You met me at the worst time possible, you know. I was a much nicer person before I got this promotion." Admitting this to him, she also admitted it to herself for the first time.

"You're still nice enough," he allowed. "At times, anyway."

She ran her finger around the sensitive curves of his ear but then stopped her teasing caress, remembering something. "You're not going to send out that roll of film of me stark naked to be processed, are you?"

"Don't worry. It's right here," he assured her, tapping the breast pocket of his khaki bush jacket. "That's one roll of film I'll take a great deal of pleasure in developing myself."

"I should never have posed like that," she said with regret.

"Don't be silly, darling." He gave her his sweetest smile. "We'll put those photos in our private album, and they'll warm us in our old age."

She thought that was the nicest thing he'd ever said to her. Maybe that was because it was about the only definite thing he'd said about a future together. She resumed her fingertip roving around the curves and valleys of his ear.

He shivered. "If you don't stop that, I'm going to pounce on you," he warned hoarsely.

"You didn't stop when I begged *you* to," she reminded him. "Besides, you can't pounce on me, can you? Unless you want to make a spectacle of yourself. Face it, Chuck. You're my captive, thousands of feet above the ground. The plane won't land for hours, and I could tease you to death by then." She leaned closer and bit his earlobe.

"At least I'll die a happy man," he sighed, reaching up to flick off the reading lights above their seat.

Their conversation ceased from then on, except for an occasional endearment. As the plane carried them east through the clouds, they were in a heaven of their own making.

They indulged in the lost art of prolonged kissing. It was supremely exciting—and frustrating. Thinking they would explode from their pent-up desires, they would break apart, breathe deeply and then resume the sweet torture all over again. The enforced restraint made them both dizzy with delight and more than a little crazy. But as much as they wanted to, they couldn't stop.

The hours seemed to fly by even faster than the jet's speed, and when the plane landed in New York they were still up in the clouds. But then reality set in. Chuck had to claim all his equipment in the baggage area, and as Keely waited for him nearby she almost dozed in her seat, suddenly overcome with exhaustion. She fought it off, though, and helped Chuck load all his paraphernalia into a taxi. At that moment they both sorely missed Zinko. The silver cases took up all the trunk space and the back seat, too, and they were forced to sit up front with the cab driver, who was swearing under his breath.

By the time the taxi came to a screeching halt in front of Keely's apartment building, it was 4:00 a.m., New York time. Although she told him it wasn't necessary, Chuck insisted on accompanying her to her door. He leaned against it while she searched her purse for her keys.

"I could fall asleep standing up," he said. He took her keys from her, opened the door, then went inside to make sure everything was all right. Joy was across the hall, spending the night with Mrs. Alphonso. He turned on the light in Keely's bedroom and looked longingly at her bed. "Let me spend the night with you," he appealed. "At least what's left of it."

He looked as bone-weary as she felt, and there was nothing she would have liked more than to tuck him into bed and join him there. But she couldn't take the chance of having her daughter finding them together. In a few hours Joy would be awake and getting ready for school. She would be coming back to their apartment to dress and collect her books. Besides, Chuck had left all his valuable equipment in the waiting cab. Keely reminded him of this.

He gave her a regretful look and then a long parting kiss. "I love you," he whispered hotly into her ear. He went out the door before she could reply in kind.

She went into the kitchen and made herself a cup of coffee. It made little sense to go to bed now, she decided. She wanted to spend some time with Joy before school, and then get to the office early.

Besides, she was no longer sleepy. Chuck's parting declaration of love rang sweetly in her ears, and she knew the echo of it would keep her awake. Twice now he had told her he loved her. As much as she had yearned to hear those words, they had come unexpectedly and caught her off guard. Ironically, she had not voluntarily stated her love to him yet. Although he had guessed it, those three simple words no longer came easily to her, except with her daughter. The only other man she had confessed her love to had been Royal LaRoux. And he had found her love too binding.

Joy was surprised and delighted to find her mother waiting for her when she returned from across the hall, but she wouldn't eat the French toast Keely had prepared for her. She had already eaten breakfast with Mrs. Alphonso. And neither did she have time to chat with her mother for very long. A girlfriend from school had acquired a new puppy, and Joy was going to meet her in Central Park to walk it before classes.

Keely objected to this. The idea of two young girls walking in Central Park alone did not sit well with her. Tears welled up in Joy's light green eyes, and she pleaded for permission. Keely held firm. She would not allow it.

"You never let me do anything fun!" Joy shouted. "I wish you'd stayed in California." With that, she ran into her bedroom and slammed the door.

She remained there, no doubt pouting, until it was time to leave for school. She gave her mother a curt goodbye before she left.

As hurt as she was, Keely understood Joy's anger. Their relationship was not on firm ground right now because of Keely's long hours at work and constant traveling. It was unfortunate that the first thing she had to do when she returned home was deny Joy something she really wanted. Not that she regretted her decision. Her daughter's safety was more important than winning popularity points with her. Still, it was not a happy homecoming, and Keely didn't like being cast in the role of spoilsport. She refused to believe, though, that her daughter really wished she had stayed away. They would sit down and work things out that evening, Keely promised herself. She also promised herself to leave work early.

But Keely's day at the office was hectic. The quarterly financial report one of her staff members was supervising came back from the printer with so many typos and errors that she could not allow it to go out to stockholders. If she had been there to oversee the proofreading, that would never have happened. But she had been in Providence, instead. Where she had started her affair with Chuck Dickens, she reminded herself.

This made her feel guilty, even though she knew it had nothing to do with the problem at hand. It had been Wellfleet's decision, not hers, for her to supervise all photography shoots. She ordered that corrections be made and the financial report reprinted. The publication would cost almost double to produce now, which would not look good for her department. And in the end it was she, not her apologetic manager, who would be held responsible.

Next she discovered that Plack had gone over the allotted advertising budget, doubling their corporate ads in a weekly business journal without her approval. She knew well enough whose approval he had wanted to win, though—the pretty blond ad rep's. His expense account was also way out of kilter. Too many lunches at too many fancy restaurants for no good reason. If he thought he could get away with that, he was dead wrong. She would have to challenge him, even though he knew about Chuck and her. She had no choice if she wanted to keep her authority as department head. As determined as she was to confront him, her hand still shook when she depressed her intercom buzzer and asked her secretary to call him into her office immediately.

"Plack called in sick today," Edith informed her.

Keely didn't believe for a moment that he was ill. He was playing cat and mouse with her, she decided. In a way, though, she was relieved. Due to lack of sleep and mounting tension, she was not at her best this morning.

"I know you're very busy, Keely, but if you have a free moment, I'd like to talk to you," Edith added.

"Sure. Come right in." If there was one person on her staff Keely would always make a free moment for, it was Edith. The secretary had proven herself to be more than competent, and was devoted to her job. Like Keely, she wanted to do the best work possible at all times. Also, like Keely, her motivation was her self-satisfaction and pride.

When Edith came in she gave Keely a close look, then frowned with disapproval. "Your trip with Mr. Dickens must have been exhausting," she commented dryly.

Was Keely imagining it, or did she discern a little snicker at the edges of Edith's firm mouth? Had Plack already started spreading his gossip about her and Chuck spending the night together? Keely told herself to stop being so paranoid. If Edith had heard any rumors, she would come right out and state them frankly. One of the traits Keely most admired in the older woman was her no-nonsense directness. Edith, a born New Yorker, reminded Keely of the folks she'd grown up with in Vermont.

"All this traveling is running you ragged, my dear," Edith continued. "You should have taken the morning off."

It became obvious to Keely that Edith was nothing but concerned. She rubbed her throbbing temples a moment and then managed to smile. "Taking the morning off is a luxury I can little afford right now."

"It seems the last thing you need is another problem, Keely." Edith twisted the beaded chain that her bifocals were attached to.

"What is it, Edith? Please tell me," Keely insisted.

Edith shook her gray head slowly. "Peter Plack and I had quite a confrontation the other day. I came in early and caught him going through your desk. I threatened to call a security guard if he didn't leave your office immediately. Then he threatened to get me fired." She sighed deeply. "I'm afraid our threats to each other were exploding like firecrackers."

A few exploded within Keely right then, but she remained outwardly cool. "You were completely in the right, and I'm grateful, Edith."

Edith nodded. "I thought so, too. But he said he'd report my insubordination to Mr. Wellfleet." She began nervously twisting her beaded eyeglass chain again. "If I got fired, I'd lose my pension."

"You won't get fired," Keely insisted. "As a matter of fact, when your review comes up next month, I plan to recommend a raise for you and a change in title from secretary to administrative assistant. You're indispensable to me."

Edith looked relieved as she patted her smooth bun. Then she frowned again. "Oh, dear." She hesitated. "After such accolades I hate to ask you if I can leave a little early today. Mr. Hamilton is in the hospital again. He had a little setback." Although they had been married forty years she always referred to her husband with reserved formality.

"Oh, Edith, I'm sorry." She sensed that her secretary was playing down the seriousness of her husband's heart condition and her own grave concern about it. "Take the rest of the day off, and go to him right now."

"I'll just finish typing some letters first and—"

"*Now*, Edith," Keely broke in. "Since when is a job more important than someone you love?"

Edith gave her a grateful look and departed.

Later in the morning Chuck called and asked Keely if she was free for lunch. Her heart tugged at her to accept. The hours since they had parted seemed like days. But she had to refuse. There was simply too much work to be done. He suggested dinner that evening, and again she had to refuse. It was imperative that she spend some time alone with Joy and bridge the gap between them. She invited him to dinner the next night at her place. He couldn't make it, though. He would be tied up preparing for his gallery show, he explained.

It seemed the only time they could manage to see each other would be work-related. Chuck was scheduled to take the president's picture for the annual report the following afternoon. They were both disgruntled over the difficulty of getting together when they hung up.

But when he entered her office the next day, a little early for his appointment, it was as if time had stood still since they had last seen each other, and they took up right where they had left off. He went around her desk, scooped her up and held her tight. She melted into his solid warmth, and even their hearts seemed to touch. She wanted to stay in the charmed circle of his strong arms forever but forced herself to step away. "What if someone sees us?" she cautioned.

Pretending alarm, he glanced around the room. "You mean Big Brother may be watching?"

"More like bigmouth Plack. Not that it would matter, I suppose, since he already knows about us."

It really didn't matter to Keely anymore. If she had used poor judgment in getting involved with Chuck while they were working together, she had chastised herself enough over it. Long after his work on the annual report was completed, their relationship would still be going strong. At least Keely was beginning to believe it would. Whenever she thought of the future, Chuck was part of the picture. She didn't know exactly how he fitted into it, only that he had a place in it.

"Where's this Plack's office?" Chuck asked, his gray eyes narrowing menacingly. "I think I'll have a little talk with him."

"Please don't, Chuck!" The last thing Keely wanted was a confrontation between them at Citation headquarters. "Let sleeping dogs lie," she urged. "I have a feeling you were right about Plack deciding against gossiping about me. It would only call attention to his own conduct, which could hardly stand the scrutiny."

"Oh, really?" Chuck arched an eyebrow. "What has he done that's so awful?"

"He cheats on his wife!" Keely spat out. "He even propositioned *me*."

Apparently Chuck didn't share her shocked outrage. "Is that so amazing? You're a very beautiful, sexy woman, darling."

Keely frowned and brushed back her hair impatiently. "You're missing the point, Chuck." And she found it disturbing that he was. "He has a wife and children."

Chuck shrugged. "That doesn't automatically make a man a saint, you know."

His blasé attitude made her muscles tense. "You and I seem to have different values," she said in a tight voice.

His easy smile faded. "Now hold it, Keely. We were talking about Plack, not me. And I wasn't excusing or approving the man's conduct. I just made a simple comment about human nature."

He looked directly into her eyes, and his were sharp and clear. He was right, of course, she decided. They hadn't been discussing his values at all. He was simply more sophisticated than she was, she concluded. That certainly didn't mean that he would cheat on his wife. If he had one, that was. Which he didn't. She felt foolish about getting so upset.

"Let's not waste our breath discussing Plack," she said hurriedly, touching his arm to make amends. "Let me brief you on this photo session with Wellfleet."

"Brief me?" Very subtly Chuck moved his arm from her touch. "I've had a lot of experience taking mug shots of chief executive officers, you know."

He was already getting defensive, she noted. And he hadn't even met the abrasive president yet. She feared that they would surely rub each other the wrong way. "Wellfleet expects to be treated with deference, Chuck," she warned. He snorted at that, but she continued anyway. "And he's very self-conscious about his weight. Maybe you could photograph him at a special angle or something to make him look slimmer.''

''What do you think I am, a magician? The camera doesn't lie. If the man's fat, he's fat.'' Chuck tugged at his beard. ''Dammit, I hate this sort of assignment. The last thing I want to do right now is photograph some vain, self-important corporate bully. Taking product pictures is bad enough.''

If he scorned it so much, then why did he do it for a living? It was on the tip of Keely's tongue to challenge him about it, but she wisely remained silent. Chuck was in what she now thought of as his king-of-the-jungle frame of mind, and she didn't care to aggravate the big cat further. Nobody told Chuck Dickens what to do, he would roar. She knew the scenario well enough by now. She smiled and said nothing.

Chuck saw her smile. ''You think I'm a temperamental egotist, don't you, Keely?'' There was humor rather than challenge in his voice. His expression was self-deprecatory.

She had expected more anger, but it seemed that the only predictable thing about Chuck was that he would always be unpredictable. Right now he seemed amused by his own outburst.

''Don't worry, Ms. LaRoux,'' he said. ''I won't be rude to your boss. I'd never do anything to jeopardize your job.''

''I know,'' she replied softly. He had always come through for her, and she believed he always would. She stood on tiptoe and gave him a light kiss on the cheek. Even this brief skimming of flesh thrilled her. It didn't take much to make her simmering passion for Chuck boil over, she had to admit.

He grabbed her arms, not allowing her to step away from him. ''Let's lock your office door and make love,'' he suggested in a husky whisper. He had an uncanny way of reading her mind.

The very idea of it shocked and excited her. He pressed his body against hers persuasively, and she was more than ready to succumb to the temptation. They had not made love since California, and that seemed light-years away now.

The sound of Edith's typing in the other room drifted into her ears and brought her back to her senses. "There isn't any lock on the door," she gasped.

Chuck groaned with regret and released her, giving her a wistful look.

Flustered, Keely straightened the bow on her ivory blouse and smoothed down her blue serge jacket. She felt completely undone. She couldn't believe she had been about to go along with his bold suggestion. Something about Chuck brought out the daredevil in her. It was a side of her nature that she had kept in complete control for over ten years.

"You're a devil. You really are, Chuck," she said in a trembling voice.

He laughed. "Tell me the truth, love. If there was a lock on your door, we'd be making love right now, wouldn't we?"

She blushed, embarrassed over her own intense desire and his awareness of it. It still upset her that she had actually considered such folly right here at Citation headquarters. She looked away from Chuck's knowing eyes and studied her watch. She had trouble focusing on the numbers. It took her total concentration.

"It's time for our appointment with Wellfleet," she announced, trying to sound businesslike. "Where's Zinko? Isn't he going to assist you?"

"He's waiting in the lobby with the equipment. I'll call him up as soon as I chat with Wellfleet for a while. I like to put my subjects at ease first, let them warm up to me."

The possibility of Armstrong Wellfleet's warming up to the likes of Chuck Dickens seemed highly unlikely to Keely. Wellfleet distrusted anyone who didn't fit into the corporate mold. And the bearded Dickens, dressed in his casual, wrinkled working clothes, certainly didn't.

She was tense when she led Chuck out of her office and down the long hallway to the elevators. She wished Chuck had at least worn a tie, an article of clothing he apparently found as offensive as a noose.

The elevator was crowded with Citation employees, and she and Chuck were pressed toward the back of it. He cupped his hand beneath her full buttocks, and she felt the intimate massage of his fingers through the twilled material of her skirt. Shocked, she shot him a reproving glare, but his face remained impassive and innocent as he stared straight ahead. His hand, though, became more audacious. As affronted as she was, Keely experienced a warm rush of pleasure and had to stifle a moan.

To make him desist such scandalous teasing, she stepped on his foot, digging her heel into his boot. At the same time, she nodded and smiled to a vice president on the car who glanced in their direction. Chuck, meanwhile, had a handful of her in his grip and was squeezing hard. Flushing bright red, she removed her heel from his foot. Her temperature rose with the elevator, but she kept her cool as Chuck continued to furtively fondle her. What infuriated her most was that she was getting a thrill out of it, and Chuck no doubt knew it.

"Okay, you had your fun. Now behave yourself," she hissed when they exited the elevator and headed toward Wellfleet's office suite. Chuck's only response was a wink.

But he did behave himself, more or less, and the photography session with the president went far better than Keely had expected. Both Dickens and Wellfleet seemed to appreciate the other's slight edge of antagonism.

Having spent a month photographing Citation products, Chuck was well-acquainted with the company and easily led Wellfleet into a discussion about business. That was all Wellfleet needed to let go, and as he expounded on Citation's high-tech future, he hardly noticed Spike Zinko, in his Donald Duck T-shirt, setting up the camera tripod and lights. Chuck kept on talking to him as he took his formal portrait behind the vast oak desk. Although he wouldn't smile, Wellfleet almost seemed to be enjoying himself.

But just as Keely was beginning to relax, Chuck suggested trying a few candid shots of the president standing by the window, using only natural light. Wellfleet readily complied.

"Just gaze out the window and think of the whole damn city as your empire," Chuck suggested to him.

That did the trick. A beatific smile edged up Wellfleet's stubborn lips. But Chuck wasn't quite satisfied.

"Oh, and sir," he added politely, "suck in your gut. You're not hiding it behind that big desk of yours now."

Keely gasped and wished the thickly carpeted floor would open so she could fall through it and disappear. No, she wished *Chuck* would fall through it. She steeled herself for Wellfleet's wrath but instead heard something she had never heard before: the sound of Armstrong Wellfleet laughing.

"Thanks for reminding me, Dickens," he said, patting his ample tummy. "Don't want the stockholders to think I'm a fat cat, do I?"

Keely's mouth dropped open. It was not an especially clever joke, but at least it was an attempt at one. Which meant that he was still in good humor. Chuck snapped away, capturing Wellfleet at his best, his eyes looking outward, toward the future, his smile gleeful *and* his gut sucked in. The perfect image for the first page of the annual report.

Chuck knew what he was doing, all right, she had to admit. He had humored the difficult man through some stodgy, predictable shots behind his important desk until he felt comfortable, and then somehow managed to bring out the natural best in him to record on film.

Keely had intended to leave with Chuck and Spike once all the equipment was packed up, but Wellfleet instructed her to stay. So she thanked Chuck formally and shook his hand before he departed. As Wellfleet watched, she did not even blink when Chuck tickled her palm with his thumb.

"For a man who needs a haircut and shave, that Dickens acts pretty damn sure of himself" was Wellfleet's first comment to Keely. He motioned her to sit down and leaned back in the big swivel chair behind his desk. "How are things going with you and him?"

"We're proceeding right on schedule," she replied with a straight face. "He's been very accommodating."

Wellfleet grunted. "He's a real professional. I spotted that right off. I admire that in a man."

In a woman, too, Keely hoped. "We'll wrap up the annual report photography early next week at the cable plant in Jasper, Vermont." She was really looking forward to that. She wanted to show Chuck where she had been raised.

He nodded his approval. "What about the California trip? How did that go?"

"Without a hitch, sir." She didn't think it necessary to mention that Chuck had used an untried assistant. In the end, everything had worked out fine.

"I'd like to see pictures he got of the X25 today," the president demanded.

"But we just returned from the West Coast early yesterday morning. The film hasn't been processed yet."

Wellfleet's thick eyebrows meshed when he frowned. "I hope you're not dragging your feet on this one, Keely."

Dragging her feet! They had barely touched ground, Keely thought, keeping a lid on her anger. It seemed that whatever she accomplished was never enough. "I'll see to it that the slides are on your desk as soon as possible, sir," she replied in a cool, calm voice.

"And I want you to arrange a big press conference in two weeks to announce the X25," he told her.

"That's pretty short notice," she replied as her heart sank.

"Any longer than that and we risk having UltraTech get wind of it and announcing their system first," Wellfleet countered. "You can handle it, can't you, Keely?"

It was more a demand than a question. Keely's shoulders began to slump under the weight of this additional responsibility, but she threw them back. "I'll get right on it. Is there anything else, Mr. Wellfleet?"

"One more thing." Wellfleet swiveled in his chair to gaze out his wall of windows. "While you and Dickens were in California, Peter Plack reported something very disturbing to me." He paused.

She paled but said nothing. She had no intention of denying her relationship with Chuck, which she was sure Wellfleet was about to bring up. She was prepared to tell him it was none of his business.

"It concerns that secretary of yours," Wellfleet went on unexpectedly. "Peter informed me that she was uncooperative and very rude to him while you were away."

Keely experienced an instant's relief, quickly followed by indignation. She stiffened, raising her chin. "Mrs. Hamilton reports to me, not Plack."

"True, but do you want a secretary who won't cooperate with your managers?" Wellfleet continued to gaze out the window, his jowly profile toward Keely.

"It's Plack who's unwilling to cooperate, sir." It was not the most opportune time to bring up this problem, but she felt she had no choice.

He swiveled to face her again, scowling. "I don't get that impression at all. Peter makes it a point to be helpful to me, especially when you're traveling, Keely."

Oh, she just bet the little worm did. She was about to explain the situation when Wellfleet checked his gold quartz watch.

"I have a board meeting now," he said, standing up. "Start arranging that press conference, Keely. And I want to see copy and layouts for the annual report soon. I also suggest you think about getting a new secretary. This is the second time I've mentioned this to you, and I don't want to have to again."

He nodded goodbye, dismissing her. With every ounce of self-control she had in her, Keely remained silent and left his office. Inside, she was screaming with frustration.

When she returned to her own office she put on a good face for Edith's sake. She would never tell her about Wellfleet's thinly veiled ultimatum. She was determined that Edith would remain her secretary. She was also determined to get that troublemaker, Plack, out of her department. She realized, more than ever, that it wasn't going to be easy to convince Wellfleet that Plack was inept and hostile. He would be more inclined to believe her once she had proven herself in her new position. It was obvious that she was still on trial as a director, and it was trial by fire. Wellfleet was pushing her to the limit. Clay Johnson had never been under this kind of pressure. Wellfleet had never expected enough from him, but he seemed to expect too much from Keely.

Well, it did no good to complain about it, even to herself, she decided. No matter how difficult the situation was becoming, she wasn't going to fail. Gritting her teeth, she bent over her desk and began listing the tasks ahead of her in order of priority. The problem was that they were all of equal and immediate importance. She had a lot of late nights and long work weekends ahead of her. She closed her eyes and rubbed her aching neck. When would it ever end? And to what end was all this hard work leading her?

Her most comforting thought at that moment was that she would be seeing Chuck the next evening. She and Joy would be attending the opening of his gallery exhibition, and then he wanted to take them both out to dinner. That he had included Joy in the invitation filled Keely with warm appreciation. She thought it was time that the two most important people in her life got to know each other better.

Chapter Eleven

Why *can't* I have a glass of champagne like everybody else?" Joy demanded of her mother when they arrived at the gallery.

"Because everybody else is an adult, that's why," Keely told her firmly, steering her toward the back of the room. "We're here to look at Mr. Dickens's photographs, not to guzzle champagne."

But it seemed as if everyone else gathered in the crowded gallery was there to have a good time. There were kisses and handshakes and laughter all around, with Chuck at the very center of it. Keely wasn't even sure he had seen Joy and her come in, he was so busy holding court. He had smiled and nodded in their direction, but for all she knew, it could have been at someone in front of or behind them. He had made no effort to extricate himself from a gaggle of admirers, most of them women.

Tilting her head from side to side, Joy made a big show of looking at the black-and-white photographs hanging on one wall. Most of them were abstract studies of light and shadows or common objects photographed at odd angles and perspectives that made them look strange. "Hmm," was the only comment she came up with. "Are people actually going to buy this stuff, Mom?"

"I don't think that's the only point, sweetie. It's Mr. Dickens's way of expressing himself."

Keely felt completely out of her element. She wasn't at ease with this arty crowd, and as hard as she tried, she could find nothing in the photographs that spoke to her personally. Even Chuck's commercial photography expressed more warmth than these abstract compositions. She was disappointed—not in Chuck's work but in herself for not being able to relate to it. She had reached the point of wanting to share everything with him, to understand him completely. And yet he remained a mystery to her in many ways.

"Mom, come here!" Joy called from another area of the crowded gallery.

Wishing her daughter would learn to keep her voice down in public places, Keely followed it. Joy was standing in front of a panel of individual portraits. The subjects were of all shapes and sizes and ages and had nothing in common except for the fact that they had all been captured in a moment of laughter. The effect of the grouping was sheer jubilation, and it made Keely smile. This she could relate to. This reflected the Chuck she knew and loved.

"Those kids look just like Mr. Dickens," Joy said, pointing to a photograph of a handsome boy and girl with blond hair and high cheekbones posed with a jack-o'-lantern. All three had gap-toothed smiles. And except for the missing baby teeth, the children did look amazingly like Chuck. Keely stared at the picture as Joy moved on.

But then her attention was distracted when Joy called to her again. "Wow, Mom! Look at this. A picture of YOU!"

Keely's heart almost skidded to a stop. The only photographs Chuck had ever taken of her were at Point Lobos during their California trip. Holding her breath, she joined her daughter and looked at the full-color portrait.

It was of her, all right, freckles and all. Her mouth was open, she was frowning impatiently and her finger was pointed at the unseen camera—or the man behind it—accusingly. She was wearing her simple Brooks Brothers suit and looked rather severe, except for her eyes, which sparkled with irritation. Keely remembered now when Chuck had taken the picture. It had been at their first shoot together in Duane, South Carolina. Chuck had asked her to stand in for Selma while he got the lighting right, and at the instant this picture was taken she was telling him how much she disliked posing for him.

She glanced at the other portraits surrounding hers. They were candid shots of ordinary people going about their daily business. Farmers. Waitresses. Traffic cops. Construction workers. From small towns, big cities and the country in between—wherever Chuck's travels took him. He had a knack for capturing people at their best, doing what they knew how to do well. The stark simplicity of the photographs was eloquent.

Her eyes returned to her own picture. Keely LaRoux, corporate executive. How self-important she looked. No, that wasn't quite right. She looked like somebody trying to look important but who was really defensive and tense. The picture was taken B.L.C.—Before Loving Chuck. But the attraction was already there. She could see it reflected in the glittering eyes of her captured image. He had captured her, all right.

"What do you think, Joy?" she asked her daughter.

"I don't like it," she replied flatly. "You're really much prettier than that, Mom. Except when you're mad at me about something. Then you look just LIKE that. But if this Mr. Dickens is supposed to be such a great photographer, he should have made you look prettier."

A deep, booming laugh that Keely knew well erupted behind them. "They say the camera doesn't lie."

Both Keely and Joy turned around to face Chuck.

"Oh, Mr. Dickens, I didn't mean that you weren't a good photographer," Joy said. "I mean, I meant . . ." Her voice faltered.

Still laughing, Chuck patted her shoulder. "You're absolutely right, Joy. Your mother is beautiful. But that's not what I was trying to show in this picture. That would have been way too easy."

"What exactly were you trying to show?" Keely asked him pointedly.

He shrugged. "Whatever you see, Keely. No more or less than that."

But she was no longer interested in her picture. All she could see at this moment was the man she loved standing in front of her. She always flushed when they met, even when they had been parted for no more than a day. His height, his looks, his voice, his manner made her blood race. They had from the first time she'd laid eyes on him.

She reminded herself that she was not the only woman on earth to appreciate Chuck. He had not been created uniquely for her, although she wished he had been. If beauty was in the eye of the beholder, then many pairs of female eyes in the crowd were beholding him right now. Not that he had gone to any special trouble to attract the attention. He was dressed as casually as ever, as if this important opening-night exhibition of his work was just one more stop in his constant travels. Still, his tan tropical wool pants, which could have used a good pressing, and his rough Irish knit sweater seemed designed especially for him. The pants accented his long, muscular legs, and the bulky sweater made his wide chest and broad shoulders look even wider and broader. Keely was not at all surprised that so many staring women found him appealing.

He was taking her in with the same deep reverence as she was him. His silver-gray eyes were as bright as strobe lights. "You look lovely tonight, Keely."

She was wearing a simple knit V-neck dress of periwinkle blue. It did justice to her figure, hair and eyes. She had wanted to look her very best that night and murmured a thank you, hoping she did.

Chuck forced his eyes from her and turned his attention to Joy. "And you look lovely, too, Miss LaRoux," he said politely.

Joy beamed. "Mom made me wash my hair and wear a dress instead of jeans. How much longer do we have to hang around here before we go to dinner?"

"Joy!" Keely admonished. "Mr. Dickens has to circulate and talk to all his guests before we leave."

"Oh, I've done enough circulating this evening," Chuck said. "As a matter of fact, I've done enough circulating for a lifetime. Maybe it's time I left the party for good and settled down. What do you think, Keely?"

His voice was light, but his eyes were quite serious. Keely did not look away from his steady, inquiring gaze. "If you think you're ready to, Chuck."

Joy shuffled her feet, impatient with the secret messages her mother and Chuck were sending.

Chuck leaned down and whispered to her, as if they were coconspirators. "Come on. Let's all sneak out the back door."

He took them to a restaurant a few blocks away. It was small but elegant, and the owner/chef came out of the kitchen to personally greet Chuck and seat him and his two guests. It was obvious that he considered Chuck a favored patron. He recited, in a heavy French accent, the special dishes he had prepared that evening. None of them appealed much to Joy, who requested a hamburger and french fries.

"Very good, *mademoiselle*," the chef said in an offended tone.

Chuck mollified him by ordering more elaborate fare for Keely and himself and a bottle of his very best champagne.

"Coke for me," Joy added before he left them.

"My daughter, the gourmet," Keely said ruefully. "Joy isn't too adventurous when it comes to food, I'm afraid. I know exactly how that poor chef feels. She turns up her nose at all my special dishes, too."

"Mom even tried to get me to eat snails once. YUK!" Joy made a face to emphasize her disgust. "She's always cooking crazy foreign food, but she ends up giving it away to our apartment neighbors. What she needs is a restaurant like this. Or at least somebody else to cook for besides me."

"I'm willing to volunteer," Chuck offered. "I love your mother's cooking."

"Then you should move in with us, Mr. Dickens." Joy's color rose as soon as she realized the impropriety of her suggestion.

Chuck laughed. "Actually, you may be seeing a lot more of me from now on, Joy. Your mother and I have become very good friends."

Joy's eyes began to twinkle. "Like boyfriend and girlfriend, you mean?"

"Mr. Dickens and I enjoy each other's company," Keely quickly put in. She was a little annoyed with Chuck. Now Joy was going to jump to all sorts of romantic conclusions, and they hadn't really established where they stood with each other.

Joy clapped her hands, delighted. "It's about time you had a boyfriend, Mom."

Keely winced but remained silent.

After dinner, when Chuck escorted them back to their apartment, it was Joy who insisted he come in for a cup of coffee. Then she excused herself and went to her room, claiming she had homework to do. Joy had never in her life done homework on a Saturday night.

Chuck followed Keely into the kitchen, where he immediately put himself to use by getting out her coffee mill and grinding the beans. A warm coziness drifted through her as she watched him move about, so at home there. She remembered her nervous excitement the first time he had visited her apartment. They had come a long way since then. A little more than a month ago, he had been a total stranger. Now he was a part of her.

"Your daughter seems to approve of me," he said as he twisted the mill handle. "Even though she finds my photography pretty boring."

Keely turned on the tap to fill the kettle. "She liked you the very first time she met you, Chuck. And as far as her opinions about your work are concerned, she's hardly qualified to have any."

Chuck reached past her and turned off the faucet. "But you are, Keely. What did you think of the exhibition?"

She looked up at him. His expression was expectant and diffident. It took her aback. She had never seen him look anything less than totally self-confident.

If her opinion of his work mattered so much to him, she felt obliged to give him an honest one. "Those abstract still lifes were very slick, very technical and professional," she began. "But as clever as they were, they left me cold, Chuck. There was nothing of you in them."

She stopped, seeing his face tense, but he nodded and told her to continue.

"But I was very moved by your portraits and candid shots of ordinary life. You have a wonderful way with people, Chuck. You bring out something special in your subjects. I think that's your true talent. You somehow capture the spiritual dignity of people in your photographs." She laughed self-consciously. "Listen to me, pretending I'm an art critic."

He lifted her hand to his lips and kissed it. "You're right on target, darling. You zeroed in on exactly what I was trying to show. I want to record those fleeting, seemingly insignificant moments in people's lives and give them lasting value. That gives me so much more satisfaction than the commercial work I spend most of my time doing." He sighed heavily. "I'm tempted to live up to my name and *chuck* my career as a commercial photographer. Then I could concentrate on more serious work."

"Why don't you?" Keely's eyes were bright with excitement. "You have the talent. You have the vision. All you need is the time."

"And the guts," he added self-disparagingly. "What if I fail?"

She reached up and stroked his soft, full beard. "How could you possibly fail at anything you make up your mind to do, Chuck Dickens?" she asked gently, truly believing it would be impossible.

His eyes soaked up the belief in hers for a long moment, but then he shook his head slowly. "It's such a big step. I'm one of the top commercial photographers in the city. Why should I turn away from what I already have, even if I don't really want it anymore? I could end up with nothing.''

"Nothing? You'll always have your talent and pride, Chuck." And me, she added silently. "If what you're doing now doesn't make you happy, you have to change your life. There are so many years ahead of you. Don't waste them."

She stopped talking then. What he did with his life was his own business, she reminded herself. He hadn't asked her to share it with him. Her own pride wouldn't allow her to show him how hurt she was for this omission. She busied herself putting the kettle on the stove and turning up the flame beneath it.

Standing behind her, he encircled her small frame with his long arms and brushed the top of her head with his lips.

"Thanks for the pep talk, darling. I'll think over what you said. But right now I'm too tired and confused to think much at all."

He trailed some kisses down her neck, and his beard tickled, sending a shiver of excitement up her spine.

"I wish I could ask you to spend the night with me," she told him frankly.

"I know. Me, too," he murmured. "But I understand. It wouldn't be right because of your daughter." He turned to the coffee mill again.

"I could come to your apartment for a few hours tomorrow," she suggested boldly, wishing he had been the one to suggest it.

He gave her a sad smile. "I'm leaving for Mexico tomorrow."

"Mexico!" She stared at him, stunned.

"You make it sound like another planet," he joked. "It's a quick assignment. I'll be back Tuesday, in time for the Citation shoot in Vermont. Don't worry about that."

That was the least of her worries right now. "You're always leaving for someplace," she said almost bitterly. Always leaving her, she thought. Just like Royal LaRoux had. She understood, intellectually, that the situations were entirely different, but she had no control over her immediate emotional reaction. Anger and despair and frustration loomed up within her. "You don't have time for any kind of relationship. But I suppose that's the way you want it."

His handsome face hardened with indignation. "What about you, Keely? What time do you have to give to a relationship? You're completely involved with your own career," he accused.

"Not out of choice," she objected. "This new position has put a lot of extra pressure on me right now."

"You accepted it, didn't you? It must have been what you wanted."

"I thought I did," she said, turning away to take the whistling kettle off the stove. She took the opportunity to blink back unexpected tears. The evening with Chuck had been so perfect until now. It would be such a pity for it to end with a quarrel.

He apparently thought so, too, because he began to massage her tense shoulders. "You know, we both want the same thing, darling, which is more time together," he said soothingly. "Why don't we spend an extra day in Vermont? Since you grew up in that area, you can show me all the hot spots."

Her laugh was a little thin. "There are no hot spots in Jasper. But it's beautiful around there, and I'd love to stay an extra day with you." Her expression became dreamy for an instant, then changed to one of regret. "Only I can't afford to, Chuck. I'm right in the middle of so many projects at work, and I've been away from the office too much as it is."

"I rest my case," he said sardonically, his hands stilled.

Dismay blurred her eyes as she gave him a pleading look. "Oh, Chuck, please try to understand that I want—"

"I know, I know," he interrupted, his tone again amicable as he continued massaging her back. "But why don't we drive up there instead of flying? Actually, it'll take less time. We'll have a few hours alone, and Spike can meet us at the factory."

She happily agreed to that plan. The image of driving through her beloved Green Mountains with Chuck by her side delighted her.

A short time later, when he kissed her good-night at the door, she could taste the coffee he had just finished on his lips, and a special sweetness that was his alone. It was a brief kiss, since both of them were very aware of Joy in the next room, apt to pop out at any moment.

"Call me when you get back from Mexico," she told him.

He promised, and when he closed the door behind him, she pressed her cheek to it, longing for him the instant he was gone.

Sunday passed slowly for her. In the afternoon Joy left to attend a birthday party for a school friend, and Keely put in a few constructive hours planning Wellfleet's news conference. The confines of the small apartment made her restless, though, and she took a long walk through the cold, windy city streets. She thought about Chuck in sunny Mexico. It did seem to her as if he were on another planet. She ached to be with him.

Back at work the next day, Keely met with her staff and handled a few department crises with a smooth, calm assurance that she had always admired in more seasoned administrators. Her old confidence began to return, along with a sense of accomplishment that had always bucked her up during times of stress. She really was very good at her job, she reminded herself with a mental pat on the back. But somehow it didn't seem as important to her as it once had. Citation was no longer the center of her universe.

Late that afternoon she met with a graphic artist, Zenna Burchard, whom she had chosen to design the company's annual report. Ms. Burchard's reputation as a designer almost equaled Chuck's as a commercial photographer, guaranteeing that Citation's report would be top quality.

She had expected Ms. Burchard to be a slightly older version of herself, a practical, conservative businesswoman who specialized in corporate publications. She was unprepared for the tall, raven-haired vision in bright silk and leather who swept into her office on a cloud of exotic perfume. The woman's style and absolute confidence in her own beauty surpassed age. She could have been thirty, forty, even fifty. It didn't matter. She was so striking that she was ageless.

"What a pleasure to finally meet you after our many phone chats, Ms. LaRoux," she said in a smart British accent, extending a hand snugly encased in a fawn kid glove.

Keely was almost but not quite intimidated. She reminded herself that she was the client and would have the last word in all decisions concerning the publication.

It wasn't easy having the last word with Zenna Burchard, though. She argued every point they disagreed on with a tenacity that no doubt had gotten her where she was in the business world. Keely held her own, and in the end they came up with a design concept for the report that would be dynamic without being too dramatic. She had to remind Zenna, more than once, that although Citation wanted to grab the attention of the financial community, it still wanted to be perceived as an established, conservative company expanding its markets.

"I want the design of the book to be strong but not too flashy," Keely summed up. "The provocative photographs Chuck Dickens has taken of our products will make it clear that Citation's new direction and impetus is high-tech."

"Yes, Chuck Dickens has never been anything less than provocative," Zenna commented. She slipped off her hot-pink suede jacket, as if the temperature in Keely's office had suddenly risen. "Quite a man, isn't he?"

Keely didn't like the knowing glint in the other woman's slanting amber eyes. "You're a friend of his?"

"Dear Chuck and I go way back." Zenna smiled for the first time since she had entered the office and crossed her long, mauve-booted legs. "But of course we are *just* friends. I make it a policy never to get too intimate with married men. In the end they usually go back to their little wifeys, don't they?"

Keely stopped breathing. "But Chuck isn't married."

Zenna's laugh was unpleasantly sharp. "He most certainly and regrettably is, my darling. He had the decency to tell me that when we were working on a project together a few months ago, although sparks were flying fast and hot between us."

"No, that can't be true." Confusion rushed through Keely's mind like a tornado, making it impossible for her to think straight, let alone be guarded.

"Keely, men don't lie that they're married. Only that they're *not*. He even showed me pictures of his two adorable children." Zenna's spike-lashed eyes danced with amusement, but her expression became suddenly contrite. "Dear me, it appears I've let the cat out of the bag. Perhaps Chuck wasn't as honest with you, my darling? I'm dreadfully sorry if that's the case." She stood up abruptly, slipped into her butter-soft jacket and zipped up her large leather art portfolio. The sound of the zipper closing ripped through Keely's ears. "I'll work up some new ideas for the annual report cover. I think I know exactly what you want now that we've had this most enlightening conversation." She hid a sly smile with her gloved hand and pretended a cough before she exited.

Keely remained stunned and immobile long after Zenna had left. Then she raised icy fingertips to her temples and pressed hard, as if trying to contain the growing, horrible doubt spreading through her mind. But when she closed her eyes and saw Chuck's intense, handsome face, she found it impossible to believe that he could deceive her. Still, she needed to talk to him desperately. She called his studio and asked the receptionist how to reach him in Mexico.

"Your guess is as good as mine, lady," came the bored, nasal reply. "When Chuck's on location, he never checks in at the studio. He figures he can handle any problems when he gets back and doesn't want to be bothered with them while he's away."

Would he always be this elusive to her? Keely wondered, returning the phone to its cradle. When they were apart it was almost as if he didn't exist at all, except in her imagination. She knew so little about him really, although he'd shared laughter and love and dreams with her. Was it possible to know him so intimately and yet not know him at all? Had passion blinded her from seeing him for what he really was—a liar, a cheat, a man totally lacking in scruples? No! her heart shrieked. That was not the man she loved. She closed her mind to any further doubts about him and held on to that love, very tightly, for the rest of the day.

She was exhausted when she went home that evening. She could hear stereo music blaring from behind her apartment door. When she opened it she discovered Joy sprawled on the sofa, munching from a big bag of potato chips and wagging her foot to the beat.

Keely crossed the living room and shut off the stereo with a sharp, angry twist of her wrist. "Why aren't you across the hall with Mrs. Alphonso, young lady?" she demanded in lieu of a greeting. "You know I don't like your being all alone here."

"I'm not a BABY," Joy replied, also skipping a hello to her mother. "And I like spending time in my own home, even if you don't, Mom."

"What's that supposed to mean?" Keely picked up a few potato chips scattered on the rug. When she bent down, her head throbbed.

"It means you're never home," Joy accused. "If you're not working late at the office, you're traveling. We never have any time together. The only way I ever get your attention is when I'm at death's DOOR." She stuffed a few more chips into her mouth.

Keely rolled her eyes. "You weren't dying, Joy. You had the flu. And I stayed home to take care of you, didn't I?" She grabbed the bag of potato chips from her daughter. "You're going to ruin your appetite for dinner. What would you like to eat tonight?"

"I don't care." Joy got up from the sofa and began sifting through her record albums. She chose one that Keely particularly detested and turned up the volume again. "By the way, Mom, Mr. Dickens called here a few minutes ago. I told him to try you at the office, but he must have missed you there, too."

"What?" Keely shouted over the noise. "Did you say Mr. Dickens called?" Joy nodded and began dancing to the music. "Did you get a number where I could call him back?"

Joy kept on dancing, her back to her mother, and shook her head. Keely grabbed her shoulders firmly, turning her around. "Show a little respect when I'm talking to you, Joy. Did he leave any message for me?"

Keely's voice was sharp, her face angry, and Joy's eyes registered surprise and hurt. "No, he didn't leave a message. I'm sorry, Mom. I didn't know it was so important."

Keely was immediately sorry, too, for taking her frustration out on her daughter. She gave her a hug. "Of course you didn't, sweetie. Anyway, I'm sure he'll call back." She wasn't sure of that at all.

Joy looked at her mother more closely now and frowned with concern. "You had a real hard day at work, didn't you, Mom? You look tired and pale."

"It's just a dumb headache," Keely told her.

Joy lowered the volume of the stereo immediately. "Sit down and put your feet up," she ordered. "I'll get you two aspirin."

Keely couldn't help but smile over her daughter's officious tone, which matched hers exactly when she was concerned about Joy's being ill. "So you're going to take care of your old mom now?"

"We take care of each other," Joy said. "We don't need anybody else because we've got each other, right?"

"That's right," Keely agreed weakly. Joy was simply repeating what Keely had told her often enough. She had meant it to comfort her daughter, growing up without a father. But now she herself found little comfort in the words.

Before Chuck came into her life with such impact, it had revolved around Joy and her job. He was the one who made her realize what an important part of her feminine nature had been untouched and unfulfilled all these years. It wasn't just her sexuality that Chuck brought back to full-blooming life. He also made her aware of how much she desired a man's companionship and friendship. Her deepest need of all was to be able to trust a man again.

Trust! The word twanged in her head along with Zenna Burchard's shrill laughter.

"Here you are, Mom."

Keely looked up, startled out of her reverie, to discover Joy handing her a glass of water and aspirin. She had a great deal of trouble swallowing the chalky tablets.

"Good," Joy said as soon as she had. "Feeling better now?" She plopped down on the sofa beside her mother and took her hand. "You know, Mom, we may not need anybody else because we have each other, but one of these days I plan to get married," she informed her.

"I sincerely hope so, sweetie," Keely replied. "But that's quite a few years down the road for you. You're really planning ahead, aren't you?"

"I just wanted you to know, in case you were thinking about it for yourself." Joy's childish face was as serious as an adult's. "I mean, I want you to know that you can get married again, too. I wouldn't mind at all if it was somebody like Mr. Dickens."

Keely's heart clenched tight, but she forced a smile. "Well, thank you very much for your permission, daughter." She patted the top of Joy's head and left it at that. Then she hurried off to the little kitchen to prepare dinner, hoping Joy wouldn't sense how troubled she was.

She fell asleep on the sofa that night, waiting by the phone for Chuck to call again, and awoke the next morning with a crick in her neck. It bothered her all day at work.

That afternoon a package was delivered to her by special messenger. It contained the slides of the X25 system and had been sent by the film processor Chuck used. She was relieved to receive them, since Wellfleet was so anxious to view them. She called his office and told his secretary the good news, requesting a meeting with the president as soon as possible. His secretary got back to Keely more than an hour later, informing her that Wellfleet was too busy to take a look at the slides now.

This had often been Keely's experience dealing with him. His demands were always urgent, but when she met them as quickly as possible, he would be too busy with other matters to appreciate the results.

Resigned, she set up her office projector and screen and viewed the slides herself. They were terrific, just as Chuck had predicted. He had managed to make an inanimate computer system come alive with excitement. There were shots from every angle possible, one as dramatic as the next. Each detail of the

X25 was highlighted, and it did indeed look like some revolutionary space-age advancement.

There was no doubt in Keely's mind that Wellfleet would be pleased. Since Chuck had shot ten rolls of film, the president had three hundred and sixty pictures from which to choose. It had been a long, tedious shoot, and Keely remembered Chuck's stamina, exactitude and constant creativity during it. Moonbeam Smith, in charge of keeping the strobe lights firing and Chuck's cameras reloaded, had kept right up with him. Keely, watching from the sidelines, had offered to take charge of the exposed rolls of film, but Moonbeam had insisted it was her responsibility and stored them in the deep pockets of her jumpsuit.

Gazing at the bright, advancing slides in her dimly lit office, Keely experienced a warm rush of love for Chuck. His very presence was almost palpable in the room as she remembered their time together in California. She had let down her defenses with him at last and had trusted him completely. She knew her heart could never recover if this trust had been misplaced. She longed to talk to him so he could explain why Zenna Burchard was convinced he was married. She desperately needed that explanation.

As if responding to her need, he called. Unfortunately, the connection from Mexico was a bad one, and she could barely hear him over the static. She managed to make out that he missed her and would be back in New York very late that night. He would pick her up the next morning for their Vermont trip.

"Call me tonight, the minute you get back. I don't care how late it is!" Keely yelled into the phone, trying to pitch her voice above the static.

"What? Darling, this conversation is impossible. See you tomorrow. I love you!" he shouted. And then he was disconnected.

Chapter Twelve

She was waiting in her apartment lobby for him the next morning. Her face was sallow from lack of sleep. The moment she saw a sleek white sports car pull up to the curb, she knew it was Chuck's. Of course he would have an expensive, fancy car, she thought irritably. Not smiling, she ran out, opened the passenger door and awkwardly arranged herself in the low bucket seat.

"What kind of car is this, anyway?" she asked Chuck tartly before he could lean over the gearshift and kiss her.

He looked surprised that she didn't know. "It's a Porsche."

She adjusted her bulky winter coat around her hips. "Pretty cramped inside, isn't it?"

He laughed and gave her a big kiss on her cheek. "Most women would be impressed. Or at least pretend they were."

"Well, I'm not most women, Dickens. So don't expect me to act like all the others you've known."

Chuck let out a low whistle. "I'm just going to assume your bad mood was caused by my absence and not by my current presence, darling." He went on to tell her about his assignment in Mexico, ignoring her glumness. He was humoring her, and Keely resented it.

Wanting his full attention, she waited until they had escaped the snarl of city traffic and were on the clear, open highway before she broached the subject that had been so heavy on her heart and mind for two days, wearing her down.

"I met with Zenna Burchard Monday," she began. "She's designing the annual report for Citation."

"Smart move, Keely," Chuck replied easily. "She does good work."

She didn't want to discuss Zenna's competence, though. "She claimed to know you very well, Chuck."

"I've worked with her from time to time, but we're hardly great pals." His voice was cool and casual. "I would take anything Zenna says with a grain of salt, darling. She tends to exaggerate."

"Was it an exaggeration to say you have a wife and two kids? Or do you have just one?" Keely had meant that to come out light and uncaring, but her voice cracked.

Chuck frowned, looking more perturbed than upset. "Why the hell would she say..." He paused and pulled at his beard. "Oh, yeah, I remember now when I told her that. Pretty stupid of me, wasn't it? But it seemed the only decent thing to do at the time."

Keely stared at him, dumbfounded. He was actually smiling, as if his admission was of no importance to either of them. The color drained from her lips, and she had difficulty moving them.

"Too bad you weren't so decent to me," she said hoarsely. The urge to jump out of the speeding car was almost overwhelming.

He took his eyes from the road and looked at her stricken face. "Good Lord, Keely, you believe I really am married, don't you?"

"Oh, no," she corrected in a trembling voice. "Belief involves faith and trust. What I believed was that you *weren't* married. I never did pin you down and ask you, though, did I?"

He directed his eyes back to the road. His strong profile seemed carved from wood except for the little muscle that always twitched on the crest of his high cheek when he was angry. They drove on in deep silence for a while until he spotted a rest stop ahead. He pulled the car off the road and turned off the motor. He still kept his eyes straight ahead, though, and his hands clutched the steering wheel tightly. Keely waited for him to speak. There was nothing more she could say at the moment.

"I told Zenna I was married to avoid hurting her feelings," he said in a flat, precise tone. "It was either that or telling her point-blank that I had no desire to sleep with her. No woman wants to hear that from a man she's practically trying to bulldoze into bed. I even showed her pictures of two child models an agency had sent to the studio. I claimed they were mine. That cooled her interest in me fast enough."

His story made sense to Keely. Having witnessed how tenacious Zenna could be in business, she could easily imagine her pursuing an attractive man like Chuck with the same persistence.

"I was sure there was some kind of explanation," she said as relief coursed through her. She covered his hand, still on the steering wheel, with hers.

He pulled his hand away. "No, you weren't, Keely. You weren't sure at all. You've obviously been fretting about this for days. All it took for you to doubt me was some silly woman's gossip. And then you babble something to me about faith and trust. Lady, you don't even know the meaning of those words."

His accusation cut through her heart like a serrated knife. "That's not fair, Chuck! I tried so hard to disregard what Zenna told me. But everything between us has happened so fast. I hardly know you."

He closed his eyes. "If you don't, then no one does," he said in a hollow, hopeless voice. When he opened his eyes again and looked at her, they were the ominous gray of stormclouds. "I have never been more open with a woman than I've been with you, Keely. I've tried in every way I know how to show you who I am. I've expressed my love for you time and time again, even though you fought me every inch of the way, from the very beginning. Love isn't something you fight against, dammit!''

His booming voice filled the car, and Keely shrank into the soft leather of the bucket seat. She had seen him impatient and short-tempered before, but never this angry. For once she had no quick, heated retort to fling back at him. The echo of his angry voice receded, only to be replaced by another awful silence between them.

And then, as if to fill it, raindrops began falling on the roof of the car, the sound as sharp as bullets. "I hope this tin can of yours doesn't leak," Keely said, trying for a joke to break the tension between them.

It didn't work. Chuck's stormy eyes only deepened in color. "Maybe it's a tin can to you, Keely, but I'm very proud of this car. I had to struggle to get established as a commercial photographer, and about ten years ago I bought this Porsche as a symbol that I had finally made it."

His injured yet rather superior tone made Keely defensive. "Ten years ago my symbol of success was meeting the rent on time," she told him.

That just about did it for him. He exhaled with such force that she was sure his hot, angry breath would fog up the windshield.

"I wonder if Joan of Arc had red hair," he mused in a deceptively calm voice. "Both of you being such great martyrs, Keely, you may have had that trait in common, too."

She took his sarcasm to heart but didn't let it defuse her own just anger. "You're hardly a saint yourself, Chuck Dickens. I don't think you've been as open with me as you claim to be."

"What do you want from me, Keely? Didn't I go out on a limb and tell you I loved you?"

"You make it sound as if you did something dangerous," she replied. "As if love is a risk that may not be worth taking."

He thought about that for a moment. "It is risky," he answered. "Especially with a woman who refuses to trust me."

Keely threw back her head in frustration. "How have you earned my trust, Chuck? You're with me one moment, gone the next. I don't hear from you for days. And then you call and expect to pick up exactly where we left off. Which is *where*? I have no idea where I stand with you."

"You're the woman I care about most in the world," he replied in a voice filled with wonder that she didn't appreciate such a position.

She buried her head in her hands. She truly believed that he cared about her now, at this very moment, but she also knew that would be cold comfort late at night when she was alone in bed.

"That's not good enough," she told him. It came out a muffle under her hands.

But he heard it clearly enough. "And the way you're so quick to distrust me isn't good enough, either," he answered hotly.

She took her cold hands from her pale face. "So where do we stand now?" she asked him bluntly. Apprehension fluttered in the pit of her stomach, almost making her sick.

"Obviously not together," he answered and then swallowed hard. "I think the problem is that I rushed you. I saw you, I wanted you, and that was that for me. But I understand now that you needed more time. Time to build up your trust in a man again. I don't know." He paused to run his hand through his beard. "Maybe you haven't gotten over the hurt of your marriage."

"That's not true!" she objected vehemently. "You're the one hurting me now!" That hadn't come out quite right. What she'd meant to say was that she loved him so much that she ached from it and all the uncertainty it aroused in her.

He flinched as if she'd struck him. "That's the last thing I want to do, Keely. What I want is a woman who believes in me completely."

If only she could! She turned from him and pressed her hot forehead against the cool side window. "Obviously I lack that qualification."

"Oh, Keely, please." He touched her stiff shoulder. "Don't turn this into a job interview, dammit. All I'm trying to say is that we may have gotten too involved too quickly. We need some time to let things settle between us."

She lifted her forehead from the glass and turned to him with a brave smile. "You're suggesting we end our relationship, aren't you, Chuck?'' Every nerve ending in her body screamed with pain.

''I'm suggesting we change it. For a while anyway. Maybe we'd better try to become friends before we become lovers again.''

Was this actually Chuck Dickens talking? Was he opting for friendship in lieu of sex? Keely couldn't believe what she was hearing. ''Please be straight with me, Chuck. If you want things to end with us, come out and say it.'' Every muscle in her body stiffened as she waited for the blow.

But it didn't come. ''I don't want an ending,'' he insisted. ''Can't you understand that all I want is a new start with you? For all our intimacy, we obviously don't know each other very well.''

He was right about that. And perhaps it was her fault as much as his, she realized. She was always so defensive with him. Her greatest fear was that he would take all her love and then leave her with nothing. And now he was offering to pull back a bit and give her some breathing room, some time to adjust to the shock of falling so hard for him. It was an offer she'd be foolish to refuse.

''Okay. It's a deal,'' she said, putting out her hand. ''We'll give it a try.''

He clutched her hand in his strong grip. ''I'll try my best to be open with you,'' he promised.

He started the car and slid out of the rest area. Plunged into the turnpike traffic again, Keely watched the dull gray highway scenery slide past with unblinking eyes. She wondered what would come of their strange agreement.

They sped through a sheet of heavy rain. When they left New York and crossed the Vermont border the rain changed to sleet and then snow. They had to turn off the main highway to get to Jasper, and the winding roads were slippery and hazardous. Chuck navigated his car with expertise, but visibility was very poor and soon they were crawling through the dense snowstorm at less than fifteen miles an hour.

''It's crazy to go on like this,'' he told Keely.

"We'll never make the Jasper plant in time for the shoot today," she agreed. "I think we should stop at the first motel we see."

He nodded in agreement, keeping his eyes on the treacherous road. As they crawled along Keely spotted a hand-painted sign advertising The Bear and Elk Inn. She pointed it out to Chuck.

"Let's hope they take in people, too," he joked.

She smiled, relieved that he was in a good mood again. She hoped that once they were alone together, waiting for the storm to blow over, their own storm would blow over, too.

They drove down a long, rutted driveway to a handsome three-story white colonial house with black shutters. It was badly in need of a paint job. They got out of the car and mounted the sagging porch steps. A pane of glass was missing in one of the front windows, replaced by a piece of cardboard. Chuck knocked on the front door.

They waited a long time before the door was opened by a gray-haired woman in a flowered apron and slippers. She frowned suspiciously at the two strangers.

"Any rooms available?" Chuck asked, flashing his bright smile.

"Try the motel down the road apiece," she suggested in a flat Yankee accent.

"Sure we got rooms, folks!" an elderly man called out before she could shut the door in their faces. He shuffled toward them. He was wearing overalls, a worn flannel shirt and a fishing vest decorated with a variety of hand-tied flies. "The welcome carpet is always out at The Bear and Elk Inn, ain't it, Matilda?"

The woman sniffed. "Easy for you to be so obliging, Elwin. I'm the one does all the work around here. I just got through telling you my arthritis is acting up."

"Don't pay my missus no mind," Elwin said jovially, ushering Keely and Chuck inside. "If she can't complain, she ain't happy."

He led them down a large, drafty foyer to a check-in desk. "I'll give you the best room in the place. It faces the pond."

"Actually, we'd like two rooms, please," Chuck stated.

So he intended to go through with this, Keely thought grimly. Was the idea of a platonic relationship really a sound one? The one thing they didn't have a problem with was sex. Still, she realized that passion blurred the reality of their relationship. They would have to find out if they had one at all beyond the bedroom. And she had to give Chuck credit for acknowledging this.

He was a man who could constantly surprise her. And if she couldn't understand him, maybe it was because his emotions were as deep and complicated as her own. She was beginning to realize how very complicated he was.

There was another knock on the front door, and then it was thrown open by a man leading in his family. The mother, carrying a little girl, was followed by three boys.

"Thank God this place is open," the father said. "The motel up the road was filled. We need three rooms, please."

Elwin shook his grizzled head with regret. "Sorry, mistah. I only got one room left. This couple here just took the other two."

"Surely a place this size has more than three rooms," the man protested.

"Used to have ten, but we closed up the third floor and half the second a few years back. One room is all I can offer you."

"That will have to do, dear," the woman told her husband. "We can't risk driving any farther." She turned to the proprietor. "Do you have extra cots for the boys?"

Elwin shook his head again. "No cots, missus. But we got a few spare quilts you can lay on the floor for them."

Keely and Chuck shared a quick glance. They read each other's mind instantly. They couldn't make this family suffer.

"I think there's been a misunderstanding," Keely spoke up.

"Yes, we only asked for one room," Chuck added.

Elwin didn't so much as blink or miss a beat. "That's right, so you did." He handed over the key to Chuck and gave him a sly wink, as if to say the snowstorm had surely worked to *his* advantage. "First one to the right at the head of the stairs. Suppah's served at six sharp. Don't be late or Matilda will have one of her fits."

"This doesn't change a thing, of course," Chuck told Keely when they entered the high-ceilinged room.

She rolled her eyes. "Don't worry, *Mistah* Dickens. I'm not going to attack you."

She paced the room, not quite knowing what to do with herself. They had planned a day trip and hadn't brought overnight luggage, so she couldn't even busy herself with unpacking. She could well imagine what old Elwin thought they were up to right now. She could well imagine it herself. She hugged her arms to her chest.

"It's freezing in here!" she said, turning to Chuck with a frown.

He smiled. "Our gracious host certainly doesn't believe in treating his guests like hothouse flowers."

Keely touched the metal radiator under the long window. "Cold as ice," she reported. And since there was no suitcase to kick, she gave the radiator one. It didn't respond with so much as a hiss.

"I thought you Vermonters laughed at the cold," Chuck said.

"We save our laughter for flatlanders," she replied, blowing on her hands.

In three long strides Chuck was across the room and beside her. "Here, I'll warm them up for you," he said, capturing her hands and rubbing them between his. "We flatlanders have our uses."

She glanced at the sagging double bed with its scarred maple headboard. "Indeed you do," she murmured, remembering how he'd heated her up in California.

He understood her glance completely. "We could cuddle together under that patchwork quilt," he suggested lightly.

But he had laid down the rules, and she wasn't going to let him break them. "You mean *just* cuddle? No hanky-panky?"

He let out his deep laugh. "Of course not, ma'am. A deal is a deal. We'll keep all our clothes on. No hanky from me, no panky from you. We'll tell each other the story of our lives, and if neither of us dozes off, that should prove we're in love."

Keely immediately went to the bed, turned down the covers, fluffed up the feather-stuffed pillows and propped them up against the headboard. "Take off *only* your shoes, and come right this way, Mr. Dickens," she said, patting the mattress. "I'd be delighted to hear your life story." She kicked off her own shoes, slipped off her coat and slid under the covers.

He followed suit and joined her. "This quilt smells a little musty," he said.

"Stop stalling and start talking," she ordered.

"Well, I was born in a little log cabin and learned to read by the flickering firelight," he began. "Walked ten miles to school and back every day. Later I became president and freed the slaves."

She swatted his shoulder. "Begin again, please."

He sighed. "I was born in Boston. In a hospital. Mother didn't believe in roughing it. I was born with a silver spoon in my mouth and almost gagged on it. You made fun of my name when we first met, Keely, but where I come from it's a rather important one. Being firstborn, I had the great honor of being named after my father. He never thought I lived up to it. He predicted I'd be a great failure. He died before I had a chance to prove him wrong. In other words, he died a happy man."

She shifted uncomfortably beside him. "You sound so bitter, Chuck. You couldn't have hated him that much."

He pulled the quilt closer around them and nestled against her. "Hate him? Keely, I worshipped him. All I ever wanted growing up was for him to understand me. Then I stopped trying. I'd never be the son he wanted, I realized. I wasn't like him. It was as simple as that. We were oil and water. No, more like oil and fire. Whenever we got together, there would be an explosion." He paused to tousle her hair. "You know, like you and me."

"Except I happen to think you're great," she told him.

"Do you really?" He kissed the top of her coppery head. "You have a funny way of showing it at times, LaRoux."

She rubbed her foot against his. "Maybe. But I have other ways of showing it plenty, as you well know."

He gave her arm a squeeze. "That's true enough. What kind of name is LaRoux anyway? It makes me think of can-can dancers in Paris at the turn of the century."

She let out a spurt of laughter. "Hardly that. Roy's family were Canadian lumberjacks. My maiden name was ordinary enough. Reilly. But because of Joy I kept my married name. But don't get away from the subject, Chuck."

"Which is what?"

"Which is you. What about your mother?"

"You mean the dowager empress of the world? That's what my brother and I call her. She came from an even better background than my father. Or at least she thought so. She could trace her family back three hundred years to English royalty, and there had never been a divorce in it. That's why she stuck it out with my father, I think. So as not to blemish her precious family history."

"I see." Keely thought for a moment. "I'm sure she'd turn up her nose at me."

Chuck flicked his finger against her own nose. "How could she? You both hold those strong chins of yours too high for her to manage it. No, she'd like you, Keely. She admires strong women. You'll have to meet her sometime."

That certainly sounded vague enough, she thought. "I'm sure you don't make a habit of introducing her to all the women in your life, Chuck. They'd probably fill Fenway Park."

"A slight exaggeration," he said a bit sharply. "I don't play the field the way you assume I do, Keely. It's not my style at all. Believe it or not, I'm a one-woman man."

"Oh, really?" Her voice was equally sharp. "Then why haven't you ever settled down with one?"

"Who says I didn't?"

She turned to look him full in the face, but he busied himself readjusting his pillow. She touched his arm. "Are you telling me you were married, Chuck?"

"No, I'm not telling you that at all." He lay back again. "But I once lived with a woman for several years. At least we shared the same address. She was a model, always off on assignments, totally involved in her career. I was always on the road, too, equally involved in mine. There was no dramatic breakup. We just kind of drifted apart in the end."

"But were you..." Keely bit her bottom lip and then plunged ahead. "Were you faithful to her during the time you lived together?"

"Yes. In the way you mean I was. But I think we both cheated on each other with our time and energy. Our work came first, so we always came second to each other."

Keely considered his words for a long while as the storm howled outside. Was he warning her that they would drift apart, too? Was he dooming their relationship before it had really even begun?

He broke into her thoughts. "It could be different for us."

"I wonder," she replied, her voice filled with misgivings. "Maybe you don't want it to be, Chuck. Maybe you chose me because it'll be history repeating itself. Career pressures are already limiting our time together. You pretend to resent it, yet maybe you use work as an excuse to keep your distance from me." He began to speak, but she held up her hand to silence him. "I know you're going to say that works both ways. But I think, deep down, that's really the way you want it. Love on the run, so to speak. Excitement without commitment."

"Rubbish!" he grumbled. He made a move to get up, but she grabbed his shoulder and pulled him back. He laughed at her show of force but remained where she wanted him. "Who do you think you are, Sigmund Freud?" he asked, still disgruntled. "How would you like it if I tried psychoanalyzing you, Dr. LaRoux? You're the classic type-A super-striver who buries her insecurities under work and more work."

"Rubbish!" she echoed.

"Don't be so defensive, my dear," he said in a parody of an Austrian accent. He patted her hand. "Lie back and tell Uncle Siggy all about this unhappy childhood you keep alluding to whenever you want to show you're superior to that egomaniac Mr. Dickens."

That brought her up short. "Is that what you think I do, Chuck?" She didn't expect a reply. Obviously he did. And maybe there was a kernel of truth in what he said. Deep down she did feel she'd worked harder for her success than he had. "But I never said my childhood was unhappy," she told him. "Just poor. That's not the same thing at all. My four brothers and I learned to appreciate the most basic things in life because that's all we had. In a way, lacking material things gave us freedom. You can't buy natural beauty, and growing up on the farm we were surrounded by it."

As she spoke, her voice softened with memories. Chuck gently ran his fingers through her short hair. "You must miss it sometimes," he said.

"More and more. The older I get, the more I realize how rich I really was as a child. The California coast was quite beautiful, Chuck. But to me, this area of Vermont will always be God's country. The Green Mountains shout His praise with every season."

And then, as he continued to stroke her hair, Keely told him about her four rambunctious brothers and shared special memories about her mother's love and strength with him. It occurred to her that he'd effectively deflected the conversation away from himself, but he was such a good listener that she couldn't stop talking. It felt so good to pour out her heart to him.

"What time is it?" she finally asked, suddenly noticing how dark the room had become.

Chuck had to pull the tassled chain of the lamp sitting on the rickety table beside the bed to read his watch. "It's only ten of six," he reported. "We've got all the time in the world."

"Not if we want our *suppah*, we don't. Elwin said six sharp, remember. Or face Matilda's wrath."

Chuck pretended a shudder. "We don't want to do that. But I guess we'll have to. I don't know about you, darling, but I'm starving. All this soul-searching burns up more calories than sex."

"I'm the one who did all the talking," she reminded him, getting out of bed and doing her best to brush out the wrinkles in her suit.

"No, Keely. I told you plenty," he disagreed. "And we still have all night ahead of us. All night in the same bed without lovemaking!" He groaned. "I may be reduced to telling you all about my collection of baseball cards to keep from going crazy."

She groaned, too. "Come on, Dickens. I need some food in my stomach to fortify me for that particular revelation."

When they walked into the large dining room they were greeted by a mounted elk head over the fireplace mantel and the family of six already seated at the long table. They glanced up at Keely and Chuck, their expressions almost as bleak as the stuffed elk's.

There was no food on the table, but a great deal of clatter emanated from the kitchen beyond. Pots and pans crashed, cupboard doors slammed and finally Elwin emerged. He was wearing his wife's flowered apron over his overalls, and he was carrying a large platter.

"Sorry supper's late, folks, but Matilda's on strike," he announced. "Had to make it myself."

He plunked down the platter in the center of the table. Eight pairs of eyes stared with horror at the scorched carcass on it.

"Turkey," he informed them. "It was frozen, so I turned up the oven real high. That bird looks pretty done now, though, don't it? I'll be right back with the rice, soon as I scrape it out of the pan. Dig in, folks. Don't be shy." Elwin disappeared from whence he had come.

"At least it's not bear," Chuck said.

"Or elk," Keely added.

But the family was too hungry to find any humor in the situation. The wife declared the turkey inedible. The boys begged to be driven to the nearest McDonald's. The father reminded them that there was a snowstorm raging outside. The little girl began to cry.

Keely stood up. "Don't worry, everybody. I'll make dinner," she declared and without further ado marched off to the kitchen.

Elwin looked more relieved than surprised to see her when she entered. She took one look at the pan of burned, lumpy rice he was about to serve and told him to dump it in the garbage. Then she checked out the supplies in the walk-in pantry. She didn't find much there—a loaf of stale bread, a basket of apples, a big can of tomatoes, potatoes and leeks. There was also some brown sugar, flour and cornmeal. In the refrigerator, which was in dire need of defrosting, she discovered a container of chicken fat, plenty of eggs and butter, a slab of Vermont cheddar and a gallon of milk. And some frozen sweetbreads, which didn't require thawing before cooking.

She chased Elwin out of her way, handing him the apples and cheese to tide over his hungry guests. Then she took off her suit jacket, rolled up her sleeves and set to work. There was nothing Keely liked better than a good challenge.

Chuck came in to offer his help, and she set him to work peeling potatoes and cracking eggs. Meanwhile, she mixed up the batter for a corncake, using the chicken fat for shortening as her mother had done. She made a creamy sauce to cover the sweetbreads. If the boys asked, she would tell them it was chicken.

They didn't. When the meal was served, within the hour, everybody ate heartily. Keely had used the potatoes and leeks in two savory French peasant omelets and the stale bread and brown sugar in a scalloped tomato casserole. There was Apple Pan Dowdy for dessert, served hot from the oven as soon as the dinner plates were cleared away.

Elwin, who had joined them in the feast, had two helpings of everything. When the meal was finished, he urged Keely to stand up and take a bow. Everyone applauded when she did, and her face flushed with pleasure at their appreciation.

Elwin invited them into the parlor after this satisfying meal. It was a spacious, well-proportioned room with centuries-old paneling, wide-beamed wooden floors and a large stone fireplace. But it was shabby and a little dreary, and Chuck suggested brightening things up with a fire. He even volunteered to brave the storm and go out to the woodpile for fuel. He came back with his big, strong arms loaded with wood, snow caught in his thick hair and beard. He looks like the lord of the manor, Keely thought.

Soon a cheery fire crackled in the hearth, and the bleak, rundown Bear and Elk Inn became a cozy, welcoming place. After some pleasant conversation, the other guests took their sleepy children up to bed, leaving Keely and Chuck alone with Elwin. He gave them a wink and brought out a jug of applejack.

"Tonight was almost like old times here," he said, pouring them each a glass. "When my parents ran the Bear and Elk, it was one of the finest inns in Vermont. But me and Matilda have let things get run down, I admit. She'd like me to sell the place and move us to Florida."

Keely leaned forward in the sagging sofa, interested. "It's a lot of work running an inn properly," she said. "Maybe it's getting to be too much for your wife."

"Yep," Elwin said, and stared into the fire. "And I ain't much help, or so she claims. Says all I care about is fishing, which is true enough, I s'pose. Down there in Florida, you can fish all year round. If I could get the price I want for this place, I'd sell tomorrow."

Chuck took a sip of his applejack. "And how much would that be?" he asked. When Elwin told him, he nodded. "Sounds fair to me."

Keely and Chuck finished their drinks and bid Elwin goodnight. When they returned to their room he gave her a big bear hug.

"You're a real trooper, Keely LaRoux," he declared. "I don't know how you managed it, but that was a terrific dinner. You would have made a great pioneer wife."

She laughed. "That's the first time that word ever crossed your lips, I bet, Dickens."

"What word? Pioneer?"

"No, sweetie. *Wife!*"

"And that's the first time you ever addressed me with an endearment, darling. Sarcastic as it was, it sounded good."

And *wife* had sounded pretty good to her. "We make a good team, don't we?" she asked him. "Despite our little run-ins, we work well together. We've already proven that with the Citation project." She began pacing the chilly room again. "Why, I bet we could even make a go of this inn if we put our minds to it."

"Aren't you getting a little carried away with your success tonight?" he said, grabbing her arm to make her stop pacing. "One meal and you think you're an innkeeper. It's damn hard work running a place this size."

"I've never been afraid of hard work." She smiled up at him. "After running a farm, this would be a piece of cake. I'm an excellent organizer. A superlative cook! I know about advertising and publicity. People would come here in droves!"

"There's no drove station hereabouts, is there?"

"Don't joke, Chuck. I'm serious. This is an excellent location. Tourists come through here all year round."

His gray eyes narrowed. "You really are serious, aren't you? Do you really think we could start a new life for ourselves here?"

"Why not give it a shot?" She'd picked up the incipient hope in his voice, and her own pushed it forward. "Our old lives aren't so great right now, are they?"

He released her arm and began his own pacing. "I could work on my book here," he mused.

"What book, Chuck?"

He halted midstep and turned back to her. "Oh, it's just a crazy idea. Some publisher saw my gallery exhibition and suggested I put a book of photographs together. My real stuff. The pictures I care about. But who would want to buy that?"

"That publisher apparently thinks people would. Oh, Chuck, don't assume you'll fail. You've proved your father wrong already." She stood in the center of the room, pale with intensity, gazing at him.

"But what about your own career, Keely? You'd have to give that up if we moved here."

"You mean my *job*?" She shrugged. "Cooking for those people tonight gave me ten times more satisfaction than Citation ever has or could." She met his surprised stare and locked gazes with him. "And loving you, Chuck Dickens, has opened a world of new possibilities for me. I'm willing to take the gamble with you beside me."

He backed away from her, as if stunned. Bumping into the bed, he sat down hard on it. "You're saying that you're willing to give up everything to take a chance with me?"

"Yes! I think we can make it together."

He stretched out his long arms to her. "Come here," he said.

She complied, once again walking into the magic circle of his arms. He caught her up and brought her into the comfort of his lap. He gave her the softest, most gentle kiss possible.

"You really do have faith in me," he said. His fingers moved over the planes and recesses of her face, as if he were a blind man discovering it for the first time. "This changes everything, you know," he finally said. "I find that a bit scary, don't you?"

She shivered inwardly, because she truly did. But she wouldn't allow herself to show that to him. "Does it change our little agreement not to make love for a while?" she asked in her husky voice. She wanted him so much at that moment.

"Oh, yes. That too."

He kissed her again, this time passionately, and pulled her across the bed with him. The old bed squeaked and swayed alarmingly as they made love, and the boards finally caved in. But that didn't stop them.

Keely awoke alone again. She shifted to get more comfortable, but that was impossible. The mattress beneath her dipped to the floor. Then she remembered the sharp crack of the bedboards breaking. She laughed aloud.

"So what's the big joke?" Chuck asked her, coming into the room with a breakfast tray.

"Maybe it's not so funny," she replied with a broad smile at the sight of him. "We managed to break Elwin's bed last night."

"Don't worry. I already paid him for it. He was very understanding."

"Oh, I just bet he was, the old coot." Keely did her best to prop herself up and patted her lap. "You can put down that tray right here, mistah. But I should warn you, I could get very used to having you serve me breakfast in bed. And bad habits are hard to break."

"Why bother to break this one?" he asked in his lightest voice, laying the tray across her thighs. "I like serving you in bed."

Her elfin face turned up to his, and she wrinkled her upturned nose impishly. "So you do, Mr. Dickens."

Her body began to tingle with the remembrance of his knowing caresses, and she looked away, turning her attention to the tray on her lap. There was a plate of thick flapjacks on it, a slab of Canadian bacon and a large pitcher of maple syrup.

"Is this all for me, or will the Green Mountain Boys be coming in to join me?" she asked Chuck.

"I guess dear Matilda got carried away trying to make amends. It's her way of thanking you for cooking dinner for everyone last night."

"*Dear* Matilda?" Keely raised questioning eyebrows.

"She really is an old dear, you know, once you get past her craggy exterior. She and Elwin and I ate breakfast down in the kitchen together this morning."

Keely plunged a fork into the soft mound of pancakes and brought up a big bite. "That must have been cozy."

"Actually it was. We had a long talk. And then they showed me around the place so I could see it in the daylight. There's a leak in the attic, but the cellar's bone dry. All in all, a good solid construction."

Keely stopped eating. Her heart began beating a little faster. "What do you think? Is it a good buy?"

"Oh, no doubt about it." He walked to the window and pulled up the yellowed shade. Sun filtered through the dingy lace curtains. "I walked around the property, too. It's a wonderland out there today after the storm. The pond was frozen and buried under snow, but I believe Elwin when he says it exists. I even believe there's trout in it. When I was a boy I used to dream of fishing in my own pond."

If there hadn't been a tray balanced on her lap, Keely would have leaped out of the bed to hug him. Instead she gently set the tray aside. "Now you could have that dream, Chuck," she told him softly.

"Except I'm not a boy anymore, am I?" He turned to face her, a frown creasing his high forehead. "Dreams are one thing. Reality is another. I can't give up everything for some pipe dream you have, darling."

Keely experienced a sinking sensation in her stomach that was in no way caused by Matilda's pancakes. "You're saying we should continue the way we are," she said flatly.

"Is that so awful?" he asked. "We're in love, aren't we? We can work out ways to spend more time together."

"You're afraid," she declared coldly. It was the last thing she thought she would accuse him of, but it was as clear as ice to her now. "For all your fancy talk about friendship and love and what you need from a woman, you're afraid of committing yourself in any way. You never have, and you never will!"

She threw aside the patchwork quilt and got out of bed, not even noticing that she'd upset the tray. Although she was stark naked, she stood before him, hands on her hips. He looked away from her.

"Listen to me!" she ordered. He turned back reluctantly to face her. She breathed hard a few times and then went on. "You want things to stay the same between us because you're not risking anything. You can take off whenever you want to. Fine! Take off!"

But he didn't budge. "You can't tell me what to do, Keely. Don't ever think you will." His eyes glittered dangerously.

"Get out of my life right now! Why wait? You're going to eventually." Disregarding the dangerous gleam in his eyes, she threw the door of their room open, her full breasts heaving from the effort of her grand gesture.

He pulled her away from the open door, kicked it closed and easily tumbled her backward onto the bed. He towered over her, angrier than she'd ever seen him. "Okay. You're right. I am afraid," he said in a voice so low she barely heard it.

"Afraid of *what*?" she cried, hot tears burning her eyes.

"You," he answered point-blank. "My feelings for you. I don't think I could bear to lose you, Keely, but I don't know how to keep you, either. You're asking too much of me right now. You're asking me to give up success and risk failure."

"No," she protested, shaking her head against the rumpled sheets. "I don't want you to give up anything, Chuck. I just want us to have more."

He captured her face in his hands and pressed his fingers into her soft cheeks. "Stop crying," he demanded. "I need your strength and common sense now, not your tears."

She could give him that much and more if only he'd accept it. She wiped the tears from her face. "I thought you really wanted to change direction, Chuck. I thought you wanted to give up travel and get down to serious work. I even thought you wanted us to have a life together.''

''I do!'' he insisted. He sighed deeply. ''One of these days.''

''That day may never come,'' she warned him. ''You're thirty-five years old, and it hasn't yet. Are you going to be moaning about your life-style and living out of a suitcase when you're fifty? Seventy? You'll probably die on the road in some strange bed, regretting you never took the chance to do what you wanted with your talent.''

''That's a pleasant thought,'' he said grimly.

''Well, you asked for it. But you're right about one thing. I can't expect you to believe in *my* pipe dreams. I'd love to run an inn like this. And I'd be damn good at it. I even have enough money saved up for a down payment.''

''Money's not the problem,'' he interrupted quickly. ''I've always had plenty of that.'' He laughed without humor. ''Maybe it's the guts I lack right now.''

''And I've always had plenty of *that*,'' she told him. She got up and began collecting her clothes. ''Now I'd better get dressed. We've got a shoot to complete at the Jasper plant.''

Their conversation had come full circle and was going nowhere, she realized. ''I hope Spike managed to brave the storm and shows up with the equipment.''

''Don't worry. He won't let us down,'' Chuck said. He paused and went to the window again and gazed at the snow-covered pond. ''The way I've let you down, Keely,'' he added softly.

She didn't answer him and continued to get dressed. She wasn't going to deny that he had. But she wasn't going to accuse him, either. She'd expected too much of him, that's all. That wasn't his fault but hers.

Before they drove away from The Bear and Elk, though, Chuck stopped the car at the end of the driveway to give the inn one last look. Icicles hung from the eaves and wide porch cornices, the roof was covered with a thick frosting of snow, and the proud old edifice sparkled like spun sugar in the sun.

"It sure is a pretty place," he conceded. "But the first thing I'd do is trim that big oak on the left. Next storm, a falling branch could do real damage to the roof."

He pulled out and sped off without saying more. But a little flicker of hope ignited in Keely's heart. For a moment there he'd sounded like a real property owner.

And at that moment Keely wanted two things more than she'd ever wanted anything in her life: she wanted Chuck beside her, and she wanted that inn. But she also realized she might have to settle for one without the other. Even if she couldn't make Chuck change his life, she could still change hers. It didn't make her happy, but it was something she'd have to think about long and hard.

"So we're heading for the place where the famous Keely LaRoux got her start," Chuck said, breaking into her reverie. "You must be excited about seeing old friends at the Jasper plant."

"I doubt many of them will remember me," she said. "It'll be good to see Mike, though. We were really close growing up. He's the oldest of the boys. I always think of him as a kid, but here he is, foreman of a Citation plant." She shook her head in amazement.

"I'm looking forward to meeting him," Chuck said simply.

Chapter Thirteen

Spike was already there to greet them when they arrived at the Jasper plant. Keely couldn't help but give him a big hug. He really was a darling, dependable young man, appearances to the contrary.

"Whoa, take it easy in the clutch, Ms. LaRoux. I'm a married man now," he told her in a jubilant voice.

She stepped back, laughing, thinking he was joking. But then she saw that his funny face was quite serious and almost handsome with the glow of love.

"You married Angel Proctor," she said. "That lovely caterer in Providence."

He nodded. "Her name's Angel Zinko now."

"That has a certain ring to it," Chuck said dryly. "Why didn't you invite me to the big event, buddy?"

"Hey, I tried reaching you, man. But you were off somewhere like always. Anyway, it all happened so fast. I told you guys it was love at first sight. So why waste time?"

Chuck slapped his assistant's narrow shoulders. "Congratulations, Spike. I wish you and Angel the best."

Spike looked a little uncomfortable. "This is going to be my last shoot with you, Chuck. Angel wants me to stop knocking around and start concentrating on my music."

"She's right," Chuck said. "You should. It's time you lived up to your talent."

Keely gave him a sharp look. Easy enough for him to give good advice to someone else, she thought. But her expression softened when she turned back to Spike. "Tell Angel I think she's one lucky lady," she said, and, ignoring his blush, she stood up on tiptoe to reach his cheek and kiss it.

"Well, come on," Chuck said gruffly, hiding his own sentiments. "If this is your last shoot with me, you're going to work damn hard on it, buddy."

They entered the production area, and the first thing Keely noticed was a big banner hanging off the ceiling pipes. Actually it was a sheet with the words WELCOME HOME, KEELY painted across it. People she'd worked with on the production line years ago rushed forward to greet her. She blinked back tears, unprepared for such a warm, enthusiastic greeting. She spotted her brother Mike hanging back from the welcoming crowd around her. He wasn't one for showing affection in public, but she knew that the banner had been his idea. She walked over to him, deep affection in her eyes. He held the same for her in his soft brown ones.

"Hey, Keely girl," he said almost shyly. Instead of kissing her in greeting he tousled her hair. That used to drive her crazy when they were kids. "Don't you look like the big-shot executive?"

"You're doing all right yourself, kiddo," she said, tweaking his ear. That used to drive *him* crazy. "I see you're wearing a tie now that you're the plant foreman here."

He smoothed it down self-consciously. "Only 'cause you were coming. Citation's been pretty good to us, hasn't it, Keely?"

She remembered back to the time long ago when she was assembling motor parts and he was sweeping the factory floor. "We deserve what we got," she told him. "We've been good to Citation, too. Don't ever forget that, Mike. We Reillys work hard for our pay."

They often talked on the telephone and had just had a conversation the night before when she called to say the storm had delayed them. But she hadn't seen her younger brother since Christmas and couldn't hold back any longer. She took him in her arms and held him tight.

He patted her back, heartily but clumsily. "I got fresh coffee in my office," he said. "And Stella baked a batch of your favorite cookies, too. She was hoping you could have supper with us tonight."

A longing to see Mike's wife, Stella, and their two boys swept through Keely, but she shook her head with regret. "We've got to get back to New York tonight."

"We?" Her brother glanced behind her and took in Chuck Dickens with interest.

"I drove up with Ms. LaRoux," he said.

Keely hurriedly introduced them to each other. "We've been working together. Chuck's the annual report photographer, Mike. And this is Spike Zinko, his assistant."

Chuck seemed a little put out by such an abrupt introduction. "Why don't you and your brother have a little visit while Spike and I set up," he suggested.

"Join us for coffee first," Mike invited.

"I'm sure family talk would bore Mr. Dickens," Keely said, quite certain that it would.

"I wouldn't want to intrude." He walked away and began directing Spike, who was positioning the strobes.

Mike gave his sister a quizzical look, but she only shrugged. Chuck's unpredictable moods had already drained her, and she wasn't going to let their problems ruin her brief time with Mike. She was beginning to think, with a hopelessness too deep to acknowledge right now, that their problems were insolvable. But she tried to push that depressing thought into the very back of her mind as she and her brother chatted in his small office.

He showed her pictures of his two boys and their new puppy. She showed him pictures of Joy and mentioned how much her daughter would love a dog of her own. Mike wondered if his niece was getting enough fresh air and exercise, living in the city.

"I wouldn't move to New York for all the dough in the world," he said, munching on one of his wife's pecan cookies. "Not that I'm saying you shouldn't have done it, Keely girl. You had to, I guess. But don't you ever miss it up here?"

"I always have, Mike. I may surprise you one day and move back."

He looked surprised enough at her just saying it. "And give up that fancy job of yours? Nah, you don't turn your back on success. It ain't American."

"But starting fresh is. What I'm doing now doesn't make me especially happy, Mike. And Joy resents my long hours away from her. You know The Bear and Elk Inn off Route Seven?" He nodded, giving her a closer look. "It's for sale, and I'm thinking of buying it." She flushed with excitement and waited for her brother's reaction.

It was a long time coming. Mike never jumped at the idea of anything new. "It used to be a fine inn as I recall," he finally declared. "But it's gotten run-down."

"That's exactly why I can afford it," she told him.

"Having two brothers in construction and one an electrician could come in handy then," Mike went on. "And I know a saw from a hammer myself. Didn't I build my own house? Yeah, we four could help you out, Keely girl. You did plenty for us growing up. And if Ma were still here, she'd remind us."

Keely couldn't talk for a moment, she was so overcome by his offer. She swallowed hard, her throat constricted by emotion. "Oh, Mike, I never meant to imply that you or the other kids would have to help me."

"We're not kids anymore, sister. We're grown men. And we're family. We were all too young to help you out back when Joy was a baby and Royal took off, but we sure as hell can now." He noticed the tears welling in her eyes. "Hey, if you start blubbering, the deal's off."

She groped for a tissue in her purse and blew her nose. "There's no deal yet. I haven't made up my mind about the inn. But it's good to know I have your support."

"Always," he assured her. "And I know you could make a go of it if you put your mind to it. You always liked a good challenge." He picked up another cookie and examined it, as if counting the pecans. "So tell me, Keely," he said at last. "What's with you and that big bearded guy?"

"I told you, Mike. Chuck's the photographer Citation has assigned to take the pictures for the annual—"

"Yeah, yeah, yeah." He waved the cookie impatiently. "But there's a lot more to it than that, isn't there?" She made no reply. "Come on, sis. I saw the way he was looking at you. Hell, even if I was blind, I could've picked up the vibrations between you. So what gives?"

"One of us will have to eventually," she replied sadly.

Something in her eyes must have warned her brother not to press the issue, and he let it go at that. They talked about family some more, and Keely promised to come "home" for Christmas, as usual. Joy adored her four uncles and enjoyed her many cousins, and she loved the emotional upheavals of a holiday with the boisterous Reillys.

As Keely expected, the shoot went smoothly. The only complaint she had, aside from Chuck's polite coolness to her, was that it went too quickly. By early afternoon they were back in his car, heading for the city. The Vermont countryside was a glittering fairyland of ice and snow after the blizzard, but neither Keely nor Chuck commented on the breathtaking scenery.

But then Chuck pulled off the road and stopped. She steeled herself, waiting for him to tell her what was on his mind. She feared she'd pressured him too much about resolving their relationship and his solution was going to be simply to end it.

He hadn't stopped to talk, though. "Do you mind waiting in the car while I take a few pictures?" he asked her. "It's so beautiful here, I can't resist."

"I'll walk with you," she said.

"No. Not in those silly high heels of yours, Keely. You'll get your feet all wet. I'll leave the motor running so you won't get cold. I won't be long."

She watched him disappear down the road. She knew he'd be back shortly, but her insides constricted when she lost sight of him. It had gotten to the point where she missed him the very moment he was no longer within touching distance. The thought of parting with him for weeks on end made her almost sick. But if that's the life he was determined they have together, she resolved to accept it. She promised herself not to complain about it anymore. If it was a choice of accepting his nomad life-style or losing him completely, then she would have to accept.

But another part of her, indestructible even in the face of her bright, searing love for him, rebelled against such a compromise. She was willing to change her whole life for the good of one shared with him. Shouldn't he be willing, too? And if he wasn't, how much did she really mean to him? This question was left dangling like a noose in her mind when he returned to the car.

He kicked off the snow on his boots and got in. "I got some great shots," he said.

He tossed his camera bag into the back and gave her a long, searching look. "You know, when you introduced me to your brother," he said at last, "you acted as if I meant nothing to you. Nothing at all but a business acquaintance."

She didn't tell him that Mike had known better. "How did you expect me to introduce you? Mike, I'd like you to meet the man I'm having an affair with? I don't think that would have gone over very big with him."

"That description doesn't go over very big with me, either," Chuck said. He stepped on the gas so forcefully that the car skidded. But he twisted the wheel and swerved it back onto the main road again.

In the silence that followed, Keely bit hard on her bottom lip. Would she never learn to go easy with him? she asked herself. What about her resolution to *accept* things between them made only a few minutes before?

"I'm sorry, Chuck. That was a low blow. Loving you seems to bring out the worst in me at times."

He let out a harsh laugh. "I'd hoped it would bring out the best."

"But it has!" she protested, and those tears that had lately become so familiar to her sprang back into her eyes. "I've never been so happy and miserable in my life."

He nodded with understanding. "Me, too, Keely. What a fine pair we are. I've waited all these years to truly love someone, and she turns out to be a red-haired virago who gives me no peace or sympathy. Not exactly my concept of tranquillity forever after.''

"You just described death, not love," she pointed out to him.

He nodded. "So I did. And tranquil you're not, lady. I've never felt so alive as I do when I'm with you. For better *or* worse."

That had a vague ring of a marriage proposal to her, but Keely slammed the lid on that hope. Chuck had already dashed it earlier in the day at the inn. But she still managed a brave enough smile. "You take me for what I am, Dickens, and I'll do my best to take you as you are, too."

"Fair enough," he replied and drove on toward the city and the frantic life that awaited them there.

Once they reached Manhattan they got caught up in traffic. Chuck's sports car weaved in and out but then came to a full stop behind a bus exuding smelly fumes.

"I might as well get out here," she said. "My office is only a few blocks away."

"But you're not going back there today," Chuck objected. "Let's go to Lawley's Bar for a drink. We have things to talk about, Keely."

"Oh, Chuck, I really do have to check in at the office now. How about tonight, though? Come over for dinner."

He groaned. "I can't. I have to meet with a client about a fashion shoot in Barbados next week."

She got a vivid image of tall, gorgeous models in teeny-weeny bikinis. "That should be a pleasant trip. Maybe you can send me a postcard."

"Why don't you come with me?" he suggested. "We could stay on for a few days and finally relax together."

"What about my daughter? I can't just leave her again. I'm with her too little as it is."

Chuck waved away that problem. "Bring her along. I like Joy, and she seems to like me. I'll teach her how to scuba dive. I'll teach you both. We'll have a great time, the three of us."

"Joy and I can't simply take off like that, Chuck," she told him as calmly as she could, keeping the impatience out of her voice. "She has school. I have work. Unlike you, we need a little stability in our lives."

He heaved one of his great sighs. "I want a normal life, too, Keely."

"You could have fooled me," she said flatly. But then she relented. "Why don't the three of us have Thanksgiving together? I'll cook a really special meal."

He looked away from her. "I'll be in Japan then. I made the commitment months ago."

"I see," she said, her hand on the door handle. "And where will you be at Christmas? Tibet?"

"I never travel on Christmas day," he assured her.

"Well, we'll be in Jasper," she told him. She turned to get out of the car. "See you around, Dickens. If you can fit me into your busy schedule, that is."

He gripped her arm to prevent her from leaving. "That's not fair, Keely. You of all people should understand how work sometimes gets in the way of other things."

"Other *things*? You mean me?" She was hurt to the core. She felt completely excluded from his life right then. "Let go of my arm," she enjoined. She didn't want to cry in front of him again.

His grip tightened. "I'm not going to let you leave angry."

But his car was blocking traffic, and a cacophony of horns blared in protest. He released her arm and shifted gears.

"You have no choice," she said. She jumped out of his car as it began to move and hurried to her office building without looking back.

The next morning she was depressed and bleary-eyed as she hunched over her desk. Chuck hadn't called the night before. She hadn't really expected him to. It seemed there was nothing left to talk about. She'd stayed awake all night, staring at ominous shadows on the ceiling above her bed. And now, opening her desk calendar, she glumly noted it was Friday the thirteenth.

That, too, seemed ominous, although she wasn't superstitious. Well, maybe she was just a little. She remembered that as a little girl she used to wear her underpants inside out on this particular day. Why she thought this would ward off bad luck, she had no idea. Sensing it was going to be a bad day, she had the sudden impulse to go to the ladies' room and turn them inside out once again. She didn't act on the impulse, though. She wasn't a silly little girl anymore.

Edith came in with the morning mail, as usual. What wasn't so usual was that Edith wasn't smiling. "I have something to tell you, Keely." Keely tensed and nodded for her to go on. "I'm quitting, dear," Edith blurted out. "I'm giving you two weeks' notice, of course, and I'll do everything I can to help you find and train a replacement."

"But no one can replace you, Edith." She resolved to beg her secretary to stay if she had to. Edith was the only person she completely trusted at Citation.

Edith shook her head and smiled sadly. "Everybody here is replaceable, Keely. But I want you to know how much I've enjoyed working for you."

"Then why are you leaving me?" Sparks flew into her green eyes. "It's because of Plack, isn't it? He's been causing you too much trouble. I'll take care of him, Edith. He goes. You stay." And to hell with what Wellfleet thinks about it, she added silently.

But the older woman kept shaking her head. "I would never do anything because of little Peter. He's far too unimportant to me." She ran a hand across her pale face. "But my husband is very important to me. He needs me at home with him, Keely. His last heart attack was more severe than I was willing to admit at first. But it's become clear to me that our time together is most precious." Her voice cracked, and she paused a moment to regain her composure. "I know you're going through a tough time at work, dear. I wish I could stay and help you. But you're young and resilient and can manage without me in the end. I don't think Mr. Hamilton can anymore."

Keely leaped up and hurried around her desk to hug Edith. "It's right that you should be with him," she said. "Don't worry about me for a minute." Her own voice snagged. "But I'll miss you, Edith. You're the one true friend I have here."

Edith patted her back, more accustomed to giving comfort than receiving it. "No, I won't worry about you, Keely La-

Roux. You'll do just fine. You always have. I remember when you first came here. You were as green as your big, wide eyes! But smart as a whip and ambitious. So determined to get ahead. And you did. Just look where you are now.''

The trouble was that Keely didn't want to be where she was anymore. But she wasn't going to burden Edith with that. She embraced her again and wished they could have shown more affection for each other over the years. But affection was an alien emotion in the sleek, cold offices of Citation.

''What a touching scene,'' Peter Plack commented from the open doorway. His smirk held nothing but disdain.

The two women broke apart. ''Come back later, Plack. I don't have time for your nastiness now,'' Keely told him.

''Time for others, but no time for poor me. I guess I'll have to stand in line behind Chuck Dickens. Tell me, Keely. Is he a hard act to follow?''

Her face heated with rage. ''I said to get out, Plack.''

Instead he leaned against the doorjamb. His eyes had a dangerous gleam in them. ''Not before I bid farewell to Mrs. Hamilton. I managed to overhear you were leaving our happy Citation family, madam.'' He bowed formally. ''And not a moment too soon, I might add. Mr. Wellfleet has been trying to get Keely to fire you for weeks.''

If she'd had a gun, Keely would have shot him on the spot. But Edith actually laughed. ''How funny you are, Peter,'' she said. ''A vicious little boy dressed up in a man's three-piece suit. Do you think I'd take anything you had to say to heart?''

She turned back to Keely, told her she'd be taking inventory in the stock room and then walked past Plack without further consideration of him.

After Edith left it took all Keely's self-control to keep herself from slapping Plack across his smug face. His needless cruelty enraged her.

''You're the one who's fired,'' she told him through clenched teeth. ''You've given me plenty of reasons, but telling Edith how Wellfleet felt about her was the last straw. Clear out your desk and leave within the hour, Plack.''

But he was in no rush. He studied his manicured fingernails for a long moment. ''A lot can happen in an hour, Red,'' he said. "I came to inform you that Wellfleet wants to see you immediately."

"About what?"

Plack smiled like the cat who'd just swallowed the canary. "Go upstairs and find out for yourself, love."

Unable to tolerate his presence a moment longer, she pushed past Plack and stormed out. As she rode up the elevator she resolved to have it out with the president if he didn't support her for firing Plack. If Wellfleet expected her to take on all the additional responsibilities he'd been throwing her way, then she had a right to demand competent managers to help her. And to top it off, the position she'd held before her promotion hadn't even been filled. It wasn't fair.

In this frame of mind she strode into Wellfleet's office, shoulders back, chin out. But her bold entrance was missed by the president, who was holding a newspaper in front of his face.

She cleared her throat, and he lowered the paper to reveal a glower that almost made her gulp. Something was terribly wrong. He threw the paper across the desk toward her.

"Read it and weep," he instructed.

Keely sat down heavily and picked up the paper. The article he'd circled in blood-red reported that UltraTech had announced a revolutionary new computer. The description that followed perfectly matched the one for Citation's X25 model. So UltraTech had beaten them to the punch after all. The rushed trip she and Chuck had taken out to the California plant for product pictures that would be used in Citation's own announcement was all for naught. UltraTech had stolen their thunder.

She raised her eyes to meet the president's and tried to look sympathetic. Deep down she'd always disliked the idea that Citation had a spy in the competitor's camp, though. It had bothered her more than she wanted to admit to herself.

"They announced their new computer sooner than we expected," she said.

"And why do you think they did that, LaRoux?"

His glare was so angry that she almost shrank away from it. She could understand his disappointment but not why it was directed at her. She and Chuck had done their jobs, just as he'd demanded.

"Why don't you ask your friend Dickens why they did?" he went on in a deceptively calm voice. "He's the one who tipped off UltraTech about our own plans. He was kind enough to give them detailed pictures of our X25 so they'd know what they were up against. Not that kindness had anything to do with it. It was greed that motivated him."

"Don't be absurd," Keely said, forgetting who she was talking to. "He would never do that."

Wellfleet slammed down his beefy fist on his desktop. "He would and he did, you foolish woman! UltraTech paid him plenty for those negatives of our prototype. I warned you to be careful about this assignment, LaRoux. But you were too busy sleeping with the man to keep your mind on business, weren't you?"

Keely blanched but kept her head high. "Plack got to you with his gossip, I see."

"Are you denying it?"

She refused to do that. She wasn't ashamed of what she'd done. She loved Chuck. "No, I'm not," she replied softly. "But that's entirely my business, not Citation's."

As Wellfleet studied her proud, resolute face, the anger in his own diminished a bit. "Oh, Keely, it *is* company business now. I don't believe you were in on Dickens's espionage, but by trusting him you caused Citation great damage. You let me down, and I can't abide that."

She pressed icy fingertips to her pounding temples, trying to get her thoughts together. "It's possible that UltraTech moved up their production schedule and their announcement had nothing to do with someone tipping them off," she pointed out.

"But someone did. I know that for a fact from my informant there."

"Why assume it was Chuck Dickens?"

"Who else, Keely? You?"

She stood up on shaky legs. "I'll talk to him. We'll get to the bottom of this, sir." That's all she could think to do now. She desperately needed to talk to Chuck.

Wellfleet slowly stood up, too. "We've already hit the bottom on this," he said. "The X25 isn't big news anymore. Citation remains a step behind with its high-tech products. Might as well put a picture of a lawnmower motor on the cover of the annual report." He shrugged. "Not that it's any concern of yours anymore, Ms. LaRoux. You're through here, you realize."

And in a blast of understanding, she suddenly did. She wouldn't be given a second chance—or even a chance at all—to vindicate herself. It had already been decided that she would be the scapegoat. Her ten years of hard work meant nothing now. As the president had so succinctly put it, she was through.

"I'm sorry," he said. "I have no one else to hold responsible for this but you. I can't even have Dickens prosecuted. Then I'd have to admit I had a spy at UltraTech. But you're still accountable for your lack of good judgment." A fleeting glimmer of regret passed over his heavy features. "As of today Peter Plack will take over your duties as director. I wish you luck in the future."

And that was that. He turned away to look out his wall of windows as if she no longer existed. And for a horrible moment she felt as if she didn't, as if she were nothing. All she had to hold on to was her dignity, and that's what she walked out with.

She rode the elevator all the way down to the lobby, not stopping off at her own floor. She couldn't endure going back there to get her purse and coat. It was Plack's office now, and she had no doubt he'd already made himself at home in it. She refused to allow him the satisfaction of gloating at her.

But pride had its price, and she had to walk the thirty blocks to Chuck's studio, having no money to pay for a cab. Her only protection from the cold was her suit jacket, but she was oblivious of the temperature. All she could concentrate on was placing one foot in front of the other and getting closer and closer to Chuck. He would explain everything. He would make everything all right again once he held her in his arms. That's all she knew for sure. The rest was a blur of confusion. Her safe, secure world at Citation had shattered into a million pieces.

She'd never been inside his studio before. She stopped by the receptionist's desk and asked for him in a tremulous voice.

"He's not in, lady. And I don't know when he will be."

Keely recognized the twang immediately. So this was her telephone nemesis, Trudy, in person. She was much more attractive than her voice. And there was a look of concern on her face as she regarded Keely.

"Hey, you look kind of sick," Trudy said. "Can I get you a drink of water or something?"

"No, thank you. I'll be fine. I'll just wait here for Mr. Dickens, if you don't mind."

"It may be a long wait. Maybe Mrs. Dickens can help you."

Keely swayed slightly. "Did you say Mrs. Dickens?"

"Yeah, she came in from Long Island to help out at the studio today. Her office is the last door down the hall."

Unable to speak, Keely nodded and went in the direction the receptionist had indicated. She proceeded down the long hall in the slow motion of nightmares. The walls seemed to sway and the floor to undulate, but she kept her balance and made it to the last office.

The door was open. A woman about her age, with silvery-blond hair, was sitting behind a desk marking contact sheets with a grease pen. The pen was red. The woman's fingernails were painted a pale pink. There was a charming little mole on her porcelain-smooth left cheek. Keely noticed all these details with a vividness more intense than reality.

The woman glanced up. "Hi. Is there something I can do for you?" Her voice was as sweet as a flute.

"Are you Mrs. Dickens?"

"I sure am. Come in."

Keely stepped into the office, afraid her knees would buckle. "I'm Keely LaRoux," she managed to say.

The woman smiled, her lovely blue eyes friendly. "Oh, yes. The Citation account. Chuck mentioned you to me. Seems you've been working together quite a lot lately." There was nothing in her tone or face but open friendliness.

What a nice woman, Keely thought through a haze of sheer pain. "I'm looking for your—" Her voice broke. She couldn't say the word *husband*. "I'm looking for Chuck."

Mrs. Dickens laughed. "Someone's always looking for Chuck. He took off again last night. He should be back this afternoon, but he still asked me to come in and cancel all his shoots. What an impossible man!" But there was more fondness than criticism in her voice.

Keely lowered her eyes, unable to look at the other woman. Because, in truth, *she* was the other woman. Her attention was caught by a picture of a boy and girl on the desk. They were the same handsome children Keely had noticed in a photograph at Chuck's gallery exhibition.

"Are these your children, Mrs. Dickens?" She knew the answer was yes. Nightmares had their own predictability.

Sure enough, Mrs. Dickens nodded assent. She even picked up the picture to give Keely a closer look. "That's Tina the Ballerina, as Chuck calls her. She's eight. And little Chuck is ten. He looks just like the big one, doesn't he? A real Chuck off the old block!" She laughed at their silly family joke.

Keely gave her a wan smile. Would this nightmare never end? Or would the monster in it finally make his appearance? Because that's who the man she loved was. A monster. A lying, cheating, deceitful monster. Maybe he had betrayed her by selling the Citation film to UltraTech. But that was the least of his crimes. And the most horrible part of this whole horrible dream was that she still loved him.

It was this realization—that she did still love him—that made Keely wake up. Her nightmarish doubts dissipated as she let her love for him pour through her. At this crucial time, when it was most difficult for her, she truly believed that Chuck Dickens never had and never would let her down. He'd demonstrated this to her in so many ways that she'd refused to acknowledge before. But now the truth of it hammered home with every beat of her heart.

Her sickly smile changed to one of wide understanding. "You're Chuck's sister-in-law, aren't you, Mrs. Dickens?"

Frowning, the other woman nodded. "Of course. Who did you think I was? His mother?"

"Hardly!" And then Keely laughed so hard at the absurdity of it all that tears ran down her cheeks. Catching Mrs. Dickens's deepening frown, she stifled her giggles. "I'm sorry to act so silly," she said hurriedly. "But I had a big shock this morning, and I'm just coming out of it, Mrs. Dickens."

"Please call me Susan. And tell me what happened."

"I got fired, Susan," Keely announced almost gleefully.

"But that's terrible! Is that why you want to see Chuck? Can he help you out somehow?"

"Oh, he already has," Keely assured Susan, holding tight to her belief in his love for her. "Would you please tell him I stopped by and would like to see him as soon as he returns?"

"Of course I will, Keely." Chuck's sister-in-law gave her a warm smile. "I have a feeling that I'll be seeing a lot more of you and we'll become friends."

"Me, too," Keely told her, taking the hand Susan offered.

It wasn't until she'd left the studio that she remembered she didn't have a cent on her. Although she didn't exactly relish the idea of pounding concrete again, pride would not allow her to go back and ask Trudy or Susan for cab fare. And so she hoofed it another fifteen blocks home. By the time she reached her apartment building her feet were blistered from her business shoes, elegant pumps not designed for hiking. She resolved never to let pride interfere with her true desires ever again. It occurred to her how many times it had in her relationship with Chuck.

She let herself into her apartment with the extra key Mrs. Alphonso kept for Joy, kicked off her shoes and sank down on the sofa like a deflated balloon. Getting fired was rather exhausting. She was thankful she had a few hours to herself before Joy came home from school. She didn't much look forward to telling her daughter that she was unemployed.

There was a pile of paperwork on the coffee table. Work she'd brought home from the office the day before. At least she wouldn't have to worry about that anymore, she thought in a sudden rush of freedom. She swept the papers off the table, and they fluttered to the floor.

She was free of Citation! Sweet relief coursed through her. It didn't even matter to her that Peter Plack had replaced her there. She knew he wouldn't last long in the position. He couldn't handle the work and responsibilities that went with the title. Without Edith and the rest of the staff supporting him, he was doomed to failure.

But that happy thought soon faded, and Keely began to worry about what she was going to do next. The relief she'd felt only a moment before changed to apprehension. She'd never been unemployed before. It scared her. She pushed herself off the sofa and headed for her little galley kitchen. Whenever she had problems to work out, she cooked. It was like therapy to her.

She threw herself into making a blueberry pie, Joy's favorite. She wondered if Chuck liked it, too. There was so much she still didn't know about him. Wellfleet's accusation that he'd sold pictures of the X25 to Citation's competitor flickered in her mind. Though she smothered the thought, Chuck's own words came back to haunt her. Take what you can, he'd advised her. He was always so disdainful of the corporations that paid his high rates.

She began rolling out the pastry dough with quick, light strokes. It calmed her, and the moment of doubt instantly passed. No matter how damning the evidence was against him, she couldn't believe he'd willfully hurt her. She never thought she'd be able to put her trust in a man again, but now realized that she had. It had taken the Citation crisis to vividly bring this home to her. Loving Chuck had changed her. Until he'd come into her life, she never knew how much love she was capable of giving to a man. And even now, with her career in ruins, she felt better about herself than she ever had. Perhaps she'd given her heart away reluctantly, but she truly believed it was in safekeeping. She finished making the pie with total peace of mind.

And when Chuck knocked on her door, as she knew he would, she opened it wide to him, her smile wide, too.

"You sure don't look like a woman who just got fired," Chuck said. "I rushed over here as soon as Susan told me. Did she misunderstand you?"

"Oh, no. I got the ax all right. Come on in. There's a blueberry pie baking in the oven. I hope you can stay long enough to have a piece."

"Of course I'll stay. I came to comfort you." He took her hand and pulled her to the sofa. "But I certainly didn't expect you to be calmly baking a pie!"

"But I love cooking more than anything. Except making love with you, that is."

He was clearly puzzled by her lighthearted attitude. "Are you really okay? Maybe you're still in shock. After all, you just lost the most important thing in your life."

She laughed. "No, I haven't. He's sitting right here beside me."

He took her into his arms and held her close. "You don't know how good that sounds to me, darling. But I'm here to make *you* feel better. Don't you want to talk about it? Tell me what happened?"

And so she did. She told him everything, including Wellfleet's accusations of his part in it. As he listened, the small muscle in his cheek began to twitch.

"Moonbeam Smith," he pronounced very precisely.

Keely comprehended immediately. "She hid the rolls of film in that baggy jumpsuit of hers. I told you she had shifty eyes."

"And I was too pigheaded to listen to you." Chuck took her hand and held it in both of his. "I'm so sorry, Keely. But I promise you one thing. She's not going to get away with it. I'll make sure the truth comes out."

"I don't think either Citation or UltraTech wants that," Keely cautioned. "All parties concerned were unscrupulous."

"To hell with what they want! What about our own reputations? It's especially unfair to you, Keely. When I think how devoted you were to that damn company, and then kicked out like that, it makes my blood boil."

Keely touched his face, and she could almost feel his anger subsiding with her gentle touch.

"I feel more relief than regret over the whole incident. I'm glad I'm through with Citation," she told him. "But you're right, Chuck. You have to clear your name. You can't let this affect your business with other corporate clients."

"It's the principle of the thing that matters to me, not that," he said quickly. "I don't even want any more corporate assignments. I'm changing the direction of my career once and for all, Keely. No more traveling."

"Do you mean it, Chuck?" The moment she asked, she sensed that he really did.

"I'm tired of it," he said. "Tired of running away from what I really care about because I'm afraid of failing at it. It's time I led my own life and stopped being influenced by my father's bleak estimation of me. You made me see that very clearly in Vermont, Keely."

"I wasn't sure you were listening," she said softly.

He grinned. "You make it pretty difficult for me *not* to listen to you, lady. You can be very convincing, you know. You even convinced me you could run an inn with your hands tied behind your back."

For once she didn't speak up. She sat very still, barely breathing, and waited for him to continue. Her heart was somewhere in the vicinity of her throat.

He misunderstood her silence. "Have you changed your mind about that?" he asked apprehensively. "Don't you think it's a good idea anymore?"

"No, it's probably the best idea I ever had," she managed to say.

"That's a relief! Because I think it is, too."

"You didn't yesterday morning," she reminded him.

"I needed a little time to get used to it, Keely. But when you leaped out of my car when we got back to the city, it jolted me into action. I realized that I could lose you if I didn't face up to changing my life. I decided it was now or never, and I drove straight back to The Bear and Elk. I told Elwin I wanted to buy the inn."

Keely leaped up from the sofa. "Why didn't you call last night and tell me?"

"Because I didn't want to disappoint you, darling. Someone else had already put in a bid for the place."

Keely sank back down in a dejected heap. "Oh."

He patted her back. "Hey, I thought you were a fighter. *I* certainly didn't just give up. Elwin hadn't signed on the dotted line yet. So I checked in and spent the evening trying to convince him to sell to me instead. He said he'd sleep on it. Matilda must have snuggled up to him and put in a good word for us, because this morning Elwin took my check and gave me a bill of sale."

He took it out of his jacket pocket and handed it to Keely. She looked down at it for a long time, not reading a word. All the letters were swimming in front of her eyes. And then her tears started falling and made little plopping noises as they dropped down and spattered on the paper.

Chuck handed her his handkerchief. "I hope those are tears of joy, darling."

She stared up at him, her emerald eyes glistening. "I've never been so happy in my life."

"Except there's one little stipulation," Chuck warned her softly. "The only way I could cinch this deal was to tell Elwin and Matilda you were going to be my wife. They wouldn't have sold their place to a flatlander like me. So I had to throw you into the bargain. We could even have our wedding reception at the inn. Invite all your brothers and their clan. Is it a deal?"

"Are you actually proposing to me, Mr. Dickens?"

"I sure am, Ms. LaRoux. For the second time, I might add."

She sniffed. "You can't count that time in California. You weren't serious then."

"It was you who refused to take me seriously, if you'll recall."

"You didn't try very hard to convince me otherwise."

"I was hurt, Keely. I'd never asked a woman to marry me before. It wasn't exactly encouraging to have her scoff at me."

He'd said the words lightly, but Keely sensed there was truth in them. She lowered her eyes. "I'm sorry if I hurt you. But I was so afraid you'd end up breaking my heart that I put up barriers to protect it." She looked up at him, no longer trying to keep all her love from showing in her eyes. "And you kept knocking them down! I'm so glad you knocked them down, Chuck. You freed my heart to love you completely."

"Then you'll marry me? The answer is yes?"

"You bet it is, mister. You're not going to get out of it so easily this time."

He laughed at that. "I don't want to, darling." He stroked back her thick coppery hair and covered her forehead and cheeks with kisses. "I've been traveling all my life just to find you. I realize that now."

"We've both traveled a long way to get to this place," she told him, wrapping her arms around his big solid chest and holding him close to her.

Meanwhile another pie burned to a crisp in the oven.

* * * * *

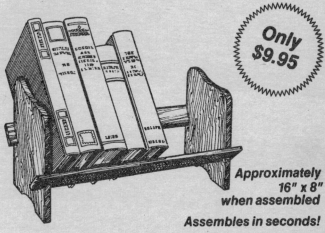

Silhouette Special Edition

COMING NEXT MONTH

#409 A CERTAIN SMILE—Lynda Trent
Impulsive widow Megan Wayne and divorced father Reid Spencer didn't have marriage in mind, but what harm could come if their friendship turned into something stronger? Reid's two teenage daughters didn't intend to let them find out....

#410 FINAL VERDICT—Pat Warren
Prosecutor Tony Adams's upbringing had built him a strong case against lasting love. Could attorney Sheila North's evidence to the contrary weaken his defenses and free his emotions from solitary confinement?

#411 THUNDERSTRUCK—Pamela Toth
Crew member Honey Collingsworth accepted the risks of hydroplane racing. Still, when her brother and dashing defector Alex Checkhov competed, churning up old hatred, she feared for their lives...and her heart.

#412 RUN AWAY HOME—Marianne Shock
Proud landowner Burke Julienne knew that to restless vagabond Savannah Jones, the lush Julienne estate was just another truck stop. Yet he found her mesmerizing, and he prayed that one day Savannah would trade freedom for love.

#413 A NATURAL WOMAN—Caitlin Cross
When farmer's daughter Vana Linnier abruptly became a sophisticated celebrity, she desperately needed some plain old-fashioned horse sense to cope with her jealous sister and her disapproving but desirable boss, Sky Van Dusen.

#414 BELONGING—Dixie Browning
Saxon Evanshaw returned home to a host of family fiascos and the lovely but stealthy estate manager, Gale Chandler. Who was she really? Where were the missing family treasures? And would Gale's beauty rob him of his senses?

AVAILABLE THIS MONTH:

Starting in October...

SHADOWS ON THE NILE

by

Heather Graham Pozzessere

A romantic short story in six installments from best-selling author Heather Graham Pozzessere.

The first chapter of this intriguing romance will appear in all Silhouette titles published in October. The remaining five chapters will appear, one per month, in Silhouette Intimate Moments' titles for November through March '88.

Don't miss *"Shadows on the Nile"*—a special treat, coming to you in October. Only from Silhouette Books.

Be There!

IMSS-1